POWER PLAY

EMPIRE STATE HOCKEY
BOOK 1

LEXI JAMES

Cover Design: @booksnmoods

Editor: Mattingly Churakos

❀ Created with Vellum

To the girls that drool over single daddies. Rex says hi.

POWER PLAY PLAYLIST

1. Cardi B- I Like It.
2. Sam Smith-Unholy
3. Mickey Valen- Chills (Dark Version)
4. Chloe Adams-Dirty Thoughts
5. Never Leave- Bailey Zimmerman
6. Justin Bieber- Off My Face
7. Miguel- Sure Thing
8. Sia- Chandelier
9. Conan Gray-Yours
10. Ali Gatie- It's You
11. Latto- Big Energy
12. Archers-Blanket Fort

PROLOGUE

REX, 5 YEARS AGO

"Your career is over."

Those words have played in my head on a constant loop since my injury six months ago, when my doctors and coaches told me I would never get on the ice again. At least not playing hockey for the NHL. I tried to ignore them, pretend none of it real. I went through with the surgery, the physical therapy, and even tried a new trial therapy that's supposed to be promising for injuries like mine.

But if I'm being honest, I've known it was over for a while, and it fucking sucks. Hockey has always been the one thing I had that no one could take from me. It's been something I've worked for since I was a little kid and have poured my heart and soul into. I'm not even sure where to go from here or what I'm supposed to be doing. It's not like I have a backup plan. Hockey was it. It's always been it. Hell, in college, I majored in fucking communications for fucks sake. If that doesn't scream "Athlete that doesn't know what he's fucking doing," I don't know what does.

But in the blink of an eye, it's gone, all because of a

stupid accident.

Now, I'm injured with no idea where to go from here. It's just me and a bottle of pain pills that will hopefully numb more than just my knee.

*O*ne year later

Laying in my bed, I stare at the ceiling, like I do every day. It's where I think the most, which is a double-edged sword. I should definitely be thinking about my next steps, or how to pull myself out of this black hole. More importantly I should probably think about cleaning my apartment, at some point. Looking around, the stench of vodka from the random empty bottles and leftover takeout containers isn't exactly a good look for anyone.

But anytime it's quiet, I end up thinking about the accident and how I lost the one thing that means the most to me.

I'm a mess. Between the prescription pills, the alcohol, and fucking a different woman as often as I can, I'm not sure where I'm supposed to go from here. Something's gotta give.

My parents have tried to help me. They even moved down here a couple of months ago to try and support me, but there's nothing they can do when I'm so unwilling to see anything positive. I'm stuck wasting away in my apartment.

In my mind everything is already over, so what's the point in trying to fight my way back? Even if I get more use out of my knee, I'm thirty-three years old. It's not like I'm exactly in my prime, just waiting for the opportunity to join another team or to get back with my old one. I'm old news. Washed up. That's a hard fucking pill to swallow, and trust me, I've had plenty of practice.

When the doorbell rings at seven a.m., I assume it's my

parents doing their usual check-in, or at least my mom. Ever since I got injured, my dad and I have had an interesting relationship. He's not mad about the injury, but he's ready for me to man up, pull my head out of my ass, and start making better choices.

Throwing on a pair of sweats, I walk to the door, passing more take-out containers and liquor bottles in my living room that I've yet to clean up. My mom's going to have a field day with this mess.

But when I open the door, it's not my mom waiting there.

I recognize the woman standing in front of me but can't seem to recall her name or where I know her from. But that's not even the worst part.

The worst part is that she's standing here on my doorstep, tears streaming down her face, holding a bundle of blankets in the shape of a baby.

What. The. Fuck.

"Uh, hi. Can I help you," I muster out, unease slowly creeping in as I battle the fogginess of my brain. Why does she look so familiar?

Maybe I've seen her around before. It's not unlikely, our apartment complex is weird.

"Rex?" she whispers tentatively.

Fuck me. Who the fuck is this?

"Uh, yeah, that's me. Who are you?"

"Miranda. We met at The Last Stop, the bar over in old town. It was, uh, awhile back."

She's obviously nervous. Why is she here if she's so nervous?

"You obviously don't remember me, which isn't exactly surprising. It was a weird night, for both of us. But I remember your name, and what you looked like, and you seemed like a nice enough guy," she says, mumbling to herself and confusing me further.

It's way too damn early for this.

"Miranda, right? It's fucking early and you're speaking too fast for my brain to process anything. What did you say you needed?"

She looks upset, but confident when she says her next words.

"I need you to take your baby."

I know I'm hungover, possibly still drunk, plus it is only seven a.m., but there's no way in fuck I just heard her correctly . . . right?

My baby?

"Uh, excuse me? I don't have a baby."

She has a strange look on her face, a mixture of sadness, embarrassment, and what seems like panic.

"So, uh, we met about nine months ago. You probably don't remember much. I mean, I was bartending, and you easily put down enough shots to forget the night, if not the week. But we ended up in the bathroom at closing time, and apparently, we didn't use protection because she's here."

She.

I have a daughter.

"Maureen . . . I . . ."

"It's Miranda."

"Sorry, I, uh, I think you have the wrong person. There's no way I'm a father, plus I *always* use protection."

It's true. I always use protection, no matter what. I mean, even when I was on the team and would hook up with puck bunnies at our games, I never forgot protection. But . . . what if I did? If my math is right, this would have been shortly after I realized my career with hockey was over.

"Okay, Rex. Well, she's here, and she's yours. This is her

bag, it has everything you'll need. You're much more capable than I am, even if it does seem like you're struggling right now," she says, glancing around my apartment, tears filling her eyes. "Look, I just want her to have a shot at a good life, and that's not with me. I don't want to be a mom; I never have." I try to stop her by putting my hand up, but she easily ignores me, continuing on as if she's afraid to stop talking. "Along with all her things, in the bag is her birth certificate and the paternity test I had done. Don't ask, but I promise you it's true. You can repeat the test, and you'll get the same results. I, uh, I also signed over my rights. After this, she's yours and only yours."

The reality of the situation starts to hit me, and I realize that there's no way my apartment is a good place for a baby right now.

"Uh, can you give me a minute? Come on in, I just need to gather my thoughts."

"I can't stay long; I have a train to catch in an hour."

"Wait. You're leaving already?"

"Yeah. I . . . I can't stay. I thought I could do this, but I can't, and honestly, this is going to make me sound like the worst person ever, but I don't want to do it. I don't want to be a mom. But I'm not evil. I don't want her to have a bad life. You're her father, her only shot."

Is she serious right now? I can't even take care of myself, and yet this woman thinks I'm able to take care of a baby that I didn't even know existed.

"Can I make a phone call before you leave?"

"Yeah, no problem."

Walking past the mess of my living room, I go back into my room to find my phone. There's only one person for me to call, and I just pray she can get here quickly.

"Mom? I need you. Now. Please come over."

1

REX

PRESENT DAY

I've been driving around this city for the last three days, sitting in interview after interview, but nothing feels fucking good enough.

When Bernard called me with a job offer, I told him no. Absolutely not. Don't get me wrong; it was an incredible opportunity, but it was back in New York, and I've refused to return since I left the NY Cyclones five years ago.

Now, he expects me to just pack up my life in Austin, Texas, and move back home? It's not as easy now as it was back then. I have more than just myself to worry about this time. I should have known better than to argue, though. Bernard was annoyingly persistent and smart enough to sweeten the deal a bit until I finally caved and accepted the job. Now I'm the new head coach for the men's hockey team at Brooklyn University here in New York.

Bernard also helped pull some strings to get Rory into the university daycare. Apparently, it's an amazing program that has a waitlist a mile long. I still interviewed almost every other daycare around us to make sure it's the best choice, but it is.

It's been exhausting traveling around New York and interviewing at least thirty different daycares this week. I'm worn out.

And the worst part is, he was fucking right and the smug look he gave me earlier told me he knew it.

The university daycare program is easily the best facility around. By a fucking landslide. Who would have thought that the hardest part about moving to New York City wouldn't be driving, finding a job, or even finding a place to live? No, the hardest part has been being a single dad and refusing to give my little girl anything but the best.

A couple of the daycares that didn't work out felt the need to tell me that I was overbearing and needed to stop trying to control every aspect of my daughter's life. They believed that if their program worked for all the other kids, why shouldn't it be fine for Rory.

But that's not the point. I want to be involved in her life, even when I'm at work. I want to make sure she's getting everything she needs. Why is it unacceptable that I want updates throughout the day, maybe even a picture or two to let me know how she is? It's not like I'm asking for a daycare camera that I can watch her with . . . although I don't hate that idea.

It also shouldn't be that fucking difficult to follow a simple menu, which I would provide. I just don't want her eating a bunch of shit. She doesn't need a lot of sugar, plus Rory and I always cook together, so she's not really used to eating takeout or junk food. Well, unless my sister, Stella, is around.

It's simple, yet everyone acts like I'm high maintenance for it. It's fucking annoying.

Why am I being judged because I want the best for my little girl?

In the end, it didn't even matter, though, because none of those facilities would have worked with the hours that I need. Being a college hockey coach makes my hours go all over the place. Sometimes we have late practice, and our games are almost always in the evening, so I needed to find a place willing to accommodate that.

The university daycare had no issues with the hours or any of the other things I asked of them. Apparently, one of their daycare teachers has been looking for the opportunity to do dance classes in the evenings, and Bernard helped push to make it work for our schedule.

It's like déjà vu. I'll be coaching at the same university I went to almost fifteen years ago, and Rory will be joining me.

It couldn't have worked out better, and I was even happier with the choice after I toured the facility and met the teacher, Claire. Claire is young—probably nineteen or twenty—but she's sweet and has a personality that I think Rory will love once they get her to open up a bit.

My daughter is a tough nut to crack, taking after me in that aspect. She always seems to have these walls in place, especially around adults. Plus, she has a lot of big feelings for being only four years old, especially as she gets older and sees other kids with their moms and dads. She's starting to notice that she doesn't have a mom and has had a difficult time understanding why. Even if her mom was only in her life for three days, it's like she's aware something's missing.

When Miranda brought her to me and told me she was mine, it took me a while to come to terms with the fact that I had a daughter, yet as soon as I did, I started making choices to ensure she had a good life. At that time, I was struggling and spiraling out of control after my hockey career ended. But Rory saved me. She's the only reason I've come as far as I have, with the help of my mom, of course.

My mom knew what I was going through and knew I wasn't making good choices, so she came over with my father to help.

Miranda waited just long enough for them to get to my apartment, but after that, she was gone.

My parents though? They moved me into their place for a couple of weeks, making sure I was in a better place while also helping with Rory however they could. My dad used that time to help me detox and figure out what the fuck to do, while my mom helped me figure out my new role as a dad.

Now, with all of that behind us, we're moving cross country back to New York for a job I almost didn't take.

I've played hockey since I was five, going on to play in the NHL with the Cyclones until I retired after my injury. I ended up moving down to Austin to do some trial rehab for my knee, which seemed promising for a while, but it wasn't enough to keep me from having to hang up my skates permanently.

But now I'm back in the hockey world, and it's surreal as fuck.

Walking into the main office, I head past the secretary in search of Bernard, the Athletic Director, who used to be my old college coach. It helps that I've known him for years, as his son Trevor and I played together since we were five. Even after my injury and my move to Austin, Bernard and Trevor never wavered and were there for me every step of the way.

Walking up to his office, I'm just about to knock when the door swings open and Bernard is standing there with his usual happy smile covering his face.

I'm not sure what Mrs. Adams puts in their food, but him and Trevor are always so fucking cheerful.

"Mr. Lockwood," Bernard says, stepping back to let me into his office, the smile never falling from his face. "It took you long enough to get back here. We're happy to have you, son."

Almost outside of my control, my face turns up into a smile. It's hard not to smile at this man, who is equal parts both infuriating and fucking incredible at his job. He has a knack for treating everyone like they're important but also like they are family. He's all about tough love and congratulating you on a job well done, but in the same breath would threaten to whoop our ass if we made dumb decisions, on or off the ice. If he had still been my coach when I got injured, I don't think my life would have turned out the way it did, and I sure as hell wouldn't have pitied myself for as long.

But, I wouldn't trade that time for anything because it brought me Rory and that little girl saved me from myself.

"It's good to be home," I tell him honestly. "We both know it wouldn't have happened if it hadn't been for your offer. Well, that and your goddamn stubbornness."

Bernard just smirks, his eyes lighting up with mischief. "You can't expect an old dog like me to learn new tricks. Stubbornness is in my bones."

That I know. You truly can't teach an old dog new tricks.

Shaking my head, I laugh.

"Well, I had hoped that by now that Mary had whipped you into shape, but I see that was just wishful thinking."

His eyes immediately light up just at the sound of his wife's name, and that brings me a stupid amount of happiness. I love Mrs. Adams; she was like our team mom back in college, always feeding us, taking care of us, and making sure we were acting right with the ladies.

"Nah, son. At least not in that way," he says with a smile. "But, let's get down to business, I know you have other places you need to be. You ready to start on Monday?"

"Yeah, I'm moving Rory here on Saturday. I already have our place all set up with our things. And I'm sure you're not surprised that you were right about the daycare. She'll start there on Monday."

"Well, of course I was right," Bernard says with a wink. "Here are your keys to the rink. You already have your office, and I think we've gone over everything else. The teams all excited, I mean with your history on the team in college, and the NHL, I think they're all a little intimidated."

"Thanks for everything. Especially this opportunity. You know, without this, I would have probably never come back.

"Rex, I've known you for thirty years. You went through a rough patch, but that doesn't make you a bad person." Bernard reaches his hand out to shake mine, I return the gesture but pull him in for a hug at the last minute. We've always been close. "Now, go have fun. I overheard Trevor and his mom talking last night when he was over for dinner, sounds like you've got some plans."

Trevor and his parents are close. He goes to their house for dinner every week, so it's no surprise he was talking to them about our plans. Trevor and I used to get into some shit when we were growing up, even more so in college. Which might be why I'm so close with Bernard, as he had to whip our butts into shape sometimes, never letting our mistakes impact the team or our futures.

"Well, that wasn't what I wanted to hear," I laugh, trying not to sound irritated. "I told them just a beer and some dinner, but of course your son never listens."

"He's just like his old man. We don't listen too well."

"Ain't that the fucking truth," I say with a laugh. We say goodbye, and Bernard invites me to the house for dinner soon before I leave to go call Trevor and figure out what plans he's made for the evening that I'm sure I'm going to hate.

2

SAWYER

Another night working here at Atlantis, which means another night of dealing with my pushy ass boss and coworkers.

Molly, the owner, and my boss, is constantly trying to push my limits, always telling me it's "for my own good."

This bitch doesn't listen.

She also doesn't take no for an answer, which is why I'm sitting here listening to her beg me to go out on the floor again.

Why can't I just tell her no? Actually, not no, but fuck no. I mean, aside from the fact that she's one of my good friends and my boss, of course.

She's pushy, but she does understand when to stop if she can tell I'm really against something. She's never forced me to do anything; she just tries to see what she can get me to try, even if it's only once. She always says it's about getting me to live a little.

"Sawyer, come on. Just try it once," she whisper-shouts in my ear as she shakes another cocktail at the bar.

I've been working for her, here at Atlantis for the last six months, and honestly, I love it. Molly took over this club five years ago, and what started as a seedy, run-down "titty bar" that no one wanted to step foot in has turned into a high-class strip club that's always packed, even on a Wednesday. She didn't change what it was or take anything away, but she remodeled the entire place and added precautions and safety measures for both the employees and the clients. Her goal was to make sure that everyone felt comfortable and safe, which obviously worked because now it's constantly packed and one of the most well-known strip clubs in New York City.

When Molly hired me, I told her that I only wanted to bartend, which honestly has been a lot of fun. I still get weird looks from people when they find out where I work, but I don't really give a shit about their opinion of me. I'm working here for a reason, doing what I need to do to follow my dreams. If they have a problem with that, fuck 'em. Besides, even if I were stripping, there's nothing wrong with it. I don't do it, but that's just because it's not really my style. Which is why I usually just leave this job out when people ask what I do. I don't have time for their judgment or pretending I actually give a fuck what they think about me.

"Why, Molly? I'm doing just fine back here bartending, plus I like it. Why does it matter? Don't you already have enough girls competing for shifts? Adding me in would just be more of a headache, so I'll make the drinks, they can serve them, and do their little dancey dance," I tell her with a wink.

Yeah, if I came out from behind the bar, I could make a lot of money, which is almost enough for me to say yes, but not quite. It'd be nice to save up what I need by the end of the year, but I'm making progress on my goal as it is. Molly keeps bringing that up every time she tries to convince me, but it hasn't worked yet. I have goals, but I'll meet them on my own accord.

But I can promise, this isn't it.

"I know you are, hun. But you never know until you try, and honestly, I think it might be a nice outlet for you. You're fucking hot. I just know they'd eat that shit up. As for the other girls? Hell, some of them need a fire lit under the ass, and you just may have the match."

"What are we talking about?" Serena, my friend and one of the dancers says as she walks up, waiting for her table's drinks.

"Nothing," I tell her quickly. Obviously too quickly, though, because she perks up, looking at Molly for answers now.

"I was just offering up a serving shift if she was willing to give it a shot," Molly says, feigning innocence, and outright ignoring my glare.

She's so far past innocent it almost feels ludicrous to joke about. I once watched her dance naked on stage with two other dancers, all grinding on each other, at a bachelor party's request. The money they made . . . Yeah, I don't think they thought twice about getting up on that stage.

"Yes! Do it, just once! You never know unless you try!" Serena yells, her eyes filled with excitement.

"Shh. Don't let the whole damn club hear you," Molly hisses, but Serena hardly pays her any attention, she's too excited.

"Come on, Sawyer. I've seen you dance before, I know you'd fucking kill it. Besides, there's also the possibility that you'll like it. It's fucking exhilarating sometimes, being able to turn these big bad men into puddles of desperation." Serena leans against the bar top, sighing dramatically. "I'm serious though, Sawyer. You really never know if you'll like something until you try it. Besides, haven't we always said we'd try anything once?" Serena says, adding a little wink with her smile this time.

That look right there is the one that gets these men eating out of the palm of her hand. The tips she brings home are proof.

Well, her smile and her willingness to set her shame aside. If she even has any. I've yet to see it.

Serena is honestly the most confident chick I've ever met, walking around this club in tiny little outfits, leaving nothing to the imagination. But it works for her, and she's killing it right now. Besides, with her looks and body, it's no surprise she's so confident. She has curves in all the right places, and her long red hair goes down to her ass, high-lighting it perfectly.

I may be straight, but I'm not fucking blind; she's a smoke show.

"Yeah, thanks, but no thanks," I say, rolling my eyes at her theatrics.

I hate that there's a little voice in the back of my mind that's disappointed I didn't say yes. What would it hurt to just try it? Just once. It's like I've said no for so long that I'm scared to say yes.

I ignore that little voice though, it's the same voice constantly telling me to branch out, open my heart up, test my limits. All of the things that have gotten me hurt in the past, so why open myself up to that again.

Besides, that little voice is kind of a slut who only thinks with her vagina, and currently, she's tired of my celibate ways.

Right as Serena is about to start arguing with me, she peers over my shoulder at a group of guys who just sat down in her section. I follow her gaze, my jaw dropping when I see them. These guys are hot, like dangerously hot, and you know they know it. Most of them have that slightly edgy look, but in a pretty boy kind of way, which most girls love; it just doesn't do it for me. They seem to be having a good time, joking around, and smiling, or at least mostly all of them are. One of the guys is staring at his friends with an interesting look. At first, he appears annoyed at their antics, but his eyes show a hint of humor, like he's actually enjoying himself.

Watching him, it's intriguing. It's like his eyes are the only part of his expression that holds the truth and his face is just a mask.

"Give me a minute. This conversation isn't over yet," she says, as she scurries off to go greet the new table.

The vibe is rowdier, more electric than it usually is on a Wednesday night. The club is always busy, but tonight you can feel the energy in the air. It's dangerous in an exciting, intoxicating way.

No one's complaining, we all live for nights like this. It makes our shifts go quick, with constant action. No pun intended.

And the tips are always very generous.

The people who come here on a Wednesday night . . . yeah, they have no issue being a little heavy-handed with their tips. They can easily afford it. I mean, if you can afford the membership for this club, you're not exactly hurting for money.

Atlantis is one of the only clubs around here with a membership nearing a million dollars. But for that price, you're only in charge of your tips when you come. You get access to the bar, and the showroom, which has private dancers and pole dancers. You also get access to the private rooms.

The best part? Customers and employees all sign NDAs. If anything gets leaked or anyone's involvement with the club is used to negatively impact their outside life, they are fined. And sued by the club for the individual. Atlantis protects what's theirs.

Taking a drink ticket, I smile when I see it's a $10,000 bottle of scotch. Reaching for the bottle, I set it down right as Serena walks over with a smile on. That's not surprising, but this one looks devious. She must know she's going to get paid out big from this table alone.

"Hey, Sawyer, could you grab five or six glasses for that scotch and run them to that table? Molly is over there dealing with something, and I like, really have to go to the bathroom." She walks away without even giving me time to refuse her. Asshole.

I know what she's fucking doing, but I'm also terrified at the prospect of her coming back to a pissed off table if I fuck it up.

"What the fuck!" I yell after her, before turning to see the table still laughing and talking with each other, except for one guy. His eyes are on me, just watching. He almost looks angry, fire reflecting in his eyes. Why hasn't he looked away?

Looking around, I notice Molly and Serena are nowhere to be found, meaning I have no fucking choice but to go serve this table. Fucking fantastic.

I look down at my outfit and sigh. While we have fewer rules than the dancers and servers there's still a dress code policy. Meaning, I'm not wearing much. I have a red lace crop top on, showing pretty much everything but my actual nipples, and some lace boy shorts. Serena said it looked hot when I came in for my shift, and honestly, I don't disagree.

Grabbing their scotch and glasses, I walk over to the table, growing more irritated as I get closer to them.

I try to ignore that my legs feel like Jell-O as I walk to the table. Looking at the guys, I notice most of them are still in conversation, ignoring everything around them. Although one guy is looking at me with a huge smile on his face, which is alarming because the man who was glaring at me is sitting directly next to him.

Setting down the bottle of scotch and the glasses, I look around and offer a smile to the guys, hoping to be able to just turn around and book it back to the bar.

"Thanks," one of the guys says as I pass him his drink. I just smile, too afraid of what might tumble out of my mouth if I open it. I may be displeased to be doing this, but I know better than to piss off the customers.

When I finally make it to the smiley guy's side of the table, he's smirking.

"Thank you, Sawyer," he says with an even larger smile. "Haven't seen you around here much before. Are you new?"

I stare at him, confused as to how he could know my name when I've never met the man, or any of the guys at the table. He must read my expression as he thankfully puts me out of my misery. "Serena told us your name. She said you were making a drink real quick but would be over to serve us when you were done."

That bitch. I inwardly wince, knowing I can't let it show on my face. She set me up. I look behind me, where, no surprise, Molly and Serena are standing at the bar together, watching me with a smile that matches this guy's.

"I'm usually behind the bar," I tell him truthfully, too annoyed to worry about what I should or shouldn't say. "My lovely friend put me up to this." I jab my thumb towards Serena.

"Nice to meet you, Sawyer. I'm Trevor. This is Miles, Harris, and Cade," he says, pointing to the guys on the other side of the booth. "And this here is my buddy, Rex. he's a little rough on the outside, but don't worry, it matches perfectly with his personality." With a point towards Rex, he gives a small wink, obviously enjoying riling his friend up.

With that, his friend looks up from his scotch to glare at him and flip him off, before turning to actually look at me with a weird combination of pure annoyance, covering up a hint of hunger threatening to overtake his eyes.

It's almost frightening. It's like all the light in this entire club is being sucked into the black hole of his eyes. It's electric.

Seeing him up close, he's even more handsome than before, in a more rugged way. His hands on the table are rough, he obviously doesn't get monthly manicures. It looks like he's spent his life using them for something other than just a desk job. I hate that I had that thought, wondering what his hands would feel like sliding over my body.

Even more though, I hate that I like it.

Shaking the thought away, I do my best to look elsewhere, but his face stops me. Yeah, his body might be built like he spends every waking moment working out in the gym. Or that he could use me to do bicep curls and . . . other things, but his face is strikingly attractive.

This man has the brightest blue eyes I've ever seen, they're almost navy. Where most people's eyes reflect the light, his almost suck it into complete darkness. His face is full of sharp lines and hard features, and although his expression is uninviting, I would still take that face for a ride.

As I pass him his drink, he continues to stare at me,

muttering a quiet grunt that I can only assume was meant to be a thank you.

"What's different about tonight if you're usually behind the bar?" Trevor asks, ignoring his brooding friend, who's now turned his glare on him.

"It's not a what, it's a who. It would be the lovely Serena."

"Ooh, the hot one?" their friend Harris pipes in with a grin.

"That would be her." I chuckle. "She's been trying to get me to come join her on this side of the bar. Apparently, she decided to take matters into her own hands. So, I guess you're stuck with me tonight." I laugh, trying to lighten the situation.

I can feel Rex's eyes on me, burning their way through my skin.

Trevor is the friendly one, the one I wish was looking at me like that. It would make this whole situation a lot easier. But no, it's the brooding, grumpy one—the one who looks like half of him wants to yell at me while the other half wants to throw me down on this table and devour me while the whole club watches.

It's confusing as fuck.

Turning towards him, I watch his eyes drift down from my face, slowly taking in my body as he goes. The feel of his eyes on me is almost enough to set me on fire right here. It takes everything in me to look back towards Trevor as he begins to talk, though his eyes are also on Rex, watching him take me in.

"Seems like we are the lucky ones. Besides, we're nice enough, right gentleman?"

The one named Harris chuckles a bit at his statement, not confirming or denying.

"Don't lie to the lady. Not a single one of you fools are a gentleman," Rex grumbles.

"Well, what about you?" I ask, staring directly at Rex.

"What about me?" he asks, looking confused, while Trevor grins.

I feel like his face should hurt at the end of the day from smiling so much. It can't be good for his health to be that happy.

"Are you a gentleman?"

My comment must surprise him almost as much as it does me. Apparently, I'm slightly willing to play the part tonight, even if it's just to fuck around with the grumpy jerk.

I'm not a huge fan of everyone's attention on me, but I guess one night can't hurt. Besides, there's pretty much no chance I'll see these guys again.

It may be terrifying and way out of my comfort zone, but it's nice to be able to pretend tonight. A part of me secretly loves being able to shock a man this damn hot. I glance at Trevor and the other guys as they watch Rex, waiting on his reaction.

"When I need to be," he says, before he finishes his drink.

I feel my cheeks flush instantly at what he's insinuating. My slutty brain is having a field day with all the images that comment puts in my head. Trevor must notice because I see him holding his drink up, trying to hide a laugh.

"Sawyer, would you grab us a round of Tequila? Top shelf, your pick," Trevor says with a smile. "Six shots, please."

"Let's make it two rounds," Rex adds.

Snapping back to the conversation, I realize they're talking to me.

"Of course, I'll be right back with that," I say before walking away.

When I get back to the bar, both Molly and Serena are smiling like proud mama bears, making me want to throat punch them for putting me through this.

"How'd it go?" Molly asks with a knowing grin.

"Hey, she didn't run away screaming or crying or try to hit me yet, so it couldn't have gone that bad," Serena says, barely avoiding Molly's attempt at elbowing her.

"Leave her alone. Besides, this is all your fault. I'm not paying L&I when she hits you at work." Molly winks at me before going back to making drinks. Looking at Serena, it's hard to stay mad at her or not laugh at her expression. She looks ready to explode with impatience, but she's smart enough not to push her luck.

She may drive me crazy, but I love her. Doesn't mean I won't actually throat punch her, but I'd do it with love.

"Sooo, how'd it go? Tell me everything," she finally says when she's about ready to explode.

"It was fine. They were all nice. The grumpy one was even kind of funny, in a dry sort of way."

"What'd they say? Did they ask for anything? I'm sorry if I pushed too far."

"They just asked for another round. Other than that, they talked to me. I think they could tell I was a little out of place."

"You say that like it's a bad thing. They have it in their minds now that if you come back to their table, they get to break you in. You know, be your first table. Show you the ropes. If you know what I mean," Serena says with a wink.

"Honestly, it's not a horrible thing in this line of work," she continues. "What can you really do wrong? It's not like you're flipping around on a pole. You're serving a table.

Worst thing that could happen is they ask you to join them in a room; easiest thing, they ask for a lap dance."

"How the hell is that the easiest thing?"

"This isn't a normal strip club, you know that. Every member is vetted. You're not going to get some perv. If they're here, they understand consent," Molly says with a smile, like that answers everything.

"I'm still not quite following you."

"They can be a little more hands on—not groping you or anything, at least not out here—but they can guide you, which makes it a little less intimidating," she says with a shrug before walking off to help a group of girls who just sat down at the bar.

"Look, I'm serious. If you don't want to do this, just tell me, but I know you've got this. And, I think you'll enjoy it," Serena says, sincerity all over her face. "But I'm telling you, men love being able to dirty something up, and with this being your first time? Who better than that group to serve?" She says with a wink.

"I'll try to play the game, but just for tonight. One table. I'll finish them up, but that's it. We can, like, debrief or whatever tomorrow, and I can tell you how much I hated it, okay?" I tell her.

"Deal."

"Promise?"

"I promise," she singsongs.

I go about grabbing the tequila shots Molly just poured while telling Serena more about the interaction, hating the smirk on her face when I get to the part about Rex.

"Okay, I know you're totally not this girl, but that grumpy one is super-hot. Plus, they're usually more fun in bed, all bossy and grumbly, throwing us around a bit. You should play it up a bit with him. Give him a little more attention than the others and see what he does," Serena says.

"I'm not even remotely interested in flirting with a guy," I tell her.

"You haven't dated in how long? And don't even try to tell me six months ago when you 'dated' Brandon. You two were study buddies who hooked up once after the semester ended. It's time for you to at least *flirt* with a guy, maybe hop on for a little ride."

"Shut up, Serena. It's not Brandon, its—"

"Oh, we all know exactly who caused your fear of attachment, your dickhead brother of course," Serena cuts me off. "He scared you away from getting close to anyone for fear of them controlling you. He tried to change you into something you didn't want to be. I know it's hard to trust anyone after your own family lets you down, but this isn't a relationship. It's just one night, hell not even that if he's like most men."

Tears hit my eyes at her impression of my relationship with my family. She knows most of it, minus a few bits and pieces, so it doesn't surprise me that she considers Max a dickhead.

"We aren't doing this tonight. If you want me to go over there, we're not talking about this. And I'm drinking, so give me a fucking shot before Molly comes back," I demand.

"You don't need to hide it from Molly. The guys ordered you two shots to take with them as well, and she poured them." She smiles before looking over my shoulder with a smirk.

"Your man is staring at you," Serena whispers conspiratorially.

Glancing back at the table, I see Rex staring directly at me as Trevor whispers something in his ear. As he notices me looking, he pauses before glancing back at Trevor and finishing their conversation.

"I don't have a man."

"No, no you don't. But I'd be fucking shocked if he didn't throw a punch or two if one of them tried to dance with you tonight. He's done all but pee on you to mark his territory with his broody looks."

"I haven't flirted with someone in months, and even then, Brandon didn't really count; he never really flirted or tried with me. It's been years, Serena, years! Flirting is not my thing."

"Well, let's make it your thing. Brush his arm a couple times, smile at him, lean over him when you're passing the others their drinks. That kind of shit. If he's as interested in you as I think he is, he'll be all over that. Even his friends have noticed him watching you. Just go have fun."

"I feel like you're sending me off into battle."

"Well, then, off to battle you go. But first, here's a shot of tequila. This one's on me." With a wink, she hands me a shot before she swats my butt, signaling I need to stop wasting time.

I've gotten used to walking in the heels they have the ladies wear here, but regardless, it's terrifying watching the shots almost spill over with every step I take.

I chose to blame the heels and not the nerves for my shaky legs the closer I get to their table.

When I reach them, they're still having random conversations with each other, not immediately noticing my return. I quickly set down their drinks, placing the extra two in the middle, before smiling and trying to turn around. But before I even think about walking away, Trevor says my name.

"Sawyer, wait. Where do you think you're going? These two shots are for you, have a seat."

"I, uh, can't."

"Here, sweetheart? At this table? I promise you can," he says with a smile I can't help but trust.

Out of the corner of my eye, I don't miss Rex's glare towards Trevor. Was it because he invited me to sit down? Or . . . that he called me sweetheart?

Shaking the thought out of my head, I set down the tray and casually lean over Rex to hand Harris and Trevor their shots, before finally setting Rex's drink down a little closer to me than necessary. Trevor must notice what I'm doing, as he smiles, a hint of entertainment glowing in his eyes.

Rex, on the other hand, doesn't say much—just a quick thank you before looking down at the shots in front of him. I just shrug it off before looking back at Trevor, who couldn't hide his devious grin if he tried.

"Have a seat, get comfortable," he says, before noticing that the others are in a full-on debate about why the New York Cyclones are the best team in the NHL. Harris seems to be poking fun at them with his rebuttals, that are obviously just to rile the others up. "Well, at least talk to us," he says, pointing at himself and Rex.

I look back to where Molly is talking to Serena. She must notice me because she smiles and nods.

"I can stay for a bit," I grab the only seat left, which is, of course, next to Rex's chair.

"Tell me something about yourself. What's something you like to do?"

"I uh . . ." I pause, thinking. This is hard for me to answer. I want to teach dance. I love dance, but after I tore my Achilles in high school, I knew I couldn't go professional.

Because of all that, I usually don't talk about it, as it brings up longer conversations that just fucking hurt. It's then I notice Rex's eyes on me, listening intently for my answer. "I love to dance. Not like the stuff here, but I used to do ballet."

I look back at Trevor, waiting for his response. He smiles but doesn't say anything.

"Why'd you quit?"

I look toward the other end of the table to see who asked but am surprised when I realize it was Rex.

"I got injured. Pretty badly," I answer. "It ended any chance of me going professional."

"What happened?" Rex asks, surprising me again with his curiosity. He has a look in his eye I can't quite discern, but I can tell he's interested in hearing my answer.

"I tore my Achilles the week before a performance, which happened to be tryouts for Juilliard. After that, I had surgery, but never quite got my full range of motion back. I can still dance, but not like I used to."

"Oh."

That's all he says. "Oh." Like I didn't just pour out my sob story to him. What a prick.

Trevor acts surprisingly quick, picking up on the tension building between us.

"Harris, don't I still owe you a birthday present?" he shouts down to the table.

"Yeah, we were supposed to go to Hawaii."

"Well, here, I'll buy you your first dance tonight. Miss Sawyer is going to help us out," Trevor says with a smile.

Harris looks alarmed for a moment, watching Rex, but he must see Trevor's smirk because he goes along with it.

"I get to take Miss Sawyer's lap dance virginity?" Harris asks with a smile. "Come over here then. Come to daddy."

The little shit has the audacity to wink directly at Rex.

Rex looks like he's about to throttle one of them. His knuckles are white from how tight he's gripping his glass.

Realizing he's not going to say anything, I start to walk towards Harris, who looks just as confused by Rex's reaction as I am. It's obvious he is somewhat interested, but not enough to follow through.

"Stop," he growls, with more passion than I've heard from him so far.

I freeze. Refusing to move, to blink, to even breathe. In fact, I don't think any of us are breathing right now.

"Come here. Now."

I'm not sure who invaded my body, or when I started listening to commands, but my body obeys that man like I'm in the military. Before I know it, I'm standing in front of him, his legs spread out, but not enough that I can't straddle him.

"Come. Closer," he growls, gesturing for me to get on top of him.

I have no idea what I'm doing as my legs straddle his, and he must notice this because he whispers something only I can hear.

"Closer," he says gruffly, like he hasn't used his voice all day.

Pulling me towards him, he leans in closely before whispering in my ear again, "I know this is your first time, so there is no way I am letting Dirty fucking Harry get ahold of you. Now, I'm going to touch you, as long as you're okay with that?"

Too nervous to respond with words, I nod my head yes.

"Use your words, baby girl."

"Yes," I respond, shocked by how breathless I sound.

Something well past excitement flashes in his eyes, but again, I can't decipher it. It's fleeting, hidden under his broody, prickly exterior, but there's a heat in his eyes. It's like he wants this. Wants me.

Without another word, Rex moves his hands from his side up to my legs, slowly gliding along my skin until he reaches my hips. Every place his fingers touch is on fire, like electricity is flowing between us.

Swallowing roughly, I look down to where he's gripping my hips, his knuckles white from his intense hold. If I didn't know any better, I would say he's close to losing control, but what he'll do next is still a mystery.

"Sit."

"But," I start trying to explain how this is a horrible idea, but his demands leave very little room for debate. If I sit on his lap, there's no chance he's not going to feel how turned on I am or that I won't feel his arousal.

"Sit. Now," he demands in my ear, before using his grip to help lower me.

I slowly lower myself even further, getting more nervous as his hands continue to grip my hips firmly. There's a bite to his grip, like he's holding on to his own control through my body.

When he begins to move me, everyone else fades away. I'm not sure if it's nerves, embarrassment, or the fact that he's rubbing his hard cock against my cunt, but I wouldn't be able to tell someone my own last name right now.

I hate that I'm enjoying this. I'm confused that he obviously is too when everything about him screams disdain.

Leaning forward, he brushes my hair back softly whispering in my ear, surprising me with his kind words for the first time.

"Are you uncomfortable?"

"No," I say, as I finally lower myself onto his lap, secretly loving the way his grip tightens as I press further down, grazing over his hardened cock.

It's obvious I didn't want to be serving their table, and if I can read anything, I could immediately tell he wasn't thrilled to be here either. Somehow, it's working though if the arousal I'm feeling is any sign. Leaning forward, my boobs graze his chest, putting them directly in his line of sight.

His eyes might be glaring, but his lips turn up on one side like he's trying to stop a smile.

"If you keep putting your tits in my face, baby girl, I'm going to lay you down on this table and make you scream for the entire club," Rex growls in my ear, causing a shot of arousal to shoot straight to my core.

The thought of him making me scream loud enough for the entire club to hear is enough to make me want to shove his face in my tits even more. But the fear of it actually happening causes me to pull back, only slightly though.

His smile has grown wider though, almost like he can hear my dirty and depraved thoughts. Maybe, just maybe, they mirror his own depraved thoughts.

Everywhere we are touching feels intense, almost intoxicating. His hands on my side are controlling my movements, grinding my body along his cock. His eyes flare, barely holding onto their blue color amidst the dark fire within. He's enjoying this more than either of us thought he would.

But so am I, and that is fucking terrifying.

Right now, none of that matters and we're just here. In this weird moment. Inside this bubble, where only the two of us exist.

That's not something I'm used to.

That's not something I'm used to liking either.

The rest of the dance is over far too quickly. Whether or

not it was actually quick, I have no idea as I was too focused on his hungry gaze.

It's his eyes that hold my stare, and the feeling that his eyes are perfect mirrors of my own that slightly scares me.

He wants this. He wants me.

Standing up, I smile at him before turning to walk away.

Tonight has been all over the place, one emotion after another, and I'm not quite sure what to do now. Do I get a drink? Smoke a cigarette? Go back to work? I don't have the slightest clue, so I sneak past the bar before the girls can see me. I rush through the crowd, determined to make it to the bathroom to touch up my makeup.

Before I even make it down the hall, I feel a hand on mine, yanking me back between a body and the wall.

"You made quite the impression back there, Sawyer," a gruff voice whispers into my ear.

I'm thankful it's Rex and not some rando pinning me against the wall because, duh, safety and all; but I'm also not so sure just how safe I am around him right now.

"You say that like it's a bad thing."

He lets an unmistakable growl out as he cages me in against the wall with his hips pushed against me, leaving no question just how turned on he is.

"I'm still not so sure it's not a bad thing," Rex responds as he slowly brings his lips down against my neck, causing me to lean into him further. Right as he begins kissing down my neck, the lounge door swings open and Serena walks through.

"Uh, shit. Sorry, I uh, I was looking for you. Just wanted to make sure—never mind. I'll see you back out there."

I can only imagine what this looks like, or if we look like as disheveled as I feel.

Rex pulls back slowly, our little bubble of lust popping

as quickly as it came. "I got carried away, I'm sorry. Forget everything that happened."

"Nothing to be sorry about, just the heat of the moment. Guess it means I did my job right."

"Right," he responds, running a hand through his hair. "Your job. Yup, great fucking job, Sawyer."

With that, he turns on his heels, leaving me wondering what the hell I did wrong and why I'm disappointed we got interrupted.

3

___

REX

"How much longer till we get home, Daddy? I'm tired," Rory says from her spot on my shoulders. Apparently, after being on a plane for the first time ever, she's decided she likes to be up high. So, according to her, if she can't be on a plane, my shoulders are the next best thing. I guess that's not surprising, because at 6'2", I'm not exactly low to the ground by her standards.

I don't mind though. I'd carry this little girl to the edge of the world if she asked. I knew this move was going to be a bit scary for her, as she's only ever known Austin as home. Thankfully, my parents are already here, which makes this transition a little easier.

"Not much longer, sweetie. Grandma and Auntie Lala are meeting us there. It's right around the corner."

I parked near the bakery my sister owns instead of the apartment because I wanted to get one of their bagels. It may be six at night, but I haven't had a good bagel in what feels like fucking forever. In hindsight, it might not have been the best decision in the world to move right across the street from my favorite bakery.

Resisting temptation isn't exactly my strong suit.

Ever since that night at Atlantis, my mind keeps drifting back to Sawyer. There's something so different about her, and I hadn't expected it.

People who work at the strip club usually fit into one of two categories. One, they like the money and the lifestyle it provides. Or two, they need the money because they're struggling to make ends meet. But with Sawyer? It didn't seem like she fit into either of those categories, and I'm not used to things feeling so messy. I don't understand her, but I want to. No, I need to understand her.

My need to figure her out has her constantly on my mind. It doesn't matter what I'm doing or who I'm with, my mind always goes back to that night.

It's unnerving. I don't like it. Yet, it's hard not to imagine her tight body in that red lace bra, grinding her little pussy in my lap.

My mind hasn't been like this since before my injury. Before Rory came into my life. I haven't let myself get close to a woman, emotionally that is, since I found out about Rory. Too scared of what damage I might do.

But that night was the closest I've been to snapping and taking a woman to my place. I've been with a few women since Rory was born, but nothing serious and nothing that included bringing them home. It's always quick, dirty, and straight to the point, whether in a bar bathroom, the back seat as our driver drops her off at home, or sometimes, at the woman's house. Those types of places were safe, no chance of someone finding out I have a daughter or of Rory finding out about any of the women.

But I wanted to that night.

So badly that I was angry with her for making me feel like this.

I wanted to bring her back to my place, lay her out on the bed and take my time, really figure her out.

What makes her tick.

What makes her burn.

What makes her explode.

It doesn't feel right to bring a new woman into my home knowing she'll be leaving in the morning. There may still be boxes everywhere with nothing unpacked yet, but it's still going to be my daughters house, a place she should always feel safe.

But I almost broke that safety. Had Sawyer stayed any longer, even just a moment, I would have been thinking with my larger, dumber head.

I don't even know what it was. Something about her had me transfixed, to where I couldn't look away. Her eyes had me under a spell, their deep, almost turquoise color sparking under the lights.

I knew at that moment that she was putting on an act, trying to "seduce me."

But that wasn't what I liked. Under her brash exterior, there was a hint of vulnerability and trust. She was letting me see something she hid from the others. She may have acted like she was in control, but she needed my support, my comfort to make it through. She was trusting me not to let her fuck this up.

I loved it. I ate that shit up. I can't remember the last time a woman looked at me like she needed me. Like she really trusted me. Actually, that's a fucking lie. The last time was when Rory's mom showed up at my front door, handing me my daughter for the first time. Before that, it was Emily, when I told her I would come back from Austin after my treatment. Her trust in me died when I texted her, telling her we were over and to lose my number.

She did, but not before telling me how much she hated me for making her wait. All for nothing.

Yeah, even I can admit I was fucking dick for that one.

Finally making our way into our building, I carry Rory onto the elevator.

"Press the top button, sweetie," I tell Rory, as I turn her toward the buttons.

When she doesn't move, I listen quietly, laughing when I realize she's fallen asleep and is snoring up there, leaning on my head.

As I press the button, I can't help but think it's hard to believe we're here. Things are slowly starting to build their way back up, and Rory is going to get to grow up in New York City, something I loved when I was younger. She's going to get to grow up with her whole family around her. She'll be in a great daycare, and I finally have a job that I'm excited about again.

As I get off the elevator, I immediately smell freshly baked cookies, so delicious that I almost walk right into my sister.

"Hey, big bro, welcome home!" Stella says with a smile, quickly quieting down when she realizes that Rory is asleep on my shoulders. "How long has she been sleeping?"

"Just since we got here. One moment she was talking, the next she was asleep."

"It was a long trip for her, she's probably exhausted. Her room is all ready. Want to go put her down?"

"Yeah, I'll be right back."

Heading over to Rory's room, I have to smile at the little touches my mom and sister must have done this morning before I got here. There are family pictures hung up, more of the boxes are emptied, and it looks like they might have gone a little crazy with the purple things.

There's a purple rug, purple bedding, purple curtains, and a bunch of different purple things hung up on the wall. How much purple can one room handle? Stella must've had a heyday with this. My mom and sister spoil Rory rotten.

She looks so little as I lay her in her bed. Back in Austin, she slept in her crib with the side off. With the move and all the changes that we were already making, I figured it would be best to just transition her to a twin bed. Hopefully, when she wakes up in the middle of the night, I still agree with that statement.

By the time I make it back out to the kitchen, Stella has the cookies out of the oven and everything cleaned up again. She may be a pain in my ass, but she's a thoughtful one. Plus, she bakes really well. Might have to start getting up even earlier to get more gym time now that we live in the same state.

"Did she go down okay?" Stella asks as I sit down at the table with her.

"Yeah, she didn't even stir. It was a long trip for her and messed with her nap time, so I think she was just ready to go to bed. Honestly, even I'm exhausted. Trevor and Cade were going to stop by, but I think I'm going to reschedule. I'm so beat."

"Not a bad idea. I mean, you only have tomorrow before you start work again, and Rory going to preschool. Maybe one night after work we can all grab drinks, catch up. I miss those lovable idiots."

"Deal."

Stella stands, her way of saying it's time to go, which secretly I'm thankful for because I'm ready to lay down and fall asleep. I'm crashing on the couch tonight, so I'm even closer to Rory in case she wakes up in the middle of the night. Don't need her first night in a new bed and a new house to be something she's never seen before and to not know where to find me.

Shit. Maybe it wasn't the smartest thing in the world to change her bed too.

"I'm going to head out, let you guys get some rest," Stella says, leaning in to give me a hug. "It's nice having you back in the city."

"It's nice to be home. I'll see you soon, okay?"

"Yep. What day did you need me to pick up Rory from daycare?"

"Thursday. We have a late game that day, but they aren't starting their night classes for one more week. Is that fine?"

"Not a problem, we'll just head back here and watch trashy tv."

With a wink, she slips past me and heads out the door.

My sister is going to be the reason I get gray hair long before Rory is. She's a handful and a half, and I pity the guy who decides to put up with her craziness. Walking over to the fridge, I'm thankful to see that they stocked up my beer; my dad must've been with them.

I didn't have many guilty pleasures back when I played hockey professionally, but sour candy and beer were the ones I could never give up. Grabbing a beer, I head over to the couch and turn on hockey. It'll put my mind at ease and probably help me fall asleep faster.

~

Sunday goes by quicker than I would have liked. After I woke up with a full beer still sitting next to me and the sun shining through the window, Rory and I got up and made breakfast together. We're meeting my parents near Central Park for dinner so they can see each other before she starts daycare on Monday. To say I'm a little nervous is the understatement of the year.

When we were still in Texas, I wasn't working much, so I spent most of my time with Rory between trying different therapies on my injury. If I did need to be away from Rory, it was usually my parents who would watch her. My parents absolutely adore my little girl and spoil her at every opportunity they get.

It surprised me a bit to see my dad act this way. Growing up, my sister and I were always spoiled a bit by our mom, while my dad was more of the disciplinarian. I expected it to be somewhat of the same thing, my mom being very hands-on and my dad in the background.

Boy, I was wrong.

My father dotes on my little girl like she's everything he was missing in this world. She has him so wrapped around her tiny little finger, and I love watching him turn to mush for her, even if that means she's even more spoiled than I want.

Starting tomorrow, Rory is going to a new daycare, except when I have away or late-night games, then my parents or Stella will watch her, which is a relief even if I know it might be a little challenging for them sometimes. Now that my parents are back in New York, my mom is starting up her fundraisers for the arts again, while my dad un-retired and has gone back to work in the corporate world. Having a three-year-old in that house might be a little different than when they were both retired in Texas.

But we'll figure it out.

We *always* do.

he first week of practice has gone just as I expected it to. On one hand, some of the players were difficult because they were pissed their old coach retired or they were annoyed that they didn't get a more experienced coach. I may have thirty years of hockey experience, ten of which were in the NHL, but to them, they just see that I've never coached before. On the other hand though, some of the players knew about my time here with the hockey team as well as in the NHL, so they were excited. It helped that one of the captains of their team, Max, was stoked to have me here.

Max and I were able to meet on Monday before I met with the rest of the team, so he got an understanding of what some of my goals for the team are and how I'm going to get us there. Last year, they didn't have the best season, winning less than half of their games. They had great players and great skills, but they weren't working together. With a few minor changes and some switches to which players are on the ice together, I think we have a lot of promise for the post-season. After I told Max all of this, he was honest with his thoughts, and told me that some of the players were going to take issue with these changes, but he agreed that it could work.

By Friday, I'm exhausted from running drills, getting ready for games next week, and figuring out Rory's daycare schedule. Never have I truly felt like a single parent doing everything on my own. In Texas, my parents helped whenever I needed them to. When Trevor texted me, saying he and the guys were going to some small bar tonight, I texted my sister, asking if she wanted to come have another sleepover with Rory. After their last one, Rory was so happy that she didn't stop talking about her Auntie Lala for days.

Getting out with the guys and having a few beers will hopefully help take the stress of this week away a bit. If not, I'll just laugh at my friends because when you put them in a room with some alcohol they become total idiots.

45

4

SAWYER

This has been the absolute longest week of my life, and I want nothing more than to crash on my couch with a bottle of wine and watch shitty TV. Unfortunately, I promised my friends that I would meet them at the bar down the street. Even worse, one of them is my roommate, so there's really no way out of it without absolute bloodshed.

When I reach my apartment door, before I can even unlock it, it swings open. No surprise, it's Cassie standing there with a glass of wine and a smirk that tells me this isn't her first glass of the evening.

"You're late, bitch," she snaps playfully. "Go grab yourself a glass and come sit on the patio. I already have the wine."

"You're bossy today."

"You say that like today is any different than yesterday. I'm bossy. It is what it is." She shrugs and walks out to the patio.

As much as I want to tell her that I'm too tired and just want to sleep, I'm pretty sure she'd kill me if I left her alone tonight. Heading to the kitchen, I set down my things before grabbing a glass. Before I even make it to the patio, Cassie starts telling me the day's gossip.

"So, you'll never guess who I ran into on campus today."

"Oh, please don't tell me you ran into the whiskey guy again. I can't use that kind of bad luck. We're trying to have a fun night."

"Ew, why did you have to remind me of him? I could have gone the rest of my life without thinking about that night."

That night will go down in history as the worst night either of us had in college. A guy was flirting with both of us and thought he would impress us by chugging a bottle of whiskey and eating three of those gas station nachos. We ended up having to clean it out of her car, and it reeked for weeks.

The worst part was that he still tried to kiss her after vomiting all over her car.

Nacho cheese and whiskey is not a sexy smell.

"So, who did you see?

"Max. He came over to the science building to talk. Mentioned that he had been trying to get ahold of you."

It's been almost a year since I refused to let Max control my life any longer. A year since he convinced my mom that I was being reckless by trying to open my own dance studio in New York. He told me that if I didn't get a safe degree, which he believed to be either teaching or medical for some odd reason, that I was just wasting my time and my mom's money. So, he convinced her to stop paying for my school and then got all distant. After that, things haven't been the same between him and I.

"Next subject," I say, walking out onto the patio and filling my wine glass. Full to the brim.

"You might be able to get away doing that with Melissa, but not with me. What's going on?"

"Max has been blowing up my phone lately, trying to get me to go visit my mom. He basically wants me to forget about everything that happened, yet he's not willing to make any changes to his controlling bullshit. Plus, my mom's still acting like a doormat and letting him make all the choices for her. He still has her convinced that I'm ruining my life and making one bad decision after another, at least that's what she tells me."

Max is frustrating, not because he doesn't care, but because he doesn't know how to show it. He thinks making sure I do things the way he wants me to is showing his love, when in reality I'm following my dreams, and he should be proud.

"So, what'd you say?"

"Nothing. I've ignored him." I shrug, walking to the balcony.

We live in one of my favorite parts of New York. I love our view of Central Park and getting to go for runs around there. Especially since there is a little food cart tucked away, where only locals can find it. They make homemade ice cream and have fresh waffle cones. It's my favorite part about our morning runs—we always finish with ice cream.

Don't judge me. They have coffee ice cream.

At night though, the views are even prettier. There are lights up all around the park, and you can see the skyline. Cassie and I frequently come out here and have a bottle of wine, whether it's to relax or to vent. It's our favorite spot.

Which is probably why she's out here if we're talking about this tonight. Soften the blow.

"Honestly, I hate to say this because I know your brother cares in his own fucked up way, but good for you. Your brother is a prick. A controlling prick, and he needs to be knocked down a peg. Or ten," Cassie says, before clinking her glass with mine.

"I know he is, and I know he needs to hear that. But it still fucking sucks that he doesn't trust me to make my own choices."

"I know. I really do. Want me to kick him in the dick for you?" she deadpans.

I can't help but laugh. This bitch is crazy enough to do it.

"No, but can we change the subject? Have you heard from the girls?"

"Yeah, Melissa said she was still going to meet that guy from the cringe app or whatever it is she's been on. Apparently, after the last guy, she wants to have an escape plan just in case. So she wants us to be at the bar in like an hour, just in case."

Our friend Melissa has been on a dating app kick these past couple of weeks. But ever since one of the guys turned out to be a total weirdo and asked if he could smell her deodorant, she's been sort of creeped out.

"Yeah, I guess that makes sense. Probably not the worst idea. But I refuse to change; what you see is what you get tonight. Honestly, I don't give a shit tonight."

Cassie stands up and makes a show of looking me up and down slowly, like she's checking me out for the first time. She just stands there, smirking and gesturing for me to spin around, which, surprisingly, I do for her.

"I'd still do you," she says before walking towards the door inside with her glass of wine. "Now let's head to the bar early. I want a shot and to kick your ass at pool."

"Yeah, you wish."

Looking down, I'm glad I'm at least wearing one of my cuter outfits, with a black tee and matching beanie and my favorite jeans that are just a tad too tight and ripped to be considered appropriate for everyday wear. My worn-out black Converse have seen better days, but they're comfy and good for walking around campus, so they'll work for the bar we're going to tonight.

Guess it's time to go scope out the new weirdo Melissa found this time.

~

Once we get to the bar, Cassie and I immediately grab a shot and head to the pool table to wait for everyone else. By the time Melissa shows up for her date, I've already kicked Cassie's ass at pool three times, each time sending her to buy us another round of shots. When Gwen showed up, she decided to play some music but ends up in a jukebox battle with a guy determined to hear only country music. Gwen, on the other hand, hates country music and only wants to hear alternative rock, so when he put on "Achy Breaky Heart," she shrieked and ran back to get more quarters.

"Want to play another round? Except this time, the winner buys some greasy food. At the rate we're taking these shots, we'll be asleep by ten," I say as Cassie keep her eye on Melissa with her date. At least this one is going better, she seems like she's actually enjoying herself.

"Where's Gwen? Have her play this round. I'm heading to the bathroom. But I'll order some fries and get us another round of drinks for when we play again."

"She's still over at the jukebox, trying to cancel out all the Garth Brooks and Carrie Underwood that dude keeps playing. I'll wait for her here though, it's entertaining to watch. When you grab that stuff, would you order some nachos, too? Pleaseee," I whine.

"Yeah, I guess. Needy bitch," she grumbles, walking away.

"Yeah, well...we both know you were going to lose the next round anyway."

After Cassie leaves to the bathroom, I stand against the pool table and people watch, which happens to be my favorite thing ever. Growing up, Max and I used to do this whenever we were out in public. We would try to make up people's life stories and decide what job we thought fit them. Max always came up with these ridiculous stories and random ass jobs that would have us cracking up. I think he did it on purpose just to make me laugh.

I can't help the moment of sadness that comes from remembering the good times with my brother. I miss them, and I just wish he was more like that now. I wish he didn't feel the burden of my dad leaving, but I guess you can't change the past.

Scrunching my face up, I push down the feelings and get back to looking around the bar. There's a guy by the bar who is covered in oil and grease and has dirty hands. Making me believe he's probably a mechanic or works on some type of equipment. There's another lady who brought her briefcase with her and is dressed in a pantsuit, probably a lawyer or a business-woman. Although if Max were here, he'd say she's an undercover prostitute and her briefcase is filled with various levels of weird ass sex toys—but that's Max for ya.

I'm so lost in people-watching that I don't notice the guy heading in my direction until he's standing right in front of me. He's got a flirtatious, sexy smile that I have no doubt gets all the girls' panties wet, but not mine. I can't place him, but I feel like I know him from somewhere.

"Hey," he starts, but immediately pauses when a look of recognition crosses his face. "Wait, don't I know you from somewhere?"

"I'm not sure. What's your name?" I ask, trying to figure out where I've seen him before. He looks too old for it to be from campus, but I can't quite tell.

"Harris."

"Sounds familiar, but I'm still not sure. I'm Sawyer," I say, reaching my hand out to shake his as a couple more guys head our way with drinks in hand.

"Harris, what are you doing over here bothering the lady. Let her play pool in peace," a happy voice comes from behind us. Why does that sound familiar too?

I turn around and it's Trevor from the other night at Atlantis. Looking back at Harris, I realize that's why I recognize him. He must realize it out too because he's smiling so big it probably hurts. He's also looking at me like he knows something I don't, and it's terrifying.

Turning back, I smile at him. "Hey, it's Trevor, right?" I ask as he leans in to give me a side hug.

"Yeah, good memory. How are you?"

"I'm good. We were actually just trying to figure out how we recognized each other, but you just helped us solve that mystery." I laugh before turning back to Harris. "And by the look on your face, you remember too?"

"Oh, I remember," he says with a wink and a mischievous grin.

Harris, Miles, and Trevor are all here, but I don't see Rex or their other friend who I can't remember the name of.

"So, Sawyer, up for a round of pool? Or are you waiting on someone?" Harris asks, looking around the bar.

"I'm in, I was just waiting for my friend Gwen, but she's still over by the jukebox, and I don't see her leaving anytime soon. Go easy on me though, I'm a sore loser." I laugh, it's unfortunately true. "Is it just you and I, or are we going to play teams?"

As I finish asking my question, I glance at Trevor, who's looking over my shoulder intently.

"Teams. Harris, get your own partner," a gruff voice from behind me says. I would recognize that intense, raspy voice anywhere. It's been the voice whispering dirty words in my dreams nearly every night since I first heard it at Atlantis.

Rex.

I spin towards him, surprising myself with just how quickly I move, almost knocking the drink out of Trevor's hand, but he just laughs. It's nearly impossible not to smile at seeing him again, especially when he looks this fucking hot. He may still have on his grumpy face, looking like he hates the world, but hot damn, the man rocks a pair of jeans so fucking well.

It's not often that you see a man look this hot in a pair of Vans, dark jeans, and a black t-shirt that fits like a glove. He looks damn good tonight with his muscles on display making me question if he ever leaves the gym.

Fuck. This is Rex.

The same man I gave a lap dance to a few weeks ago.

Now he's here, in front of me, showing off all his delicious muscles that were hidden underneath his jacket the last time I saw him.

Fuck me.

I bet Rex is the kind of man who could lift you up, slam you against the wall, and have his way with you. He's probably the kind of guy who takes control. The kind of guy that does more showing than telling, and I fucking love the image that makes in my head. It's so fucking hot imagining him manhandling me. Tossing me around with ease.

I must have been staring at Rex without saying anything for a while, because I hear chuckling behind me. Obviously, Trevor finds this amusing.

"Hi," is all I manage to muster out to Rex as he stands next to me holding a cue.

"Hello, Sawyer," Rex says. "Are you breaking, or am I?"

Harris and Trevor are setting up the table, while Rex and I are off to the side talking.

"I'll break," I say without hesitation. "Wouldn't want you to fuck it up."

He stands there with his hip leaning against the table and his ankles crossed, just watching me with an eyebrow raised. He probably thinks I'm just bullshitting him and have no idea what I'm talking about.

"After you, then. Don't fuck it up."

"How about you worry about your own shots instead of mine," I respond with a wink.

Stepping up to the table, I see that Cassie is back, chatting with Rex's friends, while Gwen is still fighting over the damn jukebox. She must have lost this round because an old Alan Jackson song starts playing.

"What is this shit they're playing on the radio?" Rex groans.

"That would be *Alan Jackson*. The guy over there at that table in the back keeps playing country, while Gwen has tried to line it up so that all we hear is *AC/DC*, *Zeppelin*, or *Def Leppard*. Seems she lost this round. Must've been out of dollars."

"Fuck this," Rex says before pulling his wallet out. "Tell her to come back over here and get this. Buy out the rest of the night. I can't listen to this bullshit any longer."

Looking down at the table, Rex lays a $100 bill down, which I just stare at.

"I'm serious, go get her."

"I'll go give this to her, then maybe she'll actually come back over here instead of awkwardly flirting with the bad music guy," Cassie says from across the table next to Miles.

All I can do is stare at Rex. There's something about him I can't quite decipher. He's grumpy, for sure, but I get the feeling that's not all. It feels like it's a façade, something for people to see on the outside, not allowing people to truly understand or get close to him.

It's intriguing.

Snapping back to reality, I realize everyone is still waiting for me to break. Lining up my shot, I hit the cue ball, causing the balls to scatter. Three balls go into the pockets, each of them striped. Looking up at Rex, I see he's watching me. There's a glimmer of something in his eyes, but I can't quite figure it out.

"Damn, girl. I guess I should have asked you to go easy on me," Harris says from across the table.

"Guess you're solids," I tell Rex.

"You guys let her break? Dumbasses. I've already lost three games against her. Had to buy a round each time. At this rate, I'll be broke by the end of the night, so I guess I should be thanking you for giving my wallet a break," Cassie says, chuckling as she comes back from the jukebox.

"I never said if I was good or bad," I respond with a shrug. "You just assume because I am a chick that y'all would win. A little sexist if you ask me."

With a wink, I walk back over to Rex.

"So, did I fuck it up?"

"Not yet. The games not over though."

If I didn't know any better, I would say there's a hint of

amusement in his voice, but it's covered up by his bad attitude.

I'm not sure how to break him out of his shell or why I feel like it's my right to do so. But fuck, I want to know what he has hidden underneath the armor he shows the world. And maybe a little of what he's hiding beneath his clothes . . .

Harris makes a shot before missing the next one, meaning it's Rex's turn. I knew from the level of confidence he had when talking to me that he knows what he's doing, but I didn't expect him to be this good. In two shots, Rex is able to knock three more balls into the pockets before missing on his next shot.

"You guys are no fun to play with," Trevor says, faking a whine.

"I didn't decide the teams, he did," I say, pointing at Rex, who just shrugs.

"Not my fault you suck at this. Maybe if you spent less time flirting and more time focusing on the game, you might figure out how to make a decent shot."

"But flirting means I actually get laid, so maybe you should give it a try sometime," Trevor counters.

"Fuck off and take your shot," Rex grumbles.

Trevor shoots and misses—no surprise to Rex—and it's my turn again. We each take turns, going back and forth a few times, with each shot getting a little trickier every time. With so few of our balls and so many of theirs, it becomes more and more challenging to make our shots. After two more turns, we are down to just the eight ball, and it's my turn.

Looking at the table, three of their balls are still on the table, each sitting in front of a pocket like they're guarding it from our shot, which they are. Making all our shots that much harder.

But that's not my style. I don't like to make everything easy on myself. I love the hard work. I walk around the table once, looking at all my possible shots, before deciding.

The eight ball is at one end of the table, while the cue ball is at the other end. Of course, their balls are in front of the pockets near the black ball, meaning I need to hit it hard enough to bring it back to this end of the table.

Difficult? Yes.

Impossible? Absolutely not.

"Bottom left pocket," I say, gesturing to the pocket I plan to hit it into.

"Seriously? You expect us to believe you're going to hit the cue ball from down here, hit the eight ball, and magically angle it enough to go into that pocket." Trevor snickers.

Harris has to chime in of course, giving us his two cents, "You forgot to mention that she somehow won't hit our balls in. Or scratch."

"Shut up and let her play. We didn't ask for your commentary," Rex says, still staring at the table, probably trying to figure out how to talk me out of the shot.

Walking over towards Rex, who happens to be standing right where I need to be for the shot, I get ready to aim.

"Good luck," he whispers quietly, almost too quietly for me to hear, telling me the words are for my ears only.

"I don't need luck," I tell him with a wink before leaning forward to aim. I can feel his body just inches away from mine as I lean forward, and my ass goes backwards. If he were just a step closer, my ass would be touching his lap. Out of the corner of my eye, I watch Cassie and Cade talking, both watching us intently.

I hit the cue ball and watch it smash into the eight ball

before perfectly taking the path I described. As the eight ball goes into the pocket, the cue ball stops just short of falling in after it.

"Holy fuck," I hear Trevor say. "Guess this round is on us, Harris."

"No shit. This one's on you. Did you even make a damn ball?" Harris yells back.

"Yup."

"The cue ball doesn't count, asshat."

The two of them walk away towards the bar, continuing to give each other shit as they go.

Turning around, I go to make another smartass remark when I see Rex is watching me. I want to know what he's thinking; crawl inside his mind and decipher what the looks he keeps giving me mean, but with my luck, there would be a fucking obstacle course inside his brain.

"Good game, partner," I tell him with a sweet smile as I slide between him and the table to grab my drink.

"Yeah . . ." he mutters. "Where'd you learn to play pool?"

"An old boyfriend," I joke.

I might just be seeing things, but for a quick moment, I think I see a flash of jealousy. Or maybe it's annoyance at my mention of another man.

"No, I'm just kidding. My brother and I used to play all the time growing up. Our parents had a table in our basement. We used to try to make the most challenging shots for the other person. I always won."

"Interesting. Well, apparently, all the fun paid off. You play really fucking well."

"You're not too bad yourself."

Cassie walks over with a grin.

"You couldn't hold back, could ya? Had to show off a

little bit?" she says to me before turning to Rex. "I'm Cassie, this showoff's best friend."

"Nice to meet you, Cassie. I'm Rex."

"Can I steal this one from you for a moment, Rex?" Cassie asks.

"Steal away. I'm grabbing another beer," Rex says as he walks away.

Cassie doesn't wait long before grabbing me and pulling me towards the bathrooms. Trevor, thankfully, notices I still have the cue in my hand and takes it from me.

"Where are we going? Why are you pulling me? Hold on, is Melissa fine with her date?"

"Shh. No talking for a minute. Melissa checked in thirty minutes ago, they went back to her place."

Yanking me into the bathroom, she immediately turns to me.

"Who is that, and why the fuck haven't you told me about him?" she demands.

"What?"

"That guy?! It's obvious you guys know each other."

"Are you talking about Rex?" I ask, dumbfounded.

"YES."

"Oh, I, uh...met him a couple weeks ago at work," I stammer.

"You didn't think to tell me about it? He's fucking hot! And his friends? Holy shit. Part of me wants to be pissed that you didn't say anything, but the other part of me understands why you would keep those guys hidden away. That sounds like one fun night, if you ask me. Not that Rex seems like the sharing type."

"What do you mean?"

"The way he looks at you, he's very obviously into you.

He watches you when he thinks no one else is watching. He's very good at keeping his friends away," she explains.

"Bullshit! It's probably just his face, he's always grumpy. At least he was the two times I've seen him."

"The looks I'm seeing him give you have nothing to do with being grumpy and everything to do with wanting to lay you down on that pool table and fuck you till you can't remember a single guy you were with before him. He seems a little possessive, in a hot way," Cassie says, fixing her hair in the mirror.

"You're reading into everything way too much. If anything, he tolerates me, and his friends are the nice ones," I tell her.

"Hah. Okay. Mark my words: that man wants you. Now let's go out there. I want to see how all this plays out," she says with a wink.

As we head out of the bathroom, part of me wonders if there might be some truth to what she's said. The two times his friends have tried to hang out with me, whether it was Harris asking to play pool or them offering to buy him a lap dance, he's interfered.

I wonder what would happen if I gave Harris a little attention. Would that be enough to get Rex to lower his shields? Or would that cause him to finally explode. Either way, it could be fun.

5

REX

My friends are going to be the death of me.

Not in the literal sense—well, hopefully not—but figuratively, they are destroying me.

Trevor has reached out a couple times since I moved back home, and the last two times they convinced me to come out with them, we've run into her. I don't even know what it is about this woman, there's something different about her that I can't quite figure out, but I want to. It's enough to have her constantly running through my mind at all hours of the day. During practice, when I'm home making dinner with Rory, or late at night with my hand on my cock, imagining her small body on top of mine, or beneath. I'm not picky.

Harris and the rest of the guys would say it's because of the lap dance, which they're not wrong; it was fucking incredible. But it's more than that. There's something she's hiding, something that I can tell is screaming to be set free, and I want to know more about it.

When we ran into her tonight, I knew there was no way I would let any of the other guys hit on her. Fuck that. So, when Harris—or Dirty Harry—tried to get her to play pool with him, I stepped in and demanded we play teams.

I don't do that shit. That's got Trevor written all over it. He's the jealous, emotional, girl-crazy type, whereas I usually don't give a fuck what people do.

Interested in me? Cool, you can have one night. Not interested? Cool, I bet Harris or Miles would love to get to know you.

But Sawyer? Fuck that. They aren't touching her.

No one is. Including me. I hook up with women that I have no emotional attraction to, and Sawyer unfortunately does not fall into the category. Although, fuck, I wish she did.

"What's that look for, man? Everything okay?" Trevor asks as he sits in the chair next to me.

"There's no look. I'm fine," I snap.

"You look like someone just took your toy without asking," he snickers.

"Don't be a fucking idiot. No, I don't. I'm literally just sitting here watching you fools."

"No. You're sitting here brooding while watching Sawyer help Harris out with his pool 'technique.' I can see the annoyance written all over your face."

"I—" Before I can even try to come up with some bull-shit excuse, Sawyer leans around behind Harris to help adjust his arms for his shot. I feel the fury start in my toes and fingers and slowly slither its way to my chest until I feel like I'm going to explode. At that moment, Harris looks back at me and winks.

It takes everything in me not to get up and rip him away from her, but Trevor's laugh stops me. Looking at him, I see a light in his eyes that I want to extinguish. He thinks this is fucking hilarious. I wonder how funny he'll think it is when I kick Harris's ass and make him deal with it.

It wouldn't be the first time, and it sure as hell won't be the last time. After all, we are hockey players. We're used to kicking people's asses, and on occasion getting our own asses handed to us. But that's how we solve things. That's why, when you're watching hockey and there's a fight, most of them end in a pat on the arm or a smile and laugh. It solves our issues.

"Why are you laughing now?" I ask, my knuckles turning white around my beer.

"Because you're going all caveman over a woman you've met twice. Plus, Harris is doing all of this on purpose, and you know it," Trevor says, nodding towards Harris.

"I. Am. Not. A. Caveman," I snarl.

"Yeah, you're doing a great job of proving that."

"Shut up, Trevor."

"I'm just glad to see you're capable of more than just a blank stare towards a woman, especially someone as hot as she is."

I glare at Trevor, who immediately lifts his hands in surrender. If he doesn't stop intentionally pushing my buttons, I'm going to intentionally punch him in the nose.

"I mean for you. You know she's not my type," Trevor adds quickly.

Even I can admit he's right. She is fucking hot. But that's not even all of it. There's just something so captivating about her beyond just being a pretty face.

"Of course she's not your type. She's not your coach's daughter," I say.

Trevor glares at me but doesn't give me a response. He's a forward for the New York Cyclones and has had a crush on his coach's daughter for a while now, but even he's not stupid enough to go down that route. His coach would kill him, plus, she's a little on the wild side for Trevor.

"All I'm saying is that you're allowed to have fun, get out sometimes, and get to know someone without always feeling guilty. A date or two doesn't mean you're getting down on one knee," Trevor says seriously, more serious than most people ever see him be. "Just because you meet someone and like their company, maybe even spend some time together, doesn't mean you're doing anything wrong. Ro will always be your priority, but you still matter."

"I hear you, and honestly, I wish it were that simple. I don't have time like I used to, and any time that I do have, I spend with her. Before anything, I'm still her dad."

"But before you were her dad, you were just Rex. You're allowed to still be him. Plus, Mr. I-have-no-time, you're out tonight," Trevor counters, slowly succeeding at poking holes in my reasoning—not that I'd ever admit it.

"Yeah, but that's because Stella and her are having a girl's night at my place. It's not like I'm free all night. As soon as we're done here, I'll be heading home and resuming dad duties while Stella sleeps in as usual."

"So? That shouldn't stop you from having fun right now, should it?" he counters.

"No, but I find it pointless to start something that we all know is going to end."

"Why do you say it's going to end?"

"It's just what happens. Everyone always leaves. My past is proof, so why would this be any different?"

"Because she's not—" I cut him off before he finishes his sentence. I am not in the mood to hear that name, it's one we rarely speak of, and I know with this much alcohol in me right now that if he says it, I'm going to throat punch him.

"For the love of God, change the fucking subject. Should we talk about you and Claire?"

His eyes immediately darken, obviously not enjoying the mention of her name.

"Point taken. I'm going to go make Harris buy us all another round. I think he's gotten enough alcohol in him that he might not argue," Trevor says with a smile before walking towards our friends.

I sit there watching everyone joke around and having a good night. I feel an almost bitter envy towards them. Not in a negative way that makes me jealous or hateful of them. I just miss when life felt easier. Don't get me wrong; I wouldn't change a single thing about my life. Rory is my whole world. But it's just her and I, and sometimes being a single parent fucking blows.

My friends are the best, but they are solely responsible for themselves. They don't have anyone else relying on them for their everyday needs. It's just different. We're at different points in our lives, and sometimes I just wish I could go out and have a fun night and without worrying about what Rory is doing and if Stella or my mom gave her a good dinner.

Before getting up to go join everyone and play some games, I decide to shoot my sister a text. It's only 9 p.m., so she should be awake, but Rory should definitely be asleep by now.

Hey, Stel, how's the night going? Is Rory okay?

STELLA

Yes. Everything's fine. Rory and I are sitting here watching the Real Housewives and eating a bowl full of sour patch kids.

Picking up my phone, I immediately dial my sister's

number, only for it to go straight to voicemail. Fuck. As I start to type out another message to her, she texts me back.

STELLA

Dude. Chill. She's been asleep for almost two hours. It's just me sitting on your couch eating the sour patch kids you thought you could hide. Thought you didn't eat candy, big bro?

Don't be an asshole. You know it pisses me off.

STELLA

Everything pisses you off ;) don't make it so easy next time

Leave my fucking candy alone, devil woman.

STELLA

Have a good night! Tell Harris I said hello ;)

Abso-fucking-lutely not. See you in the morning.

My sister is such a brat, but she's one of the only people I truly trust to watch my daughter overnight. Well, her and my parents. Which is why I'm so thankful that they all live in New York. When I have away games, I know Rory will be well taken care of, and I won't be spending the entire trip worrying about her.

Looking up, I see Sawyer standing at the table with a drink in one hand and her phone in the other. Yeah, Trevor's right, she's hot. Like, really hot, especially in this outfit. The first time I met her, she was pretty much wearing nothing, and you could tell she wasn't a huge fan. Yeah, she had a killer body, but she didn't seem comfortable or confident in what she was wearing. Right now, she looks like she could take on the world, and that is the sexiest thing about a woman.

It also helps that her ass looks fucking delicious in those jeans. I want to peel them down and bite her juicy ass right before spanking her for being this tempting.

With my eyes on her ass, she looks up, a small smirk lifting from her lips, like she can read my mind and all the depraved thoughts I'm having about her body.

Busted.

Maybe my friends are right. I mean, it's not the first time they've given me a hard time about a woman. My family has also tried to get me to date. But that's a little too much for me; I'm not willing to risk bringing someone into Rory's life unless it's permanent.

That's not what this is or what it will ever be. It doesn't need to be anything more than just some friends hanging out at a bar and enjoying each other's company. And maybe a little checking out of that ass.

But it doesn't mean I'm getting down on one knee and asking her to be Ro's mom.

Instead of shying away from being caught. I revel in it. The soft blush across her cheeks tells me she definitely saw me checking her out, and she liked it. Letting a small smirk hit my face, I watch her eyes brighten just slightly under the dim lights when she notices it. Waving her over to come sit with me, I'm thankful when she doesn't put up a fight.

"Hey," she says almost shyly, like she doesn't know what to say to me when I don't have my typical dickish shield up.

"Want to play a game?" I ask, forcing my laugh down at her surprise.

"What kind of game did you have in mind?"

"Well, we've already determined that you're a fucking badass at pool, so we can either play darts or shuffleboard. Your choice."

"Well, the last time I played darts, I almost shot someone's eye out and they were behind me. So, how about we play shuffleboard."

"Works for me. Want to meet over there? I'm going to grab another beer. Would you like another, uh, what are you even drinking that's pink at a dive bar?"

"Unfortunately, Cassie ordered these. It's a Cosmo. Would you mind just grabbing me a beer as well?"

"Deal. Meet you over there."

~

*G*rabbing a pitcher at the bar, I look around for my friends, and thankfully they're all either occupied with a game of pool or, if you're Harris and Miles, chatting with a lady . . . or two. This night hasn't really gone how I expected it to when I agreed to come out, but I'm not complaining. I'd never admit it, but I'm having a good time, and it's mostly due to the woman standing at the shuffleboard table waiting for me.

Walking towards her, I can't help but grin at the little smile she shoots my way when she notices me coming. Her whole face lights up when she smiles, showcasing her gorgeous blue eyes that I want to get lost in. She seems so genuinely happy that it's almost contagious.

Almost.

"I grabbed whatever they had on draft. I think it's Coors or something," I tell her while pouring and handing her a beer.

"That's just fine with me. I'm not picky."

"Just on what fruity drinks you like?" I smirk.

"Well, I, uh, yeah, I really hate those. The headaches the next morning sure as fuck aren't worth it, and they just don't taste good. I'd prefer a beer or tequila."

"Really? I had you pegged as a margarita girl, blended of course. Or that wine, you know, the pink stuff?"

"Rosé?" she asks, raising her eyebrows enough that I feel like an idiot for not knowing.

"Yeah, that one. I figured that'd be the type of shit you'd drink."

"Well, you missed that one by a mile. I can't stand that shit, especially the pink stuff." She smirks as she makes fun of me. "Plus, I prefer my tequila with salt and a lime."

I find myself having a hard time looking away from Sawyer. Talking to her is so enjoyable, and if I'm being honest, I'm nervous that once we stop, it'll pop this bubble we're in. It's different than I'm used to, in a good way. Normally, the more I talk to a woman, the more I'm ready for the conversation to be over. But with Sawyer, the more time I spend with her, the more time I want. She gets more and more interesting the longer we're together, and she's so down to earth it's shocking. I've spent my whole life running away from puck bunnies, so it's exciting to find someone who's the exact opposite.

Plus, I don't even think she knows who I am. She hasn't once asked what I do for a living or implied she knew who we are, so it's nice not getting attention from someone because of my NHL career. It's part of the reason I only ever spend one night with someone. I hate the attention I get when I know it's only because of my past fame. One night stands usually only care about your first name if they even want that.

"You get cooler and cooler the more I learn about you," I

blurt out, surprising myself with the admission, and by the look on her face, she's just as shocked.

Fuck. I usually play it much cooler than this.

"Ready to play?" I ask, trying to quickly move past my comment and onto safer ground.

"Yup, I'm ready to kick your ass."

"Have you ever even played shuffleboard before?"

"Nope. But how hard could it be," she says, confidently. "You take this puck-thingy and slide it down the lane. Easy-peasy. I'm sure I'll kick your ass at this too."

Spoiler alert: she did not kick my ass, and this game was not "easy-peasy" . . . for her. It only took three rounds, but she finally managed to at least keep the "puck-thingy," but only when she barely pushed it at all.

"Okay, this rounds on me, ya know, to celebrate," I say.

"I'm not one to deny any celebration, but what exactly are we celebrating?" she asks, looking slightly confused and little drunk, her eyes becoming hazy from the last round of tequila we just had."

"We're celebrating that you're no longer total shit at this game, just mostly," I tell her, covering my face to try to hide my smirk before grabbing her hand and leading her towards the bar before she can yell at me.

The second our hands touch, I feel a shock of electricity that has me almost pulling my hand back, but I hold on. She must have noticed it as well because she stiffens up momentarily and her eyes haven't left our joined hands as I continue leading her to the bar. It's almost one in the morning now, and the only people left in the bar are our friends, although everyone has kind of broken off to do their own things.

Grabbing us some shots, I pass one to Sawyer before getting us both a lime.

"You know, I almost didn't come out tonight. Every part of me wanted to stay home after my busy as fuck week. But I'm glad I didn't. Tonight's been more fun than I expected. I figured I was going to be stuck babysitting my friends, but running into you guys has been a nice treat," Sawyer says, apparently becoming more talkative as she drinks.

But I secretly like that about her too.

It may have been a roundabout way to give a compliment, but I'll take it, even if this isn't a date. And it's not a date. I've just really fucking enjoyed her presence tonight, and I keep imagining taking her over to the pool table and bending her over it. I wonder if her ass would turn pink, just like the fluorescent lights above us.

I'm so fucked, and I've only hung out with her once.

"Yeah, for as annoying as they are, those guys are alright," I say. Looking over at our friends, I see Gwen talking to Trevor and Cassie, while the boys have all found a group of girls to talk to. It's no surprise that it's only Trevor and I trying to not get our dicks wet tonight.

I almost want to ask to see her again. However, the bigger, more stubborn part of my brain reminds me why that's a bad idea.

Rory. I have to think about her.

I'm about tell her I need to get going, but I know the second I do, this happy little bubble we're in will burst.

"Hey guys, I'm heading out. Are you walking back with me, Sawyer?" Cassie asks as she walks up. She doesn't even try to hide her amusement when looking between Sawyer and me.

I guess I'm not the only one picking up on the tension between her and I—I'll have to work on that unless I want Trevor and Harris to give me shit for the rest of my life.

To my surprise, Sawyer doesn't answer immediately.

That pause alone has me thinking she's feeling something too. I have a feeling that if we had the opportunity, Sawyer wouldn't be walking home with Cassie, she'd be coming home with me.

"Uh," Sawyer starts to say.

"We can all walk out together. It's probably time for me to head out as well. Trevor and I have an early morning tomorrow," I say.

"Early morning on a Saturday? Ew," Cassie retorts just as Gwen walks up.

"Did you win your jukebox battle tonight?" Sawyer asks.

Honestly, I have no idea what music played tonight. Listening to music is the last thing on my mind when Sawyer's around. A thought that pisses me off.

Gwen looks like she's almost blushing.

"Yeah, I did. Are we heading out now?"

"Thanks for coming to hang out with us," Trevor says as he walks up. He gives each of the girls a side hug, making sure to look at me and wink as he hugs Sawyer. "Ready to go, Rex?"

"Yeah. It was nice seeing you ladies. Maybe we'll see ya around."

"Yep, next Friday. Trevor and I figured that out already," Cassie says with a smile. Out of the corner of my eye, I see Sawyer start to smile as she turns towards the door to leave.

"Well, I guess I'll see you ladies then," I say, watching Sawyer sashay out the door.

I shouldn't be excited or looking forward to next Friday, but I am. I immediately feel guilty that I'm thinking about spending time with Sawyer instead of what I could be doing with Rory. Yet, despite my guilt, I'm already texting the group chat to see if my mom or sister can babysit.

Trevor is such a sneaky bastard.

6

———

REX

Saturday morning comes far too soon, and by six a.m., Trevor and I are in Central Park stretching before our run. Back in college when we played for the same team, we would meet weekly to go on runs around Central Park. It accidentally became a tradition, especially once Stella opened her bakery on the corner that makes the best sourdough bagels I've ever had. Then our tradition became a mandatory weekly meeting, scheduled and all.

I'm looking forward to the bagels even more today. The amount of tequila I still have in my body is ridiculous, and I could use something to soak it up. Thank God Stella stayed the night because there was absolutely no way I would have made it today without sweating some of this out.

"Fuck man, I can't drink like I used to. Gwen and Cassie kept ordering those stupid fruity drinks, and man, I'm feeling it today. I feel like I have straight vodka in my veins," Trevor groans as he leans forward, stretching his hamstrings.

"Me either. I didn't drink that fruity shit, but we had a couple rounds of tequila while I was teaching her how to play shuffleboard and damn, I sure as fuck feel it today," I agree.

It's true. Drinking in your thirties is nothing like drinking in your twenties. When I was in my twenties, I could drink whatever I wanted all night long and be perky the next morning at hockey practice. Now, half the time I don't even have to drink to get hung over. I just look at the bottle wrong and I'm incapacitated for two days.

"What happened to us? We used to be fun. Used to drink all night long, but now after just a couple hours of drinking, we're practically dying."

"We got old. And speak for yourself. I'm still fun," I tell him, laughing when he glares at me. He hates when I tell him we are old.

"You got old. I'm still thirty-four. Not all of us are closer to forty than thirty like you. When did we start using the word fun to describe you? More like 'grumpy' or 'growly.' Those fit better," he quips, teasingly.

"Fuck off, jackass. You turn thirty-five in like three months, and I just turned fucking thirty-seven. You act like I'm ancient, and I. Don't. Growl."

"Hey, you just did." Trevor shrugs before an annoying smirk takes over his face, which I know will lead to a conversation I don't want to have. "So, how was your night with club girl?"

"Her name is Sawyer, use it. She's more than just her job," I grumble, doing my best not to hit him upside the head for goading me or for smirking at my growl.

"I know. I was just curious what your reaction would be, and it was just like I expected."

Trevor's grin is wider than usual—too wide for someone who's been complaining about being hungover all morning.

I want to smack it off his face because I know damn well he's trying to make a big deal out of nothing.

"And what did you expect?" I question.

"Caveman with a side of possessiveness, and boy, did you deliver. Thanks for winning me fifty bucks."

"Dude, there's nothing going on between Sawyer and me," I tell him as I run my hands through my hair, pulling on the ends. "Actually, I don't know. I'm not sure what is or isn't happening, and I'm not used to that. And why the hell did you fuckers bet on me?"

If I wanted to smack him before, I want to strangle him now. Trevor's shit eating grin and the laughter that comes out of him as he stands to get ready for our run makes my blood boil.

"Yup. I bet that you'd act just like you did. Possessive and grumbly. Like you'd piss on her if you could, mark her as yours. But I know you well enough to know that you're going to fight it and refuse to go for it yourself, yet not let anyone get close," he says.

"Thanks for the visual. Just what I needed."

"Well, don't act like a wild animal and I won't have to give you those visuals."

"So, what'd y'all bet on?" I ask as I stand to finish stretching.

"Harris thought you'd avoid the topic for a bit, then crack, while Cade thought you didn't like the girl at all and that you'd do your usual bullshit and avoid feelings like the plague. Miles had no idea, as he spent most of the night flirting and not paying any attention to you."

"You all suck," I grumble.

"Nah, we can just read you better than you can read yourself most of the time. Some of us better than others obviously," Trevor jokes, before a serious look falls on his face. "Really though, Rex, you've been dealt some tough cards in the past, but you played the hell out of 'em. Don't let anything that's happened bring you down, play the field. I'm not saying you need to do anything serious."

"I—"

"Shut it. I'm not finished. No one's saying you need to bring her home to mama, or in your case, to Ro. We just want to see you happy and putting yourself out there again," he says, effectively cutting me off.

"I know. I don't know what's happening in my head. One minute, I want to hang out with her more because it's fun, the next I freak out that I'm letting someone get too close. I don't know, but I'm sure once I fucking figure it out, you'll already know." I glare. "Now let's go run, I've heard enough talking from you."

~

*A*n hour later, we're at the bagel place picking up our usual order, mine including stuff for Stella and Rory.

"Better luck next time. One day you'll beat this *old man*," I say.

"Shut up. I could literally smell the vodka coming out of my skin when we came around the last corner. I almost stopped to puke, but the hot yoga moms were right there, and I didn't want to freak them out," Trevor groans.

"Excuses aren't going to win it for you."

"We'll race again when I'm not 75% vodka. Oh, and don't forget to figure out a plan for Ro next weekend. I promised we'd all be there," he reminds me.

"Yeah, I know. It's already all taken care of. My mom asked if she could keep her for the weekend. I guess they want to make cookies and watch some movies or something. I don't know, some Halloween bullshit the girls are into."

"Right on. Look at you, being on top of everything. Does this mean you're looking forward to it?" Trevor asks, winking as he turns to leave. "Let's grab a beer after work this week, you can let me know how the first game goes," he yells over his shoulder.

"Whatever, man. I'll talk to you then," I tell him before turning to walk back to my place.

Is Trevor right? Am I actually looking forward to hanging out with Sawyer again? Well, not only Sawyer since it's a group thing, but I've enjoyed talking to her. She's been fun. And now I'm rambling like a fucking junior high kid with his first crush.

It's not a crush.

I don't even *like* her.

I don't like *anyone.*

But even as I think it, I know that's a bold face lie.

7

SAWYER

By the time Wednesday rolls around, I'm beat.

I've been doing my best to make sure I'm getting enough sleep, but sometimes it's hard to recover after too many nights of shitty sleep.

This morning, it finally caught up to me. Somehow I had managed to snooze all my alarms in my sleep and woke up to the sun shining through my window with only twenty minutes to get to my first class. Unfortunately, I had to forgo coffee, which was a real bummer for me and everyone around me. To make matters worse, my professor is a real jackass and makes a scene whenever anyone comes in late.

But now I have an hour before I need to be at the daycare, and I'm heading straight to my favorite coffee shop to get enough caffeine to kill an elephant. The smell is the first thing that hits me when I walk in. The pastries here are to die for, but it's the coffee that keeps me alive.

Walking over to the pastry case, I can't decide whether I want something sweet or savory. They have cinnamon rolls, which are always a safe choice, but they also have quiche, and who doesn't love a good quiche?

"The danishes are amazing," a low voice from behind me says.

I turn around quickly, almost bumping into the man. Thankfully, he catches me before I do, his hand firm on my arm. His grip feels both comforting and powerful, a strange mix of safety and control. It's exciting. I'm surprised by my reaction to a stranger.

That is, until I look up and see none other than Rex, the man I've been thinking about non-stop since the other night at the bar.

"Hi, Rex. You surprised me," I tell him, my heart racing. I don't know if it's from the shock of seeing him or the fact that I nearly fell into someone. Something tells me it's the latte

His blue eyes shine bright as he smiles at me for a moment before speaking. "I saw you looking at the different pastries like you couldn't decide which one to get, I figured I'd help by recommending one of my go-to's, they never let me down. I didn't mean to startle you though. I didn't expect you to be so concentrated," he says, with a boyish and almost nervous smile on his face.

"I take my food seriously," I tell him with a wink, which makes him smile even wider.

It's nice seeing Rex away from everyone, he seems more comfortable and at ease.

"I get it. I'm the same way," he says before pausing for a moment. "Are you here with anyone?"

"Nope, just me. I was just stopping in before I have to be at work in like an hour."

"How about I grab a couple of my favorites and you go find a table? I've got some time to kill too."

"Deal, but at least let me buy the coffee."

"No. Just tell me your order and go grab us a table," Rex answers, leaving no room for argument.

I quickly tell him my order then make my way over to one of the few tables left and wait.

As I sit and people-watch, I can't help but focus in on Rex as he stands in line placing our order. The barista is smiling and obviously flirting with him, but Rex keeps turning around to check on me. It's a simple gesture that is enough to have me feeling all warm and fuzzy inside.

It's not like this is a date or anything, so there's no reason why I should care if he's flirting with the barista. And yet, despite her blatantly checking him out and pulling out all the stops to catch his attention, his focus is on me. His panty-melting smile out in full force, stirring up all sorts of feelings inside.

Jesus Christ.

I'm sitting here, imagining his hands and his mouth exploring my body, his cock filling me, all the while he's in line ordering me a coffee and a cinnamon roll. What the fuck is wrong with me and why can't I keep my head out of the gutter when I'm around this man?

Next, he'll tell me to sit and call me a *good girl*, and I'll spontaneously melt into a puddle of pleasure right here in this café.

Okayyy, Daddy.

By the time I realize I'm still staring at the man, he's sliding into his seat, placing a tray between us with our coffees and practically every pastry they sell, a boyish grin plastered on his face that tells me I just got caught staring.

Passing me my coffee, Rex just smirks.

"Thank you," I say, trying to ignore the blush I feel rising up my neck. "So, what'd you get us?"

"Uh, a little of everything. I'm pretty sure there isn't a bad pastry here, so I just asked them to grab a bunch. Here, try this filled donut, it's my favorite, it practically melts in your mouth."

"I'm not really a fan of the filling inside donuts; it never tastes right, and I always struggle to swallow it. I'll try a danish instead."

"Trust me, Sawyer. I'll never steer your wrong when it comes to food or putting things in your mouth. I promise this will be the best cream you've tasted. So far." He grins, the innuendo very clear and causing my blush to intensify.

"Fine. But if it sucks, I'm spitting it out and blaming you."

Grabbing the donut from him I just look at it. I wasn't lying; I really don't like filled donuts. I'm more of a maple bar girl, but there's something about this man that just makes it so fucking difficult to say no. He sits across from me, sipping his coffee, while I practically stare at the donut like it offended me.

"Take a bite," Rex grumbles.

Finally, I go to take a bite, and the corner of his lips tilt up just enough to see he's holding back a smile. Goddamn, this man wasn't kidding; this is delicious, and the cream just melts on my tongue, a hint of cinnamon filling my mouth.

"Good girl," Rex says. "Now, what'd you think?"

I pause at his words, knowing damn well he's probably watching me practically pant at his words.

Just hearing him say that has my clit pulsing, wetness starting to soak through my panties.

"Holy shit. It's delicious," I groan as the sugary deliciousness touches my tongue. "I'll admit it; this is incredible."

He watches me, his eyes darkening as he stares at my mouth, watching my tongue as I lick the rest of the cream off my lips. Slowly leaning forward, he reaches across the table, and with one gentle finger, he swipes the extra cream off the corner of my mouth. Never taking his eyes off of me, he brings his finger back to his mouth and licks it clean.

Holy shit, that had no business being that hot. But spoiler alert; it was.

"Mm. Yep. Even better than I remembered," he grumbles before finally breaking our eye contact with a chuckle.

"You are trouble," I announce before finally reaching for my coffee.

"I've been called worse. Now eat up. You don't have long, and you need to try them all. We'll have plenty of time to bullshit next time."

The promise of a next time makes me blush.

We spend the next half-hour trying the rest of the pastries, and I'd be lying if I said they weren't all delicious. By the time I'm grabbing my things to head out to work, I'm in a full-on sugar coma with a smug-looking Rex sitting across from me.

~

"Hey, Sawyer," Sarah, my boss at the daycare, says as I walk into the office.

"Hey. How's the day been?" I ask, throwing my bag behind the desk and clocking in.

"Oh, it's been fine, a little busy though. We had some people call out, so we've been running a little bit of a tight ship. Think you'll be okay without Claire today? She's home with the stomach flu."

"Yeah, it'll be no problem. We usually only have eight kids in our room, and then for the evening program, there's just three. Wednesdays are usually our slower nights anyway."

"That's right, that starts tonight. That's so exciting! You've wanted to do this for so long, I'm so glad we're finally able to offer dance at night."

"I know, I'm so excited! Tonight, we're doing a ballet class. It's three little girls so it'll be cute."

"Oh, that's so great. You'll have to tell me all about it," Sarah says as she turns back to the computer but stops. "Oh wait, I meant to tell you, Rory's going home with her aunt tonight, so it won't be the usual person."

"Honestly, I wouldn't even be able to tell you who picks Rory up. It's a weird pick up. Claire always brings Rory out front to her dad."

"Oh, well that shouldn't be a problem tonight. Anytime it's someone new picking up, we always go over pick-up procedures to make sure they know," Sarah says with a smile. "I'm really excited about your class tonight. I can't wait to hear how it goes. If we get a big need for evening care, we can always add more night classes to our schedule."

"Awesome! That sounds great."

Heading into the daycare room, I look around to see who's here already. We have four kids here right now: Matthew, Blake, Grace, and Rory. The first three are running around playing with toys, while Rory is sitting by herself, as usual. She's been like this ever since she got here. I'm not sure if she's just naturally shy and quiet or if she's nervous, but she barely talks to the other kids. I've been working on getting her to open to me this week, little by little, but it's been a slow process. The other kids have been trying as well. They're always inviting her to come play with them, and try to talk to her, but she never seems very interested. It's hard to watch her have such a hard time adjusting. I usually end up sitting with her while she colors, and most of the time, I'll join her. That's when she seems the happiest.

Knowing that tonight it will only be Rory and two other little girls, Grace, and Madeline, I'm hoping I can get Rory to open up and become a little more comfortable with me. According to Sarah, when her dad was enrolling her in our daycare, and was really excited about the opportunity for her to participate in a dance class, so I'm hoping it's something she's excited about as well.

"Hi, Ms. Rory. May I sit down with you?" I ask, waiting patiently to give her a chance to answer.

As much as we've been slowly building a connection this week, I don't want to push too hard too fast.

Once she nods, I take a seat next to her.

"Hi, Ms. Daniels." Rory smiles shyly, keeping her eyes on her picture the entire time. "Do you want to color?"

"I would love to, sweet girl," I tell her, quickly glancing around at the other kids, who thankfully are finally sitting down at the other table playing with blocks. I grab a coloring sheet from the stack before sitting down in the little chair next to her. "I love your dinosaur, you did a great job coloring."

"Thank you. It's a triceratops. Like Cera from Land . . . time . . ."

It's adorable to watch her try and come up with the words, but luckily for her, I grew up on this movie.

"Do you mean *The Land Before Time*?"

Her eyes immediately light up.

"YES! Daddy and I watched that movie before we moved. I loved Cera, she's the best, always makes me happy. Now I make daddy watch that movie all the time. With popcorn, of course."

"You're a girl after my own heart. Popcorn and movies are like my favorite things. But when I watch *Land Before Time*, Ducky is always my favorite."

"That's my daddy's favorite too. Ducky's silly," Rory responds, before letting out the cutest giggle I think I've ever heard, while giving me the cutest smile to match.

Oh, my heart. Rory is something else and I love that she's willing to share a piece of herself with me. Her little giggles are the sweetest things ever, and I love that she finally let me hear one.

"Your daddy sounds like a smart man," I say, returning the smile when she looks up at me.

"He is. He's my favorite daddy ever. He always plays with me and lets me pick out the movie. We even cook dinner together. I only get grumpy when he won't let me have the sour human candy my Auntie Lala gives me."

Rory starts to pout, sticking out her bottom lip so dramatically it makes me want to laugh.

"Sour ... human ... candy?"

"Yeah, umm. The little candies that are shaped like people, and they're sour. Lala likes the red ones, but I only like the yellow and blue," Rory says confidently.

Who would have thought that talking about dinosaurs and sour candy would get this sweet girl to finally open up, but alas, that was the key.

"Oh, Sour Patch Kids! I love those, but I understand your daddy not letting you have lots of candy all the time." Lowering my voice to almost a whisper, I lean down by her ear, "Maybe the sour candy is something special just between you and your Auntie Lala, it's always nice to have little things you can share with the people you love."

"What's your special thing you share with your people?"

"Ice cream. I have a favorite ice cream place that's my little hidden treasure. I only share it with people I think are special."

"Ice cream! I love ice cream!" Rory shouts, causing me to laugh and the other kids to look up from their blocks.

"Maybe one day I'll bring you all some ice cream," I tell her with a wink.

"Yes, please! Please!!!" Rory says, while the other kids come over to join us.

"I love ice cream too, Ms. Daniels," Matthew chimes in.

"Oh, don't worry, Matthew, I would never forget you! I would never forget any of you. You're all special to me," I say, beaming at all the kids.

I had tried everything with Rory all week to get her to open up, but somehow chatting about dinosaurs and our favorite yummy snacks is all it took to get her smiling and playing with the other kids. Oh, and the promise of ice cream. That's something I'll need to run past their parents first.

~

Hours later, after the daycare center has closed, it's just Rory, Grace, and Madeline dancing around with me. It's honestly the most fun I've had since I started working here. Watching the girls get so excited to learn ballet made my heart so happy. Madeline and Grace were the first to get picked up, leaving just Rory and me to run around pretending we're ballerinas in *The Nutcracker*. It was adorable to see Rory play with the kids tonight, she finally seemed like she was having a good time.

"Ms. Daniels, that was so much fun. I love ballet," Rory says.

"I'm so happy to hear that, sweet girl. We can do ballet, and other dances any time you want. Plus, I think next week, we'll have another late night so we will have to plan something fun for then!" I tell her with a smile, loving the way her eyes light up hearing that.

"Yay! My daddy works at night sometimes. He goes to hockey games. But now I'm happy. This was fun!"

"Does your daddy work a lot of nights?" I ask, unsure of what he does for a living. We usually learn most of the information about the families from their kids, and Sarah tells us the important things we need to know, but what they do for a living doesn't fall under that.

"Not too many. When we lived in Texas my grandparents would watch me sometimes."

"Does your mommy go with him?"

As soon as I ask it, I wish I could take it back. Rory quiets almost instantly and looks a little lost. Fuck... me and my big mouth. I might have just undone everything I've worked on to get her to open up to me. Don't get me wrong, I adore all the kids who go to this daycare and want them all to be happy coming here, but there's something about Rory. Something that calls me to her and makes me want to get to know her. For being only four years old, she's such a smart and kind-hearted girl.

"I don't have one," Rory says.

"You don't have what?" I ask, ensuring I understand what she means.

"A mommy," she explains, seeming detached.

Damn. Who'd have thought I'd want to bawl my eyes out at work.

"I'm sorry, sweet girl. I didn't mean to make you sad."

"Oh, I'm not sad. My daddy's the best daddy ever," Rory says, brightening up immediately.

"He always spends time with me when he's not at work. He's my favorite."

"I thought I was your favorite," a voice calls from the

doorway behind us, surprising me but not Rory, who immediately jumps up excitedly.

"Auntie Lala! You're here," she says as she jumps into her arms.

"Hey, Ro! Of course, I'm here. I told you I'd pick you up when your dad has to work."

"Auntie Lala, Auntie Lala! This is my friend, Ms. Daniels! She's the best! We did ballet today, and she told me about ice cream and she's sooo pretty, just like you!"

I blush at her little declaration, secretly loving that she feels this way.

"Hi, I'm Stella, or Auntie Lala," she says with a smile, extending her hand to shake mine.

"Hi, I'm Sawyer, also known as Ms. Daniels, here at the center," I say with a smile.

"She's so nice, Lala! And! She loves the sour people like we do!"

"I see she told you our little secret. Her dads a sugar freak when it comes to Rory and doesn't like a lot of sugar in the house. So I hide some over there for our slumber party nights," Stella says with a chuckle.

"Guess that means he probably wouldn't like my idea of getting them ice cream one night."

"He's tough, but he wants her to be happy, so he'd probably give in if she asked," Stella says with a smile.

"I'll ask daddy!" Ro says, before yawning.

"I better get this one home before she falls asleep, or else I'll have to carry her."

"Of course. It was nice meeting you. Get some rest, Rory. I'll see you tomorrow," I say with a wave.

"Bye, Ms. Daniels."

Finally getting ready to lock up and get out of here, I grab my phone and check it. Surprisingly, there's a few new messages, some from this morning. Guess I didn't do a great job of checking my phone today. Ignoring the ones from Cassie, I'm annoyed to see both my mom and Max have texted me.

MOM

Good morning, Sawyer. Sunday dinner this week? I miss you and I'd love to see you.

MAX

Sawyer, stop being a child and avoiding mom because of me. She doesn't have anyone else but us and you're being selfish. You continue to make shitty choices and leave mom and I to deal with the fall out. Be at dinner this week.

Surprise, surprise. My brother trying to control me? Yeah, that tracks. I'm not sure what he really expects me to say to that. My choices don't impact them at all, but they made it very clear that if I didn't do what they wanted, or rather what my brother wanted, I wouldn't be welcome in their home.

I decided to follow my dreams, fully aware of what it would mean for my relationship with my brother, and unfortunately, my mom who always follows Max's word.

8

———

REX

Our season has only been going on for two weeks. Two weeks and the changes we've made are finally starting to pay off. After losing the first two games, we tried a couple of different things and now we've won the last four consecutively. The guys were initially pissed when we started making changes to the lines, thinking people were being punished for not being good enough, or whatever other bullshit excuse they came up with to throw a hissy fit.

The issue isn't that the players aren't good. In fact, Brooklyn University is known for having quite a few NHL prospects with some balls-to-the-walls players. The issue lies in their connection with each other on the ice. They can't read each other correctly, resulting in players being in the wrong positions, not passing to open teammates for a shot, and failing to anticipate the need to be in front of the net for rebounds.

We played around with it, trying a few different approaches to determine which players had the best chemistry on the ice and could read each other the best. A lot of the boys thought I was trying to fixing something that wasn't broken.

But it was.

Now that we've made some changes, we're running a more streamlined version of the previous strategy. It's not entirely different, just cleaner. Over half our goals have come from rebounds that our players were able to score on, whereas before there wouldn't have been someone there to even attempt a shot.

As I sit at the bar with Trevor, drinking beer and talking about hockey, I'm reminded of old times. Which hits me with a strange combination of emotions. Part of me fucking hates it. We used to do this all the time until I got injured. I was different after. It changed me. Broke me down. I stopped hanging out with everyone, and no one wanted to talk hockey with me, except for Bernard. But he's a stubborn motherfucker that I love regardless. The other part of me feels like I'm coming home. Like being back in this world has set everything right.

Guess only time will tell.

"So, remind me again why we're out so early?" Trevor asks in the middle of eating his burger.

"My mom picked up Ro as soon as she heard I needed a sitter. My parents are watching her at their place this week-end. I guess Stella is going over too, sounds like trouble for my dad."

"Oh, that poor man. Those three ladies in one place spells nothing but trouble," Trevor jokes.

All I can do is glare at him over my beer, but he's not wrong. It is fucking ridiculous. "You know how they get when they're together. It's irritating. They basically have one big girl party and ignore all my rules since I'm not there."

"There are worse problems you could have. Besides, they

all adore that little girl so much. It's good for everyone to have some bonding time, or whatever bullshit they do," Trevor says with a smile.

I know he's right.

"I know. Doesn't mean I have to fucking like it."

As we're chatting, our waitress comes back over to check on us, flirting with Trevor as she does. Trevor, of course, is his usual self—all smiling and happy, willing to play along with her. But I just want another beer. When the waitress looks over at me, I force a quick smile before ordering another beer and a shot of whiskey. We have just enough time for one more drink before heading over to the bar to meet up with everyone else.

Her and Trevor go back and forth a bit more before she finally leaves to go grab our drinks.

"What's going on with you tonight? You seem more grumpy than usual."

Rubbing my hands down my face, I sigh, feeling defeated because I really don't have an answer for him. "I'm not sure, man. Just off this afternoon, I guess." I'm not lying, I'm really not sure what's going on with me. I don't usually feel like this. Are these nerves? I'm not the type to get nervous or antsy, unless it's something to do with Rory. Yet, I can't help but wonder if this feeling might have something to do with the little blue-eyed temptress I'm seeing again tonight.

"Everything okay with Rory?" he asks.

"Yeah, she's fine."

Our drinks arrive, and my shot hasn't been on the table for three seconds before I grab it and shoot it back. That should help my nerves.

Trevor grabs his and slams it down before leaning back with a smirk that makes me want to throat-punch him.

"This wouldn't have anything to do with seeing Sawyer again, would it?"

"Man, fuck. I don't know," I reply, frustrated. "She's obviously fucking hot. And she's cool as shit. But what am I doing? I'm what? Fifteen years older than her? And I have a kid. She's getting her masters and works at a strip club. There's zero chance she'd be prepared to spend time with a man who has a kid when she's practically a kid herself."

"Don't be an asshole," Trevor chides. "She's not a kid, she's a whole-ass adult who you're making a lot of assumptions about. So, what? She's younger...who cares? Lots of young people have kids. But—"

"No. I'm not talking about Sawyer and Rory in the same subject. That's where I draw the line. You know damn well I'm not letting someone into Rory's life again just to have them abandon her. Regardless of what I assume about this, I'm not willing to watch Rory get hurt."

"Stop with the bullshit excuses. You can't live your life like that. All I'm saying is that it's fucking ridiculous to suggest that just because of her age, she's incapable of being with someone who has a kid. Who knows? She may be incredible with kids."

"It's not bullshit. When I was her age, I was partying every weekend and living off my parents. Why would I expect her to be any different?" I question. "At twenty-four, I was in no position to take on the responsibility of caring for a child, and I sure as fuck wasn't interested in dating someone with a child. I refuse to bring anyone into Rory's life—my life—until I know for sure it's going to last. So, I'm just hanging out with friends tonight. Okay?"

"We'll see. My bets on your little plan failing within the week, so let's just wait and find out," Trevor responds with a shit eating grin.

Half an hour later, we are walking into the bar to meet everyone else. Looking around, I don't see them in our typical spot, and I start to think we may have beat everyone here. That is until I hear her laugh. Turning immediately to find where the noise came from, I stop in my track when I finally see her.

Fuck.

She's dressed in skintight black pants that hug her curves like a second skin. Jesus Christ. She has black boots on and a tiny lace tank top shows off a hint of her stomach. I want to grab her and run my tongue along the little expanses of skin I can see. I imagine her pale skin reddening beautifully from my teeth.

I want to walk over there and pull her against me. Fuck her mouth with my tongue until she's breathless and begging for my cock. I want to feel her tremble beneath me, waiting for what I'll give her and taking everything like a greedy little slut. Just for me.

What the fuck is wrong with me?

It's one thing knowing I want to fuck someone. I'll have a one-night stand on occasion. But that never involves me fantasizing about them. Her body is becoming an obsession, one I'm not sure how to get rid of. Or if I even want to.

Twenty minutes ago, I was adamant about how bad of an idea this was, but now all I can think about is how to get her naked and have her screaming my name.

Sawyer must feel my eyes on her because her head snaps up, searching the room, smiling when she notices me.

I can't move. It's like my feet are stuck in place and all I can do is watch her. She's standing on the other side of the room doing the same thing. Finally, she breaks the spell, mouthing "Hi" with a smile. I feel like I'm in a trance or an alternate universe because I actually smile back as I mouth "Hi" in return.

Trevor finally splits off, heading to the bar, while I make a beeline for Sawyer, not stopping till I'm right in front of her. She's standing with all our friends, but she's the only one I can focus on. I hear Miles and Cade say hello, but I don't respond.

She has all my attention and it's fucking annoying. But I can't deny that I enjoy it.

I usually don't get too deep with women outside of the bedroom, so giving or seeking attention has never been high on my to-do list. Normally, I only care about finding the nearest bedroom to fuck in. Or bathroom. Or hell, I'll take the nearest surface. But not now. Now, I'm just looking forward to talking to her.

"Hey, stranger," she says, in a way that's equal parts shy and seductive, sending blood directly to my cock. She's sipping on her drink and chewing on her straw, making me wish I was the straw.

I haven't even kissed the woman yet, and my cock already listens to her better than me.

"Hey," I respond.

"It's good to see you. How are you?"

"I'm here. Been a long week, but I'm here," I say, pulling my hat down a bit, a nervous habit I have. "How about you?"

"I'm good. Busy week as well between classes and work, but I made it through."

"What's everyone up to?" I ask, glancing around to see where everyone is.

"Cassie and Miles are playing darts. I think Harris and Trevor are trying to talk Gwen into a game of pool with Melissa. And apparently, Trevor bought a tray of shots," she responds with a laugh.

"That's cool. You said it was a busy week of school? What're you going to school for?"

"I'm getting my master's degree in business."

"Business? I thought you said you were a dancer?"

The words must've come off harsher than I meant because her shoulders tense in response. Her eyes seem sadder now, with some of their brightness dimming just enough to lose their sparkle in the low light of the bar. She takes a long drink from her glass and looks up at me, the sadness on her face hitting me straight in the gut.

"Yeah, you're right. I was, but then I got injured. When that happened, I decided I wanted to find a way to share my passion for dance with others, so now I teach it. You know if you can't do it, teach it, or whatever bullshit people say."

"Yeah, I get that. But why business?"

"I want to have my own studio here in the city, but I want to do it my way, not how everyone thinks I should. To do that, I need my own studio, and a degree to help me succeed as a business owner."

"That's awesome. Where would you open one if you could pick anywhere?"

"Honestly, I'm not sure. I had the perfect studio over on Broadway, but it fell through. Now I just casually look when I can, but nothing too serious until I graduate in May."

I can't lie, I'm impressed by her vision. She has the drive and the plans to back it up. It's attractive as fuck to see a girl with both a dream and the determination to make it happen. Her outlook on life is also surprising at such a young age. At least, I assume she's young. She seems barely legal to drink.

"I know this is breaking like all the rules and you're never supposed to ask a lady this, but if you don't mind me asking, how old are you?"

"Twenty-four."

"Wow," I say. *Fuck, she's young.* But thankfully, not quite as young as I thought. Plus, she's pretty mature for her age, which makes it easy to hang out with her. "It's nice to see someone your age with such drive."

"Yeah, well, I've had my dream taken from me before. I refuse to let it happen again." Sawyer immediately grabs her drink and downs it like a champ. "What about you? How old are you?"

"Thirty-seven," I reply, expecting her reaction to be less than desirable and for her to be weirded out by my age. I'm surprised when she just grins.

"Damnit! I thought I had it when I guessed thirty-three. Thirty-seven, huh? I like it. It suits you."

"You thought I was thirty-three?" I ask, eyebrows raised.

"Yeah, I mean, your face isn't old. You have some lines by your eyes, and I can see a gray or two," Sawyer teases before slowly raking her eyes from my face all the way down my body, taking her time and having no shame about it. "But I mean, you're obviously in great shape, and you have this energy about you that just exudes confidence. Usually, guys in their twenties don't have that—"

Before I can even respond, a voice behind me pipes in. "BDE," Cassie says with a grin.

"BDE? What the fuck is that? It sounds like an and STD," I say, dumbfounded.

"No, dummy. Big. Dick. Energy. It's a sort of confidence some men have, but only when they have the equipment to back it up."

If I was embarrassed easily, this might've done me in. Cassie has excellent timing with eavesdropping.

"Damn, I guess I'm more transparent than I thought. I'll have to work on that," I deadpan.

Surprisingly, Sawyer is the one blushing at that, hopefully imagining what sort of "BDE" I might have.

"Well, yeah. Whatever. We're hungry so we're getting food. Are you guys staying or going?" Cassie asks.

"I'm not hungry. I'll wait till you get back here," I tell them, staying behind to save our seats while they are gone.

"I'm not hungry so I'll stay and keep Rex company," Sawyer says.

"Alright. We will be back in a bit," Cassie responds.

"Have fun."

As soon as they leave, Sawyer immediately turns to me with a shit eating grin on her face that can only mean trouble. "Want to play a game?" she asks, grinning even wider as she stands up.

"Like what? Darts or something?"

"Well, I was thinking pool, with a twist." She winks.

"Explain," I grumble, not liking the sound of this.

"Whoever makes a ball gets to ask the other person a question, and we *have* to answer. It's a rule. If you make more than one ball, you can ask more questions," Sawyer explains, a mischievous glint in her eye.

Running my hands through my scruff, I look at her curiously, weighing the options. This chick is pretty fucking cool. Free information is always nice, and I'd be lying if I said I didn't want to know more about her. But I hate sharing information about myself, so am I really willing to play a game that forces me to? She might ask questions I'm not ready to answer.

"Why the fuck not? Let's play," I agree.

"Awesome! Will you go grab us a couple shots? I'll go set up the table."

"What are the shots for?" I question.

She gives me a look that's equal parts mischievous and

seductive before smirking, as if I'm missing something obvious. "To get drunk, silly," She responds before heading to set up the table with a cute little swing to her hips.

At this rate, I'll be wrapped around her finger before I've even been inside her.

9

—————

SAWYER

I've been looking forward to tonight all week, and I'd be lying if I said it wasn't mostly because of Rex. Last week was surprisingly fun, and it was the first time in a while I've enjoyed spending time with a man outside of the bedroom. I don't date, hell the last person was Brandon, but no one since then.

It's just the population of men in general.

Any man I've ever let into my life has let me down. My father left, my brother is a loving yet extremely controlling prick, and then there's Brandon, the guy I dated for a hot minute who turned out to be a douche.

Men in real life don't compare to the men in the romance novels I read. In real life, we run from red flags. But when I'm reading a book, I want to drown in the sea of red flags.

To sum it up, I don't trust men, so the fact that I'm seeking more time with Rex is a little fucking confusing for me.

After I've set up our game, I look over at the bar where Rex is waiting for our shots, completely ignoring the two women next to him pulling out all the stops to get his attention. If I weren't seeing it with my own eyes, I wouldn't believe it. They're both throwing themselves at him, but he can't be bothered to spare them a glance. Despite their attempts at seduction, his eyes remain fixed on me the entire time.

Regardless, even with his lack of attention, the girls don't give up. Rex stands at the bar, waiting for our shots, while the girls continue trying to talk him up. I don't blame them; Rex is extremely fucking attractive with his couple days' worth of scruff and backwards hat. He's exactly what wet dreams are made of. It doesn't hurt that his muscles are on full display in his light gray shirt and jeans that fit perfectly. *Fuck.* All I can imagine is what that scruff would feel like between my legs.

If I were the insecure, jealous type, this scene would piss me off. Watching these two gorgeous women shamelessly throw themselves at Rex, part of me wonders what's stopping him. They obviously want him, but instead of taking the very low-hanging fruit, he mouths to them, "I'm with her" and directs their gaze to me. With perfect timing, our drinks arrive, and Rex grabs them before walking back to me.

Immediately, Rex starts to lay out our shots before finally looking up at me. "Game all set?"

"Yup. It's all ready," I tell him, doing my best to not let what I just watched go directly to my head. "What was that all about?"

"What was what about?" Rex responds, his face void of any emotion. Is he really that clueless?

"At the bar, with those two girls that are currently shooting daggers my way."

Looking up, he glances in their direction where sure

enough both girls are full on glaring at me, but they quickly look away when they notice him.

"That...was nothing," he says, before gesturing to the shots. "Uh, I wasn't exactly sure what your shot preference was, so I got a couple different things. We have two Jameson, two Fireball, two Don Julio, and two Patron shots."

I can't help but smile at such a simple gesture, but it's so sweet that he cared enough to do something like this. It helps that there's a faint blush on his cheeks, coupled with a small grin, making him look even hotter than usual, and is just enough to send a shot of heat directly to my core. Hot and thoughtful? Sign me the fuck up. If he's thoughtful outside of the bedroom, I can only imagine him in it.

"That's sweet. Honestly, I don't have a preference. I drink pretty much anything. But I'm partial to tequila, so good choice. Should we start with one?" I ask.

"Let's start with the Fireball. I hate that shit and want to get it over with," Rex grunts as he passes me the shot.

"We don't have to take that one. Hell, I can do them both if you'd prefer," I offer.

"Stop talking and take the damn shot so we can play this game," he demands.

We cheers, never breaking eye contact as we both quickly took our shots. It might be the fact that I've already had a few drinks tonight, but there's been a heat in Rex's eyes since he came back from the bar, that has nothing to do with the heat of the fireball. I'm not sure if it's from those girls flirting with him or from playing a game with me, but his eyes look . . . hungry.

Setting his glass down, he grabs a cue and immediately walks over to the table. "Before I break, remind me the rules again," he grumbles, putting space between our growing tension.

"You make a ball, you get to ask me a question. You make two, you get to ask two. And it works the same for me. Got it?"

"Yep," Rex says as he starts the game, sending three stripes into the pockets. With a cocky smirk, he winks at me before letting out a small chuckle, probably at my shocked look. "I'll go easy on you with the first one, I promise," his voice is all dark and growly, promising something wicked. I can't get enough.

"Well, fuck. Hit me with your best shot," I say.

Rex ponders this for a moment, but quickly hits me with a question.

"Why your own studio? Why don't you want to teach at a studio that's already open?"

"I thought you said you were taking it easy on me," I mutter. His question is difficult, as it reminds me of the day I quit being a dancer, but it was also the day I knew I wanted to open a studio. "When I got injured and the doctors told me I would never dance like I used to, I was crushed. Absolutely heartbroken. My studio added salt to the wound when they dropped me from everything, including tryouts for Juilliard. Basically, I was worthless to them, so they replaced me. It crushed me, but it also showed me exactly what I never wanted to be like. I want to open a studio that's open to everyone. Of course, we will train dancers for greater opportunities, but I also want to help young kids who have never danced before, and injured dancers who just want to feel the music flow through their body again."

"I respect that. That's a really cool perspective on a very shitty situation," he says, staring at me with a look of awe.

"Thanks," I tell him, ready to move on to the second question. "Next question?"

"If that's your dream, why do you work at Atlantis?" Rex

asks, looking both curious and nervous about my response. Luckily for me, I've answered this before, so it doesn't faze me too much.

"I need money to pay for classes and my bills. Degrees don't pay for themselves. Plus, I'm saving to get a studio."

"You can get loans for that, right?" he questions.

"Usually, yeah. For both school and business loans. But my brother's a dick, but that's a story for another day. So, I work there and have another job during the day to pay for it all." I shrug. Not much else I can do. "Last question?"

In his defense, he only hesitates for a moment before moving on to the next question. "I overheard you tell Cassie you refuse to date, and don't give me that look, you ladies are far from quiet," Rex says. He has a shy look on his face, like he's beating around the bush to get to the question. "Why? Why don't you date? You're young, attractive, and seem like a cool chick. I guess I just don't understand because when I was your age, all I wanted to do was date around," he finishes with a shrug.

"That's the issue, all the men my age do just want to date around, and the few you can find to commit are usually just controlling assholes who want to use you as arm candy or their little plaything. No thanks," I reply.

"Is this from experience or just what you've seen?"

"Both?"

A flash of something goes through Rex's eyes. It looks like anger, but I can't tell if it's directed at me or the men who have wronged me.

"Not all men are like that. Just because some men are assholes who only think with their dicks, doesn't mean that you should stop trying."

"Yeah, well, the day I meet someone who's worth a damn and is interested in me, maybe I'll consider it. But until then,

I'm done wasting my time on men who want to play games." A small shrug is all I give, hoping to end the conversation. Brandon was the last guy I dated, and it ended up being shit. "My shot now?"

"By all means, do your worst," he says with a wave of his arm towards the table.

His cockiness is almost annoying. He's standing there, leaning back against the stool, patiently waiting for me to take my shot. He looks unaffected by the whole situation, while I feel like my entire body is on fire just from his gaze.

"Shot first," I tell him, walking over to where he's standing with the shots. Grabbing the Patron shots, I pass him one. When he reaches for the shot, our fingers touch, and I secretly love the way he pulls his hand back like he feels the same electricity I do. Without any more hesitation, I pass him a lime, and we quickly down our shots.

"Now take yours," Rex tells me in a low, raspy voice that tells me he's not quite as unaffected as he's letting on.

Walking past him, I line up my shot, making sure that when I lean over to take it, my ass is nearly pressed against him. It's not my fault the cue ball is directly in front of him, and he's refusing to move like a gigantic ass tree. After making a few adjustments to my shot, I wiggle around a bit, knowing he's probably admiring the way my ass looks in these jeans. Glancing over my shoulder, I smirk when I see his eyes immediately shoot up from checking me out. A faint blush crosses his face at being caught, but I play coy. "Sorry, not a lot of room here to make the shot."

"Yeah, I'm sure. Carry on," he says, his expression unreadable other than the slight darkening of his eyes.

Refocusing on the game, I line up my shot and send a solid directly into the pocket. Without even looking at Rex, I move across the table and make one more solid before I miss on the third shot.

"That's two," I tell him with a smirk.

"You would have had three if you had held your hand correctly," is all he says in response.

Tapping my finger on my lip dramatically, I think of what question I should ask him. Why doesn't he date? Has he ever dated? What happened after his hockey injury that kept him in Texas? I decide I should be gentle with my first question and go with the safer option.

"What do you do for a living?"

"I coach hockey at the college level. Just started up this year."

Interesting. Of course, I've found someone in the same sport as my brother, even though I said I'd never be interested in someone who played hockey. I guess a coach is different enough, right? Besides, we're just hanging out. It's not like I'm interested in anything going further with him, just some fun.

"Hmm. Okay, second question. What kept you in Texas?" I ask.

I see the moment my question hits him. His whole body tensed just enough that I know this isn't the easiest question for him. "Or you could tell me what caused you to move back to New York. Whichever you'd prefer."

"That's a loaded question. Shot first." Rex grabs the glasses, passing me a shot of Jameson. Quickly clinking our glasses because everyone knows it's a crime not to cheers, we take the shot. When I look up, he's already set his glass down and is looking at me.

"I moved back to New York because of an opportunity that came up with an old friend. He offered me this coaching job, trying to help me get back into a world I missed. As for why I stayed in Texas, I was fucking up for quite a while, making one bad decision after another. There was no point in coming back when there was nothing left for me here."

I think that's the most he's ever said to me at one time. He's always so serious, almost grumpy, and gives short, quick answers, like speaking offends him. But now . . . he's talking to me. It may not be much, but it's a start.

"So, this is an exciting opportunity?" I ask, trying to push the limit just a bit and get him to tell me more.

"If I'm being honest, I would love the opportunity to coach for the NHL, so starting with college is step one. So yeah, I guess it is an exciting opportunity," he says with a smirk before standing up to look for his next shot. When he's walked a few paces away, he turns around smugly. "Don't think I didn't catch that you stole an extra question. I'll save mine for later."

Then he proceeds to shoot another ball perfectly into the pocket. When he goes to make the next shot, he surprises me by looking back. "Next time you shoot, try to loosen your grip like this. You were holding on to it too tight and the cue didn't have room to move or pivot in your hand."

Then he shoots the next two shots perfectly into their pockets before finally missing.

"Question time," he says.

"I'm ready."

"Why are you here hanging out with me? When all your friends left."

My jaw drops at his rudeness, and he looks guilty.

"Let me try that again. Why are you choosing to hang out with me instead of your friends?"

"Because I enjoy hanging out with you. It's different than

what I'm used to. It's refreshing. Even if you aren't very nice when you talk," I respond.

One step.

That's all it takes before I'm holding my breath. The next two steps he takes make me feel like I'm suffocating, unsure of what he's doing, until he's standing directly in front of me and looking down at me with eyes so dark they look like the night sky. Slowly taking a step back to try to see him fully, I'm surprised when my back is already against the table.

Shit.

I feel like I poked the bear. Unsure of what to do next, I stand in front of him like a deer in headlights.

Rex leans forward until his lips are right above my ear. I can feel his shallow breathing as I try to anticipate his next move.

"I've heard that I can be quite generous. Does that count as 'nice'?" he growls.

My breathing stops. I want to melt into a puddle at his feet, but I do my best to appear unfazed.

"And when have you heard that? I'm not sure I believe it," I respond, breathless.

Leaning even closer, I feel his lips graze my ears and slowly travel down my neck. "When my face is between a woman's legs and I'm devouring her pussy. I'm known to be quite generous then."

My breathing hitches as he takes one more step closer until he's trapped me against the table. Eyes never leaving mine, he slowly slides his hand up the side of my body, across my collar bone, before gently laying his hand against my throat. It's not in a controlling way; it doesn't hurt, but it is possessive. He wants my attention right now, and he's going to make sure he gets it.

"Get your things. We're leaving," he demands.

"Excuse me? What about our friends?" I question.

"I'll text them. Now come on," Rex growls, sounding almost pained, like he's holding something back.

"Where are we going?" I ask, unable to blindly follow him.

Rex stops walking and turns around, causing me to almost run directly into his chest. Leaning forward, he grabs the nape of my neck and smashes his lips against mine. It's quick and dirty, with just enough tongue to show me exactly what he wants to do before he ends the kiss and stares at me with hungry eyes.

"I'm about to show you just how nice I can be. Now let's go," Rex growls, smacking my ass with enough force that I have no room to argue.

10

REX

I've hung out with Sawyer twice.

Well, three times if you count the first night at Atlantis, but she was working so in my opinion that doesn't count. It's only taken two times of being with this girl for her to burrow herself so deeply under my skin that I'm afraid she'll never come out. I'm not even sure if she's aware of the pull she has on me. It's like witchcraft, or voodoo, or something, because I'm never like this, and it's uncomfortable. The most shocking part is that I haven't felt the urge to push her away yet. In fact, I've rather enjoyed spending time with her so far. I keep craving more and more time with her, especially alone time.

Which is pretty fucking obvious as I'm hailing a cab to bring her back to my place.

This is fucking weird.

I hate having people in my home that aren't family, especially if I'm fucking them, or planning to. But here I am, throwing her into a cab and dragging her back to my place. Thank fuck I cleaned up before going out tonight, or else all of Rory's shit would be out. Nothing kills a one-night stand like kid shit all over the place.

Once in the cab, I text the guys to let them know we aren't at the bar anymore if they were planning on going back.

> We're leaving. Talk to you guys tomorrow.

MILES

Just finishing up eating now. Going to another bar?

CADE

We have a good base layer in of food and booze, we're ready to get fucked now.

TREVOR

Cade, drinking wise or dick wise?

My friends are idiots. How I've dealt with their shit for years, is beyond me. But that's not my problem right now. Right now, I want to make sure her friends know she's safe so I can get her naked in my bed. Something about this woman makes me feral, makes me want to strip her naked and devour her, sink my cock into her. The number of times I've imagined her on her knees, her pouty lips wrapped around my cock while her bright blue eyes stare up at me, begging for more, is practically pathetic. I imagine gripping her hair and shoving my cock down her throat, over and over, till my come pours down her throat.

A notification on my phone snaps me out of my fantasy.

CADE

I'm not picky. Either, or both would be fine with me.

MILES

Still waiting, old man . . .

HARRIS

Leave him alone, guys. He's probably
getting his dick sucked.

CADE

You've got a point, Harris. Let him fuck in
peace.

Why am I here? You guys are annoying.

HARRIS

If you can text while she's doing it, she's not
the one, bro.

MILES

;)

Shut up. We're heading back to my place.
No, you're not invited.

Night, fuckers.

With that, I shove my phone in my pocket, ignoring the constant vibration. I see Sawyer glance down at her phone, those big mouths must've told the girls.

Those men gossip like a bunch of old ladies. Fuck, they're worse than that. I'd be surprised if the girls weren't reading over their shoulders the entire time.

I lose all train of thought when the cab pulls up outside my place. I pay them and hop out of the cab, pulling Sawyer behind me into the building and onto the elevator. The doors haven't even closed all the way before we're on each other again. Her soft whimpers urging me on and her hands gripping me tightly are a silent plea for more.

"This mouth should be a crime," I growl. "All it takes are

these sounds, the way your soft lips feel, to fill my mind with images of you on your knees, these pretty red lips surrounding my cock. It's dangerous enough that just might fuck you right here in this elevator."

Sawyer moans into my mouth, urging me on.

Spinning her against the wall, I push into her as I savagely take her mouth again. Slipping my tongue against her lips, she immediately lets me in, moaning into my mouth as I press my cock against her.

"I have fantasies of my own, you know," she whispers, nipping my bottom lip hard before gently soothing it with her tongue. "But they include *you* on your knees, worshipping me, Mr. Lockwood."

"Oh, I promise you, baby girl. I *will* be on my knees for you, but it's you who will be screaming for me. Begging for more," I growl.

Sliding my hands down, I rest one gently against her throat, a silent demand for her attention. Unable to resist, I begin pressing rough bites, followed by gentle kisses, all along her collar bone, relishing the feeling of her hands in my hair as she pulls on it and lets out a small whimper.

"Rex," her voice is nothing more than a moan at this point. Her hands still working to pull me as close to her as possible. "More, please."

"Such a needy little thing, aren't we? I bet if I slipped my fingers into your panties right now, you'd be soaking wet. Just waiting for my cock to fill you up. God, I bet you'll look so pretty with my cock in your tight little cunt. Or in your mouth. I'm not picky."

The elevator doors finally open, shattering the bubble we've found ourselves in. Pulling back, we lock eyes, our breathing heavy as we pause and stare at each other. Desire evident in her eyes, and I'm sure my own look the same.

Without a word, I lift Sawyer in my arms, and her legs immediately wrap around my waist. Her hands waste no time exploring my body and my hair, slowly driving me crazy as I finally get my door open and her inside. Slamming her against the door, I press against her, pushing my hard cock against her core.

"Is this what you want? To watch me lose control, baby girl? Is that why you've been driving me crazy since the second I saw you in that club? Your hot little body a constant tease. Just begging me to dirty it up a bit," I breath in her ear.

"Yes, please. Lose control," she practically begs.

With one finger on her chin, I tilt her head till she's looking up at me. I'm not sure if I'm more pleased with her plea for me to lose control or the fact that she actually seems excited to watch it. Feel it. "Oh, I will. Don't worry. But, baby girl, don't forget, I may lose some control with you, but I'm still in complete control in the bedroom." Her eyes heat up—a combination of rebellion mixed with satisfaction.

Fuck me, this girl gets turned on by giving up control. If that doesn't make me want to take her over my knee and redden that pretty little ass up until she's begging for my cock. I could mark her, paint her with my cum, and claim her as mine. So far, she's pretty fucking perfect.

"Touch me," she begs.

"The second this started, you gave up your control. I'll touch you when I'm ready." She wants to fight me; I can see it in her eyes. She wants that control, but fuck that. "But I promise you'll enjoy every fucking second."

I pull her in for a kiss, taking it slow and gentle, which Sawyer immediately meets with passion, trying to force the kiss further. She's practically pleading with her mouth for more. But I'm not above making her beg.

By the time I give her my cock, I *want* her begging and pleading for me to fill her up.

When she's moaning and panting from just a kiss, I turn from the door and walk her to my room. Her mouth never leaves my body, pressing kisses along my jawline, nibbling on my ear. Her teasing works, and I walk into my room and practically throw her down on my bed.

She stares up at me hungrily, her eyes slowly taking in my body as I peel my shirt up over my head before standing there, deciding what to do to her first. Do I peel off all her clothes and unwrap her like a present? Or do I bury my face in her cunt until she's come more times than she can count and is begging for my cock? Maybe I'll fill that sassy little mouth with my cock, watching as she gags all over me.

The only thing I do know is that I need to touch her. Now.

Walking closer to her, I put one knee on the bed and lean down until my mouth is pressed against hers for a quick kiss. Pulling her up, I drag her shirt off, leaving her in just a red lace bra covering those perfect tits. Fuck, it's red like that first night.

Sawyer is built like a dancer, but she has these perfect, beautiful full tits just begging for my attention. Her thighs are cut, showcasing years of discipline; her muscles defined. I can't keep myself from imagining her thighs against my face, her cunt dripping while she rides my tongue.

With one hand, I pull her tits out of her bra, licking and sucking each one until she's squirming beneath me. My other hand slowly drifts down her body. Slipping past her stomach, I get to the button of her jeans and pop them open.

"I can't wait to see this pretty little cunt of yours. Tell me, baby girl, are you soaking wet for me right now?" I murmur, switching nipples again with my mouth, one hand pinching the other.

She's watching me, her eyes dark with desire as she nods her head yes. That's all it takes for me to me snap. Unable to stop the growl that leaves my throat, I slide her jeans down her legs. Leaning in, I press my nose against the lace of her panties.

"Jesus fucking Christ, you smell delicious," I say, slipping my fingers under her panties before tearing them off.

"Rex!" she yelps, but it quickly becomes a moan as I slip my fingers inside her, my thumb pressing lazy circles around her clit.

She squirms, her body so responsive. It's fucking incredible.

"I can't wait," I whisper.

"For what?"

"To taste this pretty pussy of yours," I say. Leaning forward, I press kisses up her thighs, stopping only once I get to her core. Moving my fingers away from her clit, I almost laugh at Sawyer's cute growl of disapproval at the loss. But as my mouth latches on her clit and my fingers slide into her wet heat, the only sounds I hear are moans.

My tongue pushes against her clit as my fingers continue sliding in and out, fucking her just enough to drive her wild but not enough to let her come. Keeping this tempo up, her body starts writhing beneath me as her hands in my hair tighten their grip. When her breathing hitches, telling me she's close, I pull out, slowing down my pace, thoroughly pissing her off.

The growl that comes from her mouth is cute as fuck. She's so frustrated. Her hips begin lifting, searching for more, trying to build the friction faster, but I refuse.

"Every time you try to make this go faster, I promise I'll pull back."

"Please, Rex."

"Please what?"

"Give me more. Make me come," she whines.

"Maybe now that you've asked so nicely."

"Shut up and—"

Curling my fingers inside her, I make sure to hit that spot deep inside her that has her practically begging for more. When I suck her clit into my mouth and graze it gently with my teeth, she explodes, her taste coating my tongue, making it nearly fucking impossible to pull back from.

Watching this woman come might be my new favorite past-time.

The way her pale skin turns a rosy pink, her eyes darkening with lust. Those things, mixed with her moans and soft whimpers, make me nearly come without her even touching me.

After I work her through her orgasm, making sure to taste every last drop, I'm already craving more.

When did this woman start occupying my mind like this? I went from wanting nothing to do with a woman for more than a night to thinking about her constantly, the desire to give her orgasm after orgasm nearly controlling me.

What is happening to me?

But that's an issue for tomorrow-Rex. Right-now-Rex is only worried about tonight and this hot little thing whose body drives him crazy.

11

―――――

SAWYER

If I thought he was hot before, I was mistaken. I hadn't even scratched the surface.

We haven't even had sex yet, and I've already come twice, which is sadly two more times than I'm used to with a man. Sad, I know, but that's what vibrators are for.

But Rex is a giver, and boy, does he know how to give. Which must be why I'm still feeling needy and wanting more, craving that feeling of him.

This man is powerful, and he knows it. He's addictive and consuming, and I can't stop.

But if I'm being honest? I just want his cock. Like an hour ago. I'm over this teasing. He's proved he's a God with his fingers already, now I just want to see if he's a God with that cock of his.

But he isn't letting up, pulling every last drop of pleasure he can from my body.

"Rex, come on. Please."

"What do you want, baby girl?"

"More."

"Use your words. Tell me exactly what you want. I want

you to beg," he murmurs, nipping my thigh before planting open-mouth kisses, soothing the spot. "You look so pretty when you beg."

"Rex, please. I want you inside of me. I want your cock . . . inside of me. Please," I whimper, unable to control it as he continues rubbing his tongue slowly against my clit.

"Good girl," he says, before his tongue continues its assault on my pussy. I'm about ready to come again, my body tensing as the pleasure builds quickly, but again the motherfucker stops, his smirk telling me it's on purpose.

"You're an asshole," I grumble, my body buzzing with the need to come.

When he finally stands and his fingers find the button of his pants, he's grinning. "I know. But remember, baby girl, I promised it'd be worth it. When I finally let you come again, your whole body is going to ignite with pleasure. You'll feel me for days. Every move you make will remind you of the way I played your body like my favorite instrument. I'm going to ruin you for every other man. I'll make you crave my cock every time you want to come."

Unbuttoning his pants, he slides down his zipper before hooking his fingers beneath his briefs and sliding them down his body.

Holy shit. My jaw drops.

I was already aware Rex had BDE. It's his whole vibe, so the fact that he's huge isn't completely surprising. But the jewelry in the tip of his cock?

Yeah, that's a fucking shock. Holy shit.

He. Is. Pierced.

It takes all my effort to pull my eyes away from the metal on his dick, just begging me to come explore. When I look up, I find Rex watching me intensely, his lips turning up into a seductive grin as my eyes keep bouncing back to his cock.

He seems younger right now, wilder, more boyish than I'm used to seeing him. He seems like he's completely comfortable, standing in front of me with his cock out, just waiting to see what I'll do.

Glancing down his body, I take him in as he walks towards me. Rex is covered in tattoos, with a full sleeve on his left arm, the majority of which are hockey related, with a few other designs scattered throughout. I'm sure he has more on his back; I noticed one on his thigh before my brain short-circuited after I saw his piercing.

Sitting up, I practically beg for him to come up close and personal. I want the feeling of that metal in my mouth as he thrusts his cock down my throat.

"You're . . ."

"I'm what, baby girl?"

"Pierced . . . I just didn't expect that."

"Is that so?" He smirks. "So, you've thought about my cock before, huh?" Rex asks, his voice laced with a cocky tone. "Has your dirty little mind been thinking about my cock? What were you imagining?"

"I . . . I imagined myself on my knees, your cock in my mouth. I was sucking your cock while your hands were in my hair, thrusting in and out as you took your pleasure from me. I imagined you would use me, control me, and do whatever you needed until you were coming down my throat."

He growls as he quickly climes up on the bed, his intensity skyrocketing, sending arousal straight to my core and wetness instantly coating the inside of my thighs. His body slowly creeps up against mine, one of his hands sits against my throat. It's not painful, but it's firm enough that he has my attention.

"As much as I've spent many nights with my hand on my

cock imagining that exact same thing, I've waited too long to have you like this. We'll do that some other time," he says.

Does that mean this isn't just tonight? I'll deal with that tomorrow.

"Then fuck me, Rex. Stop teasing me or I'm going to explode," I snap, before quickly remembering the piercing, and a feeling between desire and fear hits me. "Uh, wait! I might sound really dumb, but that's not going to hurt me, right?" I ask, pointing down at his cock.

A low, cocky chuckle comes from Rex. "What are we talking about here, baby girl? My piercing, or my cock? The piercing won't hurt you, that's a promise. It's only used for good. But my cock? It may take some getting used to. But you just gotta trust me. I'm not going to do anything your body can't handle. I'll listen, I promise. I think I've proved I know your body already."

Rex winks before grabbing his cock with the hand that's not currently wrapped around my throat and slides himself through my wetness, coating himself. Every time he slides through me, he brushes against my clit, the metal rubbing perfectly against me with just enough pressure to send sparks of pleasure throughout my body.

"Question. Uh...are you on the pill?" Rex asks, never pausing his slow assault on my pussy as he waits for my response.

"Yeah. Why?" I ask, wanting to hear him say it.

"I can't help imagining the feel of this cunt on my bare cock. I promise you I'm clean; I haven't been with anyone in quite a while. I, uh...I have only ever done this once and I was so drunk I don't remember it, not that I'm proud of that. I'm clean and I trust you."

"Then do it. Fuck me bare."

I haven't even finished my sentence before he's pushing

all the way in me in one go, stretching me to my limits. My nails scratch down his back in both pleasure and pain as he continues filling me.

"*Fuuuuck,*" he growls as he bottoms out, pulling back just enough to look at me. "You okay?"

"Yeah," I say, my voice coming out in a whisper. "But I need you to move. I feel like I can't breathe with you filling me up."

"You'll be fine," he chuckles. "Just give me a second."

As I begin rocking my hips, he groans, "Sawyer, stop. If you move, this is going to be over before it's even begun, and I'm not really in the fucking mood to embarrass myself. So, be a good fucking girl and stop clenching your goddamn cunt on my cock. I'm not ready to paint you with my come just yet."

I stop, my body freezing, giving him the time he needs. I don't stop teasing him, though, as I pepper kisses along his jaw, finding the spot right below his ear and sucking gently, loving the reaction I feel deep inside of me.

As his grip returns firmly to my throat, he lifts his body up, pulling himself almost all the way out before slamming back in.

I get the feeling it's game on.

"You're being such a good girl. Waiting patiently for me to fuck you. Are you sure you're ready for more?" he questions, squeezing a little tighter.

"Yes, sir," I beg, right as he slams into me.

Repeatedly.

I'm so full it's nearly impossible to think straight. Rex is driving into my body in slow but deliberate thrusts. He's giving my body time to get used to his size, but he's not exactly being patient about it.

Fuck it's hot to see him lose control. For *me.*

"Oh, fuck," I moan when his piercing rubs that spot deep inside my body. That spot deep inside that, until now, I truly believed no man could find it. The illustrious g-spot that I thought was hidden from all men.

He doesn't just find that spot once either. It's constant, his pace quickening, his thrusts becoming more powerful as I moan beneath him, taking everything he has to give me. Needing to take my mind off the fact that I'm already getting close to the edge, I grip his hair with one hand, holding him still until I can reach his mouth.

Craving everything from him, I brush my lips against his, my tongue slowly teasing the seam of his lips and gently nipping his bottom one. It's not demanding; no, I've learned better than to expect Rex to give me things I demand.

This is a plea, a silent plea for more. I want his cock inside of me, his mouth on mine, and our hands exploring each other until all my sensations are overwhelmed. I want everything Rex has to give me. Everything my body begs for.

His mouth attacks mine. Our tongues immediately battle, teeth nipping, as soft moans slip between us, creating a symphony of sounds and feelings, all filled with pleasure. Without a word, or breaking the kiss, he slips one hand down my body, between my legs, as he grabs my knee and throws it over his shoulder with ease, immediately deepening his thrust and making it so much more intense.

"Oh god, more. Please," I moan, this new position hitting all the right spots.

"He's not here right now, baby girl," Rex growls as he slams all the way in. His one hand still holds my leg in the air, while his other slowly moves past my collar bone, back to its place on my throat.

He seems to like it there, and I'd be lying if I said I didn't too.

As he thrusts wildly into me, he squeezes harder this time, his grip firm and unyielding as he thrusts wildly into me. His eyes darken, what were once bright blue are now dark and feral. Like he's thrown all of the pleasantries and bullshit politeness out the window, leaving just this unhinged version ready to devour me.

"He's not the one you should be begging," Rex replies, his voice husky as the shift in position brings us both closer to finishing.

I thought grumpy Rex was the hottest version he could be. I was wrong. This version of him, all demanding and dominant, takes the cake. I'll pretty much do whatever this man says in hopes I might get a "good girl" out of it.

"Don't stop, Rex. Please."

"Don't come, Sawyer. Don't you dare," he says as my legs start to shake, the need to feel that release becomes overwhelming, but I try to push it down.

Grabbing his arms, I hold on tight. Right as my body starts to fall over the edge, small bursts of electricity take over my body. But before my orgasm can completely take over, he stops, pulling himself out of my body.

My nails dig into his arms, clenching his biceps with either the desire for him to continue or anger that he even stopped in the first place; it's currently undecided. Rex's hands remain still, holding firmly on my hips as he continues to breathe heavily. He doesn't say anything, just holds me still as he works to regain control.

"Flip over, baby girl," Rex growls as he leans forward, our lips brushing. "I want to see you on your hands and knees, this pretty ass up in the air waiting for me."

I moan as Rex flips me over, positioning me exactly how he wants me. His hands explore my body. Rubbing along my hips and ass, only a growl of approval letting me know he likes what he sees.

I love that he's taken complete control of my pleasure. Leaving me to trust that he knows my body well enough to play it right so we both leave this with a happy ending.

The scariest part is that I do trust him.

With one hand on my hip, he grabs his cock with the other hand and begins sliding it back and forth through my pussy. He's teasing me, purposely, as he moves slowly until I'm whimpering. In one smooth motion, he's lined up with my pussy, slowly sliding in till he's seated inside of me.

"Jesus Christ, you're huge," I shriek.

"I don't like hearing another man's name fall from your lips, especially when I'm buried deep inside of you," Rex grumbles.

It'd be cute if he wasn't currently fucking me senseless.

Looking back over my shoulder, he's gazing intensely at me as he thrusts inside, angling my body perfectly so his cock, piercing and all, grazes that spot deep inside me repeatedly. He pushes me over the edge so fast that I don't even see the orgasm coming as he shoves my face down into the pillow.

My whole body tenses, shaking with pleasure, and my pussy clenches around him, driving Rex even closer to finishing with me. I'm moaning, possibly screaming. I'm not entirely sure. I'm just thankful my face is buried in the pillow, or the neighbors would be getting a front row seat to me getting my brains fucked out. His erratic thrusts driving into me are the only sign that he's coming along with me, but when he moans my name as he fills me up, my body shivers along with him, the aftershocks of my orgasm hitting me without warning.

Neither of us moves. It takes us both a few minutes

before either of us move or say anything. I'm lost in the aftereffects of these intense orgasms. Moving isn't exactly on my to-do list right now. And if I'm being honest, I'm not sure I'm physically capable of it right now.

"I'm going to pull out. Don't move," Rex says, sliding out and surprising me as he kisses my forehead before heading to the bathroom. After a minute, he returns with a warm washcloth and begins cleaning me up.

When he's done, I'm quickly scooped up and laid down on his pillow, still in his arms.

"You good?" he asks quietly. "You're not hurt, right?"

"Nope, perfect," I mumble into his neck.

"Good. Sleep. I'm not done with this pretty little pussy yet," he whispers in my ear before gently cocooning me in his arms.

The last thing I hear before I fall asleep is him whispering against my hair.

"I'm not sure I'll ever be done with it."

12

SAWYER

The next morning comes far too quickly. I'm not even sure we slept. I notice Rex's spot is empty. The second thing I notice is the strong smell of coffee. I figure that if I follow the coffee, I'll find Rex. Thank God. Without coffee, there's no way I'll be getting out of this bed, let alone do anything productive.

Rolling over, I'm not surprised to find I'm sore. Rex wasn't lying; he can be a *very* generous man. Bossy and demanding, yes, but he lives up to his promise.

Figuring out where all my clothes are, I head to the bathroom to make myself look somewhat presentable. In the mirror, I see hickeys coating my breasts, with little bite marks between them. He sure loved my tits last night, either grabbing them, licking them, biting them, or teasing them by playing with my nipples. Rex played my body better than anyone else has, which is such a fucking shame since I don't date. I sure as hell wouldn't mind a repeat of that bedroom action again, especially with that piercing.

Once I'm finally presentable, I venture out of his room, following the delicious smell of coffee in search of a cup and

Rex. I quickly find the kitchen but stop in my tracks when I see him. He's standing at the bar, wearing nothing but a pair of gray sweatpants hung *low* on his hips. It leaves little to the imagination. It's not that I'm not aware of how incredible his body is. I felt what he's capable of multiple times last night. But seeing it in the daylight is different from using my tongue to memorize his body.

His abs are showcased, leading down to the prominent V peeking out of those sweatpants and leading straight to his cock. A cock that fucked me better than I've ever been fucked. One I definitely wouldn't complain about having again right now.

Looking away from the window, Rex smirks over his coffee, obviously catching me as I shamelessly check him out. But I don't look away. I just continue my perusal, faking a confidence I definitely don't have.

"See something you like?" he asks, right as someone knocks on the door. Immediately, his face drops.

The sound of the door opening makes me nervous. Was he expecting someone? Was the door unlocked? Is everything okay?

"Rex," I hear a woman's voice yell from the doorway. "Are you here?"

A woman with a key to his place . . . *Fuck me running.*

"Shit," Rex mumbles, setting down his coffee cup and looking at me. He must see a mixture of emotions on my face because he has the decency to look embarrassed. "Uh . . . I guess you'll get to meet my sister. She obviously doesn't understand personal space or how to use a cell phone. Sorry."

Relief fills me at the realization that it's just his sister.

"No problem, I won't stay long. I'm meeting Cassie for our run shortly. I just needed some coffee first," I tell him.

Before he can respond, his sister yells again, "Rex? You home?"

"In the kitchen," he finally grumbles, his eyes doing a poor job of hiding his annoyance. Then again, I'm not sure he's even trying.

"Mom came to pick me up. I guess Ro woke up at 6 a.m. Figured we could make some breakfast over here if you weren't back yet. Want to invite Trevor over for breakfast after your run?" she asks.

When she turns the corner and sees me, she immediately smiles. A look of surprise taking over her face as soon as she recognizes me.

"Sawyer! What are you doing here?" she squeals.

"You two know each other? Hold on. We'll get to that. Did you say mom and Ro are here?" Rex asks, sounding panicked.

Stella looks nervous at his questions, and I can't help but wonder why. But I don't have long to worry about it before they start talking again.

"Yeah, they're parking the car. I got out so I could run to the bakery," Stella explains.

"No, Stella. You know they can't come here right now. I have company, and she's not meeting Ro," he snaps.

"Whoa, chill out, grumpy. I'll call mom and tell her I left something at the bakery, but it's not like she doesn't already know her," Stella retorts, seeming slightly annoyed at her brother's outburst.

It doesn't take long for his sister to buy us some time, meaning now there's only one question left. How do we all know each other and not realize it. Stella isn't fazed by her brother's grumpiness, in fact, she just completely ignores him.

"So, what are you doing here anyways?" Stella asks, continuing to ignore her brother.

"Um, just hanging out I guess," I say.

"Does someone want to explain to me what the fuck is happening? How do you two know each other?" Rex growls.

God, something about his voice when it gets like this makes me nervous with anticipation. Leaves me wondering what comes after his words.

Stella turns and looks at Rex like he's the biggest idiot alive. I guess that makes two of us, because I'm not understanding the connection either.

"Rex, you're an idiot. You're the one who had me pick up Ro from daycare like last week. Sawyer's her teacher, so obviously I met her when I picked her up."

"What? No. Ms. Daniels is her teacher. She talks about her all the time," he says cluelessly.

"I *am* Ms. Daniels," I tell him, slowly trying to catch up. "My name is Sawyer Daniels."

Wait. If Stella is Rory's aunt, does that make Rex her dad? Motherfucker.

The look on his face says it all. This situation is fucked. Rex is a dad? And his daughter is Rory? The little girl I've gotten so close to these last few weeks.

"How do you not know who her teacher is, Rex? Don't you have to pick her up and drop her off most days? What? You think that just because you're the big, bad, new hockey coach there that you can be lazy?" Stella questions.

"No. They do things differently there. A red-headed girl comes out in the mornings to grab her from the car, then brings her out when I call. I guess I just assumed that she was Ms. Daniels," he mutters.

"Nope. It's me. And honestly, you're the only one that does drop off and pick up that way. Everyone else comes in.

Claire, the redhead you're talking about, is nice enough to accommodate you," I snap.

I wouldn't believe it if I didn't see it with my own two eyes, but Rex looks embarrassed. I'm not sure if it's because he's an idiot and doesn't do the drop off and pick up correctly, or if it's the fact that he didn't know who I was, but I'm reveling in the fact that he's not the confident one right now.

"And wait, you're the hockey coach? Where?" I ask.

"He's the head coach for the university," Stella answers for him while Rex continues to stare at me, a shocked look covering his normally neutral face.

"*Fuck.* Yeah, okay. Well, yeah. This just got awkward." I rub my hands together, a nervous tick I've always done.

"Why? I'm pretty sure there's no rule about people who work for the same university not fucking. It's a big campus," Stella says, confused.

"No, it's not that. It's, uh, my brother. He's on that team," I reveal.

"Excuse me?" Rex finally speaks up at that. "Name. Now."

Stella glares at him, and my eyebrows are raised so high, they're probably in my hair. I'm not sure what he's used to getting with that tone of voice, but it sure as fuck doesn't work on me.

"Try that again if you'd like an answer," I bite back.

Rex sighs, obviously getting irritated. "Sawyer, please. Who?"

"Daniels," I tell him.

"Max? My fucking captain?" Rex barks, his eyes darkening again, but this time with anger, not lust.

Rex looks uncomfortable, running his hand across his face and slightly pulling on his hair like he's trying to get a grip on this situation. When he finally looks at me, he's angry.

"You need to go," he says in a low, almost pained voice, his eyes matching his tone.

"What?" Stella and I both say in unison.

"I'm not introducing anyone to my daughter. You may know her at daycare, but that's not her home. She's not about to see a woman in her house who isn't family. Besides, there's no way I can hang out with one of my players sisters. It's just fucking wrong."

"Rex, you can't—" Stella starts to argue, but he cuts her off with the raise of his hand.

Standing up, I decide I'm over his tantrum. "Don't worry, Stella. He's not offending me. I really don't care about Max. That fucker can eat rocks for all I fucking care for all the shit he's put me through, I use the word brother loosely. As for you, Rex? I get that you have it in your head that you need to keep everyone at arm's length to protect your daughter, but you don't have to be such a brute about it. I wish you lived up to the version Rory shared with me. Instead, you're just a dick, acting like I'm in the wrong.

He has the decency to look apologetic for a moment, but it doesn't change anything. "Sawyer, don't make this more than it is. We had fun, but that's all it was. You have your life and your two *very* conflicting jobs to keep you busy," he says.

That alone stings worse than anything else he's said. Having him use my second job against me, like I should feel guilty about it, stings. If anything, I thought he would understand that I'm doing everything I can to follow my dreams.

"Fuck you, Rex." Grabbing my stuff, I walk out, ignoring Rex entirely. I put my shoes on before giving Stella a quick hug and walking out. "One day you're going to kick yourself when you're all alone in your bed with no one to share memories with, because that's all we were doing. Having fun, but even that's too much for you."

With that, I slam the door. On him and any emotions he was beginning to awaken in me.

~

Four hours and countless mimosas later, I've recounted the entire conversation to Cassie, who honestly seems to be more in shock than I am. She stares at me once I finish telling her everything that's happened.

"Wait. So, you're telling me that you slept with him last night and today he kicked you out?" she asks.

"Yeah, pretty much. The worst part is that the man can fuck. He's a God in bed. He did things I've only ever read about," I muse.

"Sawyer, no sex talk yet." Cassie holds her hand up, stopping me right as the waitress comes over with our food.

We ordered appetizers right away, like five of them. All of them different combinations of cheese and carbs. We've got cheese bread, cheese dip, and some jalapeño dip with chips, but obviously, we need them all.

"I'm still in shock that the man kicked you out. Like that he actually told you to leave," Cassie exclaims.

"Yep. Me too. When we woke up, everything was fine. His sister got there and said Rory was on her way up with their mom, and he told me to leave." I shrug.

"I mean, maybe he freaked out about his daughter seeing you and just overreacted. Have you thought about giving him some time and maybe he'll realize what a dumb shit he was?" she asks, giving him the benefit of the doubt.

"That's all fine and dandy, Cassie. I would have been fine if that's all it was. But it doesn't change that he then went on to tell me we were just a hookup for fun and that I should just go be happy with my two 'very conflicting' jobs. That's beyond just overreacting. That's taking shots at my character. I've dealt with that shit enough from my own family, and if I'm not going to deal with it from them, I'm sure as hell not going to take it from a guy. No matter how good he fucks."

Cassie just stares at me in between bites of her gooey cheese bread before downing the rest of her drink. We may like to work out and stay in shape, but we don't sacrifice bread or mimosas for it. Or cheese.

I don't trust anyone who doesn't like cheese.

"But this doesn't sound like him. Yeah, he's a grumpy dick, but he doesn't seem like a legit bad dude," she says.

"I didn't think so either. He was always sarcastic and had this dry sense of humor, but for some reason, I really connected with him. He may have been a dick, but he wasn't nasty about it. I mean, I shouldn't care what one guy thinks, right? Especially not someone almost fifteen years older than me. That's on me for going after someone who's a dad," I sigh.

"Um, don't shame him for being older, especially when he's a god in bed. Besides, thirty-seven isn't old, and you may be twenty-four, but you're mature."

"I still haven't told you the worst part," I tell her, not sure I'm ready to say it. It kinda gives me the ick, but it's also just more drama I don't want to deal with.

"There's more?"

"I mean . . . yeah. He's a hockey coach and ex-NHL player."

"Okay? I'm not following," she says.

"He's a hockey coach at Brooklyn U. For Max's team," I choke out.

"Well . . . fuck. That could be awkward."

"Really, you think?" I deadpan.

Of course, it would be awkward. My brother is . . . interesting to say the least. There are many ways to describe him but overbearing comes to mind first. Followed quickly by controlling, manipulative, uncompromising, and unsupportive. In the background, there's whisperings of him being sweet, loving, thoughtful, and just a pain in the ass little brother, but those voices are much quieter.

I don't think those things are entirely his fault, though. My dad left a while ago, and after he did, my mom sort of fell apart. I was dancing all the time and getting ready to try out at Juilliard. I pretty much avoided my house and my mom like the plague. With Max being home, he took it upon himself to be strong for her and help her put herself back together.

After I got injured, I kind of fell off the deep end for a while and made a lot of questionable choices with drugs, and alcohol, and partying. He decided he was the man of the house and tried to make those choices for me, but I quickly put an end to that. Max also convinced my mom that I was going to throw my life away by trying to get a business degree to open my own studio. She believed him enough that she stopped paying for college—hence the second job. They wanted me to get a teaching degree and go work at the private school my mom teaches at in the city.

"What did he say when he found out?" Cassie asks.

"Honestly, he didn't really give a shit. He was more

concerned about getting me out of the apartment before Rory saw me. I'm sure it's just another reason for him to be a jerk to me if he were to really think about it. More of a reason to not try and communicate with him," I tell her.

"Okay. I have another question . . ." Cassie gives me a look that tells me I'm going to really hate her question, but she's smart and tops off my mimosa before continuing. She knows me well.

"Definitely don't like the sound of that," I groan.

"Have you thought about talking to Max? Maybe answering one of the many messages he sends you? I know you're pissed, and he's trying to control you, but he's still your brother," she says softly.

"Yup. And my father's technically still my father, but that doesn't mean I'm going to show up at his house for dinner next week."

Now I definitely know why she filled up my drink.

"No, Cassie. I won't be talking to my brother anytime soon. I know for some godforsaken reason you have a soft spot for him, but I don't care. He's spent years trying to control me and has manipulated my mom into thinking he's right. I have nothing to say to him until he pulls his head directly from his ass. Now. Next subject, please."

Cassie looks a mix between sad and embarrassed, which isn't surprising, she's known my family for a very long time. She's seen this issue play out before.

"Alright, then let's get back to the good stuff. Tell me about his cock!"

And with that, we are back on even ground, and we spend the rest of lunch bullshitting and getting drunk, while I do my best not to think about how I had the best sex of my life only for him to turn out to be a huge asshole.

13

REX

I t doesn't matter who I'm with or what I'm doing; I can't stop thinking about the look on Sawyer's face when I told her to get out.

It's been five days, and that's all I can think about. It wasn't even that she was mad. Fuck, that would have been easier to handle. No, she looked disappointed and shocked, like she thought it was out of character for me and I had crushed her.

Which is exactly why all week I've avoided, like a coward.

Monday came, and I continued dropping off and picking up Rory like the asshole I am, still refusing to go inside. It's embarrassing that, as a grown ass man, I can't face a woman just because I'm attracted to her. Like I'm in junior high or something.

This is exactly why it's best I just avoid her. I need to put some distance between me and her magic pussy.

Thankfully, this week is busy with hockey, so I'll be able to keep my mind off of her. We have another game tonight, meaning I'll be without Rory, so right now, I'm getting some quality time in with her doing what we love most—making breakfast and eating together.

Our kitchen is a disaster with pancake ingredients all over the counters, flour scattered on the floor, and of course, all over the two of us.

"Daddy! Chocolate chips! Chocolate chips!" Rory yells.

"Sweetheart, we already added some. Keep stirring."

Putting the whisk down, she rests her hands under her chin and flashes me her widest smile, batting her eyelashes. "More chocolate! Pleeeeeaseeee, dadddddy!"

How can I say no to that?

"You've been spending too much time with Auntie Lala, you're laying it on thick," I chuckle, reaching for the chocolate chips and measuring cup. I scoop some out and hand them to her. "Here you go, sweetie. Make sure you mix them all in!"

"Thank you, daddy! You're the best daddy ever! Thank you, thank you!!!"

Rory starts to mix the pancake mix, only splashing it on the counter a bit. When we first started making breakfast together, the kitchen would be a complete disaster. Rory would end up needing a bath after, with batter in her hair and all over her and the kitchen. She's come a long way in terms of patience, and she loves eating what we make.

She still lets me do the actual cooking part, but soon, I'll start letting her help with that too. While I cook the pancakes, Rory brings the syrup and butter over to the table, helping me set the table.

"Daddy, is the pancakes done yet?"

"Yes, sweetie. I'm finishing up the last one. Have a seat. I'll bring them over," I say, nodding towards the table.

"Thank you, daddy!"

There are days when I miss playing hockey and the lifestyle that came with it. Puck bunnies were everywhere, just waiting to warm your bed for the night, and I'd be lying if I said I didn't take advantage of that. But I wouldn't trade these memories for anything. Rory is the best thing to ever happen to me, and undoubtedly the reason I was able to pull myself out of the dark place I had been in years ago.

As we sit down together and devour our chocolate chip pancakes, Rory chats about her last visit with her aunt and her plans with grandma tonight. She's a smart kid and knows just how lucky she is to have so many people who love her.

"I do ballet this week?" Rory asks, a mouthful of pancakes garbling her words.

"Don't talk with your mouthful, Rory. You know that, sweetie. But, yes, you have ballet on Thursday."

Rory chews quickly, washing everything down with her orange juice before answering again.

"How many days till that?"

"Today is Tuesday, so not today, not tomorrow, but the next day," I respond.

"Yayyyyy! Thank you, daddy! Ms. Daniels told me that we are going to work on twirling! I want to twirl! Can we get a pretty skirt for me for ballet? Ms. Daniels has a pretty purple skirt that I love. Can I match her? Pleasssssse daddddy?" she begs, batting her eyelashes.

I'm going to have to talk to my sister about what she's teaching Rory because her fluttering eyelashes and innocent look work way too well on me, I can't imagine what Stella will teach her next, but I'm terrified.

"Okay, sweetie. Maybe you and grandma can go shopping for that this evening or tomorrow. Would you like that?"

"Yes, please, daddy."

"Okay. Now let's hurry up and eat. We need to get going here soon. Remember, grandma and grandpa are picking you up tonight."

"Yup. Sleepover!" she exclaims.

Gazing at her smile, I can't help but feel so lucky that I have such a special little girl. She's a little firecracker but has the kindest heart. I'm so happy she gets to spend so much time with family; she adores them.

But now it seems she's getting a bit attached to Ms. Daniels. I regret the way Saturday had gone. I wish that wasn't how I found out that she is the teacher my daughter considers a hero—the one she's been telling me about every morning over breakfast. I also wish I hadn't found out that her brother is one of my captains.

Maybe then, I could have spent a little more time with her.

Shaking my head, I finish breakfast and quickly get us on the road to drop Rory off at daycare.

Here's to hoping tonight's game goes better than the last two.

～

*I*t feels like I had just fallen asleep when my alarm blares on Wednesday morning. We had a game last night against Penn U, and unsurprisingly, we lost. Again.

That makes three games in a row that we've lost, so I'm heading into practice early today. Thankfully, Rory was with mom overnight, so I don't have to rush around to get her to daycare on time today.

Practice is going to fucking suck.

The first thing we have to do is watch tapes and point out

all the careless mistakes we've been making, there are so many little things that need to be cleaned up; we're missing too many shot opportunities and we're losing because of it. I need them to focus and actually see it instead of just relying on my word. They have been so sloppy with the puck that it's a miracle they didn't lose by more. After tapes, we'll move to drills—lots of drills. We'll focus on passing, puck control, shooting … all of it.

To say I'm frustrated about our losses is an understatement. None of them would've happened had we controlled the puck better, and all of this shit has happened since Saturday.

Saturday. The day I was the biggest dick alive to Sawyer, who is undoubtably like the coolest chick I've ever met. *Fuck.* I can't stop thinking about her. It's useless to even try, but I can't bring myself to allow a relationship with her to happen. Rory's already too close to Sawyer, I can't risk Sawyer not taking it seriously.

There's a difference between being thirty-seven and twenty-four. When I was twenty-four, I would have turned and run if a woman told me she had a kid. Why would I expect her to do anything different? She might stay for a bit, but I guarantee it would get old.

I also need to keep in mind who her brother is. He's one of my goddamn players for fucks sake. Plus, he's one of the captains. I can't hook up with one of my players sisters. I can only imagine what would happen if he ever found out. On one hand, he might quit, which would hurt the team. He's easily our lead scorer and honestly, he's just damn good at what he does.

It would be a shame if he quit and hurt his possibilities in the NHL. I've been talking to a few teams, one team in particular about him.

And, I can't imagine letting Bernard down. If I lost one of his best players, he'd kill me.

He trusts me to protect his team and his players, which means not fucking over one of their sisters. Even if he wasn't a player and we were just friends, it wouldn't matter. You. Don't. Fuck. Your. Friends. Sister.

It's a rule. You just don't.

The second we get done watching the tapes, I have them geared up on the ice doing one drill after another.

An hour later, we're finally about to begin a few small area games when Max walks up, looking a bit nervous.

There's no way he knows.

Right?

"Hey, uh . . . coach?"

"Yeah, Daniels?" I ask, glancing up from the clipboard that has the teams on it for drills.

Max stares up at the ceiling like he's looking for an answer written up there. "Is everything alright?" He finally asks.

"Yeah? What do you mean?"

"You just don't seem yourself . . . you are kind of—"

"He's trying to tell you that you're being a fucking prick," a voice I know all too well cuts Max off.

Turning to face the voice, I find Trevor standing there with his signature smile, trying not to laugh at the shocked look on Max's face.

"Coach, that is not what I meant. I could just tell something is . . . off," Max says as he turns around and glares at Trevor. Trevor just laughs.

These two are annoying and remind me why I don't go out and interact with people often.

Doing my best to hide my annoyance from Max, I sigh. He's right . . . well, I guess Trevor's right. But I'll be damned if I tell him that. I am in a shitty mood, and I'm probably being an asshole, but that doesn't change the fact that they need the practice. I could be less of a dick about it, though. "It's all good Max. This here," I gesture towards Trevor who still thinks this is funny. "Is Trevor. He's Bernard's son and unfortunately, my best friend. Apparently, that gives him the delusion that he can talk shit no matter where we are."

"It most certainly does. About time you caught up. Besides, I wouldn't call it talking shit. I'm merely pointing out the obvious and enjoying calling you out on your shit." He retorts before turning to shake Max's hand. "I'm Trevor. It's nice to meet you."

"I'm Max Daniels. Likewise, man," Max says, seeming uneasy about this whole situation.

"Look, man, you're probably right. I'm being a dick today, well more so than usual. I get it. I've got a lot of shit going on, and I guess I let it get in my head," I say, trying to sound apologetic.

"Not a problem. I just wanted to make sure you were good. We can take it, and if they can't they need to figure that shit out now," Max responds.

"Thanks," I tell him, I'm impressed he stood up to me, but I'm not going to tell him that. Show's good leadership on his part.

"It's woman problems," Trevor pipes in, his fucking happy grin so bright that I'm daydreaming about punching the fucker right here.

"The fucking worst," Max groans. "Girl's suck."

"They're both the problem and the solution, Max," Trevor winks, unable to act mature even here.

"Shut the fuck up, Trevor. We're not having this conversation," I groan.

"Why not? Maybe you need to hear someone else tell

you you're being ridiculous and it's affecting you outside of your personal life. Besides, I'm just saying, kicking a girl out after a hookup is brutal shit, man. I thought you might've actually liked her too."

God damn. Out of anyone he could talk about this in front of, it had to be Sawyer's fucking brother.

"Damn, that is fucking brutal, man," Max exclaims.

Rubbing my brows, I find it hard not to agree with Max. Kicking her out wasn't fun. "Yeah, not exactly my finest moment. But, again, we're not talking about this. This is practice, not an afternoon gossip session, Trevor. Max, thanks for calling me on my shit. I respect that. Go get the team started on small area games with the same teams as last time. I'll be over in five," I tell him, nodding toward the ice.

With a quick nod, Max skates off, leaving me with Trevor.

"What the fuck, man?" I bark at Trevor.

"What do you mean?" he asks, clueless.

"Max is Sawyer's brother you fucking idiot. Which is why I didn't want you to bring up my 'woman problems' or whatever bullshit you'd call this," I snap, rubbing my hand down my face.

"*Fuck,*" Trevor mumbles, realization finally sinking in.

Trevor is literally the polar opposite of me, which might be why we've been best friends since we were five. While I'm known for being a dick with a piss-poor attitude and apparently sporting a constant frown, Trevor is all smiles and happiness, to everyone. All. The. Time. Except now. Right now, he looks apologetic and a little disheartened, which is confusing.

"Yeah, basically. Why do you look like I just pissed in your Wheaties?" I ask.

Trevor sighs and turns to watch the team run their games, obviously ignoring me. He's a lot like me, and just being around hockey, whether at a game or even just watching the drills, can be calming. It feels like home. It's probably time I thank Bernard again for getting me out here, and back to being a part of the ice.

"Wright needs to work on puck control. He's all over the place, which is one of the reasons they kept losing possession last night," Trevor says.

"I know. Him and Santana both need to work on it," I tell him, watching them as well. "Hey, you watched the game?"

"Yeah, we were off last night so Miles and Harris came over to watch," Trevor says with a smirk. "I made them enchiladas."

"You fucker. You know I love those enchiladas," I snap playfully.

"Yup. I do," he quips. "Make sure they're going for the rebounds. There's been a lot of missed opportunities to take shots because no one's there."

"Yes, Dad, I know," I grumble.

Ignoring me, Trevor just stares at my players. He obviously has something on his mind, which is confirmed when he quickly turns and faces me.

"Beer. Friday. After work. You and me. Meet me at Hudson's at five," he says quickly.

"I have to get Rory, I can't," I respond.

"I already spoke with Stell. She's grabbing Rory and bringing her to your place. Cade offered to help and make Rory dinner."

"Why did you plan all this out? What's so important that you went through all that shit?" I question suspiciously.

"You. You're that important and honestly, we're all worried about you. You're lucky you're just getting me going out this time and not a full-on intervention. But we'll get to all that Friday. You get back to practice, I'll see you Friday at five."

Before I can even respond, Trevor turns on his heel and walks away. But he turns back around with a grin before getting too far. "Your enchiladas are in your office. Ass hole." Then he's gone.

Shaking my head, I quickly head back to practice where they're just finishing up their first game. They rotate teams and begin quickly, wasting no time.

I spend the next hour making a couple changes to the teams that are playing, testing out different dynamics and taking notes that I want to talk to my assistant coach and the captains about. I have a feeling some of the changes might cause a little friction.

Ending practice, the guys all walk out at a much slower pace than when they all came in. They had a grueling work-out, so it's not too surprising. I know they saw the same mistakes on the tapes that I saw, so hopefully, they trust me enough to know we're making these changes for a reason. If they can take them seriously, our team could be great.

"Bye, coach. See you tomorrow," Connor Mathews, my goalie, says on his way out.

"See you tomorrow. Great practice," I tell him with a nod.

I'm finally about to walk out when I hear my name.

"Coach Lockwood. Wait up!" Max says from the locker room door.

Turning around to face him, I see him quickly heading out with his bag thrown over his shoulder. "Yeah, Max?"

"I just wanted to tell you it was great practice. A lot of the guys really liked what we did today and appreciated what you noticed on the tapes. I know they don't always express that to your face, so I just wanted you to know," Max says with a quick shrug.

I can't help it. I smile. Not a big, normal person smile, but enough that my lips turn up.

This team has been tough to get to know, and it's been even tougher getting them to trust me, so hearing this from Max means a lot.

"Thanks, Max. I appreciate it," I say, clapping him on the shoulder.

"Of course."

We turn and start to walk out, casually talking about our plans for the evening.

"I'm just heading out to go have dinner with my mom," Max tells me.

"Are you and your mom close?"

"Yeah, she's really the only family I have," Max tells me.

How is that possible?

"No siblings?" I ask, unable to hold myself back.

"I mean, I have an older sister, but honestly, she's a real piece of work. Always making one bad choice after another, so we don't really talk," Max says the light in his eyes dimming and his jaw clenching. It's a mix of emotions but I can tell he's both angry and hurt.

It feels like a hit to my gut. It would be one thing if they were close and had a good relationship, but to know they aren't even a part apart of each other's lives really makes it sting a little more that I kicked Sawyer out. Using her brother as an excuse doesn't really work if they don't even consider each other siblings.

But then again, that doesn't change the Rory factor.

"Sorry to hear that."

"All good, man. She'll come to her senses eventually. Or she won't and she'll be a deadbeat all her life. But hey, it was good talking to you. I gotta go this way," Max points the opposite direction I'm heading. "I'll see you at practice tomorrow."

"Sounds good. See you then," I say with a wave.

I continue walking towards my car, unable to stop thinking about what Max said. Don't get me wrong, I know I'm doing this because of Rory, but it was so much easier to also blame who her brother is for ending things the way I did. And what the hell did he mean calling her a deadbeat? She works harder than almost anyone I know, all while going to school. It doesn't seem like she's a deadbeat to me . . .

It makes me wonder what he knows that I don't.

But I can't think about that as I drive home to the only girl in my heart—well besides my mama—Rory.

14

SAWYER

"What time are you off tonight?" Cassie shouts from her room.

"I'm off at six from the daycare, but I have to work eight to two in the morning at Atlantis. Why?" I yell back from my bathroom. I woke up late today, so I'm trying to throw myself together as quickly as possible so I can head to my first class before work.

To say I haven't been sleeping well would be an understatement. Last night I didn't fall asleep until almost four a.m., and my first class starts at eight. Coffee will be essential today if I want any chance of staying upright.

Ever since Rex kicked me out of his house, it's all I can think about, especially since I spend almost every day with Rory. She's the happiest little girl now that we've started doing ballet a couple times a week. I can see that she's finally opening up to me. She's been telling me more about her family, especially her 'Auntie Lala,' whom she obviously adores.

Of course, I also get to hear everything about her daddy because this little girl is obsessed with her daddy. Which shouldn't come as a surprise though; I'd be obsessed with the man too. He seems to dote on his little girl, and if what happened over the weekend is any indication, he's just as obsessed with her.

I hear Cassie slowly make her way down the hall to my room. She must've been yelling at me from her bed.

"I wanted to go grab some drinks this evening and wanted to check when you'd be free. Maybe we can go out later this weekend with everyone?" she asks.

"Maybe . . . I'm not sure that's the best idea for me to go out with you guys again. I don't really want to see Rex right now."

"Oh, I understand. Don't worry about that. I was thinking just the girls going out for some drinks. That way we could find you a new dick to bounce on. Besides, Trevor mentioned that they were busy with hockey most of the weekend anyways," she explains.

"Cassie, I really don't want to find someone to sleep with. I'm busy enough as it is. I don't need to add that to my plate. Especially not after last weekend went as shitty as it did."

"Oh, please, girl. We all need some good dick in our lives. Besides, it'll help you get over Rex," she says, raising her eyebrows.

"There's nothing to get over. It was a one-night stand," I shrug.

"Lie to yourself all you want, but we all saw that tension building. I wouldn't really call that a one-night stand. Admit it or don't, but you two were starting to develop . . . something. If you don't feel like going out to find someone new, have you considered texting him? Maybe reaching out to see what the fuck happened?" she suggests.

"Absolutely not. He made it very clear that he doesn't want anything to do with me, let alone taking it further."

"Sawyer, you owe it to yourself to at least try to be happy. I know your family has done a number on you, but you're so closed off from building any sort of relationship outside of us, of course. It just makes me sad watching you go through this," Cassie says.

"Cassie, I am happy. I really am. I'm working, I'm in school about to finish my degree this year, and then hopefully I'll be able to open up the studio I've been dreaming about."

"But that still means you're doing everything by yourself!" she exclaims.

"What about you? I don't see you dating or out to bars trying to find someone to go home with. Why is it just me?" I question.

"I . . . it's different, Sawyer," Cassie says quietly. "I don't date, but that doesn't exactly mean I'm against it. I'm just not seeking it out."

Cassie is making excuses, and I feel like she's not being entirely honest with me or herself. And unfortunately, that's an issue for another day.

"Cassie, I'm sorry. Let's make time to go out this weekend. I need to leave in, like, five minutes if I want to make it to class on time," I say as I continue getting ready.

"Okay, please just think about what I said. I don't want you to miss out on things because you're too closed off to see it until it's too late. Rex seemed different, plus he had that daddy vibe that makes girls go wild over." She smirks.

She gives me a quick wink before slipping out of my room and heads towards the kitchen. Hopefully, she's making coffee so I can sneak a cup on my way out. What are annoying best friend roommates for if not for their coffee-making abilities?

I spend the rest of the day unable to stop thinking about what she said. I can admit to myself that I did enjoy spending time with Rex. It was always exciting thinking about getting to see the grumpy asshole because he was usually just grumpy to everyone else, not me.

I push that thought away because if it actually meant something to him, then he would have been a hell of a lot nicer to me than he was.

When I get to daycare, I'm happy the kids are all here today, hopefully they can keep my mind from thinking of him, even if his daughter immediately attaches herself to my side the second she sees me. We spend the next couple of hours doing art projects, having tea parties, and, of course, dress up parties.

"Ms. Daniels! Do we get to do ballet today? My grandma took me to get a pretty purple skirt, just like yours!" Rory all but squeals with excitement.

"Yes, sweet girl. We get to do ballet tonight." I smile. "I can't wait to see your pretty purple skirt. I bet it's beautiful."

"It is! I love it! Can we change now?!"

"It's not quite time, but soon!"

"Okayyyy," Rory almost whines, but walks back to the kitchen set where the rest of the kids are playing and immediately joins them with a smile.

It's so crazy to me how resilient kids are. They take disappointment in stride, usually not letting it impact their day. I wish adults were more like that, more importantly, I wish I was more like that. Instead, here I am, still thinking about Rex as I clean up the project we did earlier.

This is why I don't do hookups and have been just fine being the sole provider of my own pleasure. Well, me and my battery-operated friends—we can all use a little help sometimes. But when you involve other people, feelings get involved, even when you promised yourself they wouldn't. I don't do feelings. Don't like them, especially since they usually end with me getting hurt.

I have to stop thinking about him and what happened. It's done and I just need to move on.

As the workday comes to an end, Parents start to arrive to pick up their kids, leaving just Rory and another girl named Bailey for class tonight. They get changed into their leotards and come out when they need help with their ballet shoes before we jump into class.

"What do you think, Ms. Daniels? Do you like my skirt? It's purple! Just like yours!" Rory says excitedly.

"Yes, Rory! It's so pretty, and today we match. Bailey, your skirt is so pretty too, it's pink and purple, just like ours."

"Yes! So pretty!" Rory says.

Bailey just giggles excitedly.

I love teaching little kids' ballet. It feels like I'm passing a bit of my soul on to them by teaching them something I love so much. I haven't actually danced since I was injured when I was sixteen. After I healed from my injury, I was so upset about my dreams dying that I couldn't imagine ever getting on stage again. Since then, I no longer think about performing, but I'm still terrified of dancing and re-injuring myself. I think deep down, I'm also terrified that I won't be able to dance like I used to, and having it taken away from me permanently might be too much to bear.

I guess I've just been too afraid to find out, so I stopped doing it all together, even though I miss it like crazy.

"Auntie Lala!!" I hear Rory yell while I'm changing the music.

"Hi, Rory!" Stella yells back.

"I missed you so much!" Rory exclaims.

"You just saw me! You can't miss me that fast!"

"Yes, I can! My daddy is stinky, I like smelling pretty like you," Rory tells her, her cute little nose scrunched up.

"I'm going to tell your dad you said that, you silly girl!" Stella laughs. "Go finish dancing with your friend. I'm going to talk to Ms. Daniels for a second, okay?"

"Okay! Watch me twirl!" Rory says as she spins away, or attempts to, but ends up falling in a fit of giggles with Bailey.

"She seems like she's having fun," Stella says with a small smile.

She seems nervous, almost uncomfortable, but I'm not sure why. She's different than she usually is.

"She is. She's opened up a lot since we started doing these dance classes," I tell her.

"It has a lot to do with you, you know that, right?" Stella says, her eyes less bright than usual. Stella is always happy and bubbly, but today she doesn't seem the same. She seems burnt out.

"I just teach the classes for them. That's it," I tell her.

"No, Sawyer, it's more than that. She talks about you nonstop. She loves spending time with you, and you're the first person outside of my family or my brother's weird friends that she's actually connected with. She was introduced to you away from us, yet she opened up to you."

"What are you saying, Stella?"

"I'm saying that you've made a difference in her life, and I just wanted to point that out. I'm still pissed at Rex for what he did at his apartment. I don't want to pry, but I can't help myself. It's just who I am. I poke. A lot. Were you two just friends?" she questions.

"Yes, we were friends. I mean if you could call us that. Him and his friends came to my other job at Atlantis one night, we met there. I, uh, kind of gave your brother a lap dance," I say with a cringe.

"That was you?! Trevor and Harris mentioned that Rex got a little action at the club, but I didn't realize it was you. Thank fucking God, someone got him out of his shell," she says excitedly.

"Uh, yeah, that was me. After that, we ran into each other at a dive bar my friends and I go to, and we hung out with them a few times after that. The night before you saw me was just a drunken encounter that led me back to his place."

"Are you telling me he let you stay the night?" Stella asks, her eyes wide with shock.

"Yeah . . . look, I don't want to make you uncomfortable talking about Rex like this." Before I can continue, Stella waves me off.

"Look, I don't need all the details on my brother's sex life. I'd just be fucking happy for him if he had a real relationship that wasn't just a quick fuck, sorry to be crude. But you don't get it. Rex doesn't bring people to his house, especially not women. Before Rory, he only had one girlfriend, Emily, and it took him weeks of actually dating her before he felt comfortable bringing her to his house. Since Rory? It's ten times worse. He's been even more particular about who he lets into his home. He gives me a hard time for bringing my friends over," she finishes.

"So? It was convenient and close. Plus, we were really drunk," I say.

"No. Like, he doesn't do it. At all. He's been through a lot, but he has these abandonment issues ever since Rory's mom left. He really doesn't trust anyone outside of family. Rex doesn't date, and he's never been the best at peopling."

"Look, I don't mean to sound like a bitch, but what's the

point of this? We both saw what happened that day. Your brother kicked me out because I'm Rory's teacher. He was embarrassed about my job. Plus, my fucking asshole of a brother is on his hockey team. That's like three strikes against me," I say with a shrug, hoping we can end this conversation soon.

"The point? The point is, Rory's happy when you're around, and whether my brother likes it or not, he's been a complete and total jackass since that day, which makes me believe it might have meant more to him than he's letting on. All I'm saying is don't completely give up on him. He's slow, but when he figures things out, he has the best heart I've ever known."

"Auntie Lala!" Rory yells, thankfully getting me out of having to come up with a response.

Turning to me quickly, Stella smiles. "I hope you don't think I'm overstepping; I just miss seeing my brother happy. He hasn't been in a long time." Rory runs into Stella's arms excitedly.

"Can we go get dessert? We don't have to tell daddy!" Rory whispers conspiratorially.

Winking at me, Stella laughs. "Of course, sweetie. Let's get going."

They grab her stuff, and Rory comes and hugs me before heading out. Bailey is picked up shortly after, leaving me with an hour before I have to be Atlantis.

Part of me wants to go get changed and head over early. Maybe a night of busy work will keep my brain clear. Another part of me wants to turn on music and lose myself in the sound. Let my body move on its own accord. Whenever I used to get stressed or overwhelmed, I would dance. It clears my mind, and honestly, while I'm dancing, I don't think about anything else.

But I'm scared. I'm scared of failing, of losing another part of me.

So, I stand up.

I close up the daycare.

Then make my way over to Atlantis, hoping that a night of working with Serena will keep me busy or entertained.

~

Tonight is turning out to be exactly what I needed. Working behind the bar when it's a busy night means I don't even have much downtime, let alone time to sit and sulk. Apparently tonight must be bachelor and bachelorette night, as I'm pretty sure we have five separate groups here celebrating before signing their lives away to someone else.

Oh, well, that's their problem, not mine.

The only downside of tonight? I wish I actually had a moment to breathe so I could talk to Serena more than just in passing. By midnight, most of the parties have slowed down, and most people are watching the shows on stage, especially with one of the servers giving a personal lap dance to one of the guys from a party.

"Girl, you should try it sometime. It's invigorating," a voice says from my side.

Serena sits there at the bar, smirking while she watches me watch Clarissa on stage.

Pouring a couple tequila shots for her table, I roll my eyes. "What? A lap dance? Nah, been there, done that. Thanks to you, of course. I think I'll pass," I quip.

"Not just a lap dance but being up on the stage giving a lap dance. It's nice because you still feel safe and secure since you get to pick your victim." Serena gives a wink that I know she usually saves for the men tipping her. "But it's exciting as fuck because everyone is watching you. I've honestly never felt sexier than when I've danced on stage. Maybe next shift?" she asks, her eyebrows raised in silent question.

"Yeah, that last time didn't really work out too well for me, not exactly too excited to go for a repeat."

"What do you mean? From what I remember he had you pressed up against our back hallway before I fucking ruined the moment. Plus, I thought you said that you ended up hanging out with him again after that day," she says.

She's not wrong. All of those things happened, yet it still ended shitty.

"I mean, yeah. But we also slept together, and he proceeded to kick me out of his apartment the next day, so not exactly a win in my books," I say, finishing up another drink for her. "Here, I think this is the last thing you're missing.

"Oh, girl, we need to talk. I want to know all the details —not just the cliff notes. Let me drop these off then I'll come back."

Serena swings her hips as she scurries off to her table. What exactly is there for me to say? There're just too many strikes against me for him to be willing to hang out again.

I spend the next few minutes catching up on drink after drink while Serena makes her rounds quickly. In a slow moment, I quickly check my phone just to make sure I'm not missing anything, and I see I have a few surprising texts from Rex.

REX

Hi, Ms. Daniels. Rory mentioned a different kind of dance class for next week. I'm just checking in to see if I need to purchase anything before that class. I want to make sure she comes prepared.

Ms. Daniels? He's tasted my pussy, but now he wants to go back to formalities. What are we, fifteen again? Yeah, fuck that.

No, Rex. She doesn't need anything different. It's actually done barefoot.

Apologies for the late response, I just saw the message.

I feel like a dick sending the message. I just realized it's after midnight, and he's probably asleep.

REX

Not a problem. I'm on the west coast for a game, which you probably already know, so it's only 9 here.

I actually wasn't aware. Had you asked, you would know that Max and I don't speak.

REX

So, what is it?

Huh? Also, why is he talking to me? He hasn't seen me once since that day. Always making sure he doesn't have to see me for drop off or pick up, yet now he wants to talk?

What is what?

REX

Your favorite.

My fingers start to type a couple times, ready to tell him to shove it, to leave me alone, or to ask him what happened and why he had to be such a jerk to me. But every time I try to type, my fingers just hover over the keys, frozen. Instead, I respond to his question in the only way I know how, honestly.

> Lyrical. I loved that I got to just move to the music. My body having the free will to move as it pleases and feel the music. It was always such a release for me.

REX

Why the past tense?

> I don't dance anymore.

REX

But you teach my daughter?

> I haven't actually danced since my injury. I've been too nervous to find out I can't do it anymore.

Why am I telling him this? More importantly, why is he asking me when he so obviously wanted nothing to do with me before.

REX

I was the same after my injury. It wasn't until Bernard and Trevor practically forced me onto the ice that I skated again. Sometimes you just have to make the leap and try, especially if it's important to you.

I'm not sure it'd work out the same for me.

REX

You never know until you try.

Thanks for the advice. I've gotta get back to work.

REX

Work?

Oh . . . Why are you still working there?

Because someone has to pay for my schooling, and my brother made sure my mother won't.

REX

quit.

Serena comes back before I can overthink his comment, not that I'd know how to take him telling me to quit my job. Does this asshole really think that I'll listen to him after he was so fucking rude to me? Fuck him.

Sorry, it's my turn up on stage. Travel safe, Mr. Lockwood.

A little white lie to hopefully shut him up, then I turn off my phone and look at Serena who's watching me curiously.

"Who ya talking to at this time of night?" She asks with a knowing smirk that's annoying as hell.

"No one. Was just looking through my phone," I say quickly.

"Nice try. I was watching you text. Spill."

"It's nothing. Rex was just asking me a question about dance for Rory," I tell her. It's not a lie, that is how it started.

"At this time of night? I'm sure that's what ya'll are talking about. Don't bullshit a bullshiter."

"I'm actually not lying though. He did text me asking if she needed something for class, then we started talking about the injury . . . and I ended the conversation when he told me to quit my job here," I rush out.

Serena starts to laugh.

"I thought you said he kicked you out . . . like he wasn't into you."

"He did. He's obviously not," I snap, her laughing now pissing me off.

"You really think this guy isn't into you? Look, I know you're like relationship stupid, but this man totally wants you."

"Not only is his daughter part of my daycare, which is a strike against me, Max is also a player on his team. Oh, and get this, he thinks I'm too young for him," I respond, rolling my eyes.

"What? Does he think he's eighty or something? He's not a dinosaur."

"Nope, he's thirty-seven, but apparently that's too old for me," I reply.

"That's the dumbest thing I've ever heard. First off, you're mature as fuck, and if he's worried about his daughter, you already know her, right?" she asks.

"I mean, yeah."

"So, what's the fucking problem? It's like fifteen years, not fifty."

"Well, regardless of the age it doesn't change that Max is his player, and he doesn't want Rory meeting anyone new."

"Fuck Max. That doesn't matter at all. Your brother's a prick and I'd love to see the look on his face when he finds out you're getting dicked down by his coach," Serena starts laughing, and I can't help but follow.

"I mean, you're not wrong on that. I couldn't care less about the Max thing, but Rex doesn't agree," I sigh.

"You realize these are all bullshit excuses, right? You both are so stupid, and you obviously avoid any real feelings, so you're coming up with every excuse possible to avoid it."

"I don't think that's it," I say, shaking my head.

"Really? You obviously like the guy, you're texting at midnight. He told you to quit your job, a job where other men pay to look at you. He's a tad possessive over you if you ask me. It's fucking hot."

I can't respond. She's not wrong . . . about any of it. Are we just avoiding something because the feelings might go past just wanting to fuck?

"Just think about what I said," Serena tells me, heading back out to check on her tables, not realizing the mind bomb she just planted.

It's all I can think about through the rest of my shift, and long after, until I finally fall asleep.

15

REX

Trevor has been the absolute biggest pain in my ass these past two days. He's constantly messaging me, reminding me that we're meeting tonight. I get it.

Hudson's. Five p.m. Don't be late.

Fucking nag.

Stella came by tonight and planned a movie night with Rory while I'm gone. Cade offered to come make them dinner, and they're both thrilled. Outside of being a bad ass hockey player, Cade is an excellent cook, so we usually try to make sure he's the one making dinners if we can help it. Stella usually leaves early to work at the bakery for a few hours, so as long as I get back home at some point in the evening to be with Rory, everything should run smoothly.

By the time I get to Hudson's, it's 4:50, and as expected, Trevor is already here and has secured us a table. I spot him waving me over, and I walk past the hostess with a quick nod of acknowledgment.

I feel like I'm preparing myself for an attack, which is honestly fucking uncomfortable. Trevor means well, and I know he truly wants me to be happy, I just don't want him to come at me with his "logic."

"Hey, man! You're here on time," Trevor says happily as I sit down across from him.

"Yeah, and you're early as usual."

"Well, yeah. I'm always early. If you're not early, you're—"

"Late. Yeah, yeah, I know," I cut him off. "Your father has been breathing that down my neck for years," I tell him, reaching for the glass of scotch he ordered for me. "So, what's this all about? Why did we need to meet?"

"I just wanted to have some time to talk. You're very good at making sure the people you love are taken care of. You're always there for us. But you're shit at taking care of yourself. To be honest, I've noticed it for years, and it's gotten even worse since your injury. After you had Rory, you started putting yourself last."

"That's how it's supposed to be, man. Kids come first," I grumble, not liking where this is going. "Rory is and will always be my number one priority," I say, emphasizing my point.

"I get it, and I agree. But that doesn't mean that you can't make changes or make decisions that will benefit both of you. Rory deserves to see her dad happy," he says.

"I am happy," I growl.

"No, you're content. There's a big fucking difference, and we both know it. You're satisfied with the way things are and are determined to not let anything change. But that also means that it's always going to be just you and Rory," he pushes.

"What's wrong with that? That's all I need, and I'm all she needs. Plus, she has my parents and my sister," I respond stubbornly.

"What happens when Rory grows up? What happens when she goes off to college? Then it's just you by yourself. Don't you think you deserve to be happy? That you deserve to share your life with someone? There's also the other side of it too," Trevor says, sipping his scotch in between thoughts. "What happens when your little girl gets older and starts missing that permanent female presence in her life? She's going to want someone she can talk to, someone she can ask all the 'lady-bit' questions that come up. I mean, unless you want to talk about periods, birth control, and sex with your little girl." I can't help the growl that immediately comes from my mouth when he says that.

"Trevor. Don't."

"What? Just because you want to pretend none of that exists, doesn't make it true. It's going to happen, and at the end of the day, you also need to take care of yourself," Trevor says, his tone firm.

"What makes you think I'm not?"

"Well, for starters? You kicked a girl out of your house after sleeping with her. A girl that we could all tell you were actually starting to like, more than just tolerate."

"Trevor, you just said the problem. She's a girl. She's twenty-four for fucks sake. I'm thirty-seven. She's practically a kid," I groan.

"Shut up. You sound like a fucking idiot right now. She's not a kid. She's mature, has dreams she's following and puts up with your grumpiness better than we do half the time. Besides, you weren't such a troll around her, you started to open up and have fun, even if it was when you didn't think we were watching. Plus, the best part? Rory already loves her; Stella told me all about that."

"Are you all teaming up against me?" I ask, my frustration mounting. "Sawyer and I ended things because she's young. Her brother is a player, you know that. With her age I never know what choices she's going to make. Plus, her relationship with Rory is a factor," I explain, rubbing my hands over my stubble, which is merely a day or two away from being a full-blown beard. "What kind of dad would I be if I were willing to risk keeping her around on a personal level, knowing it could impact Rory's relationship with her? What if I did try to date her and it ends? Would her and Rory be okay? Would she leave Rory too? I can't do that to my little girl," I say, feeling defeated.

"I just have one question," Trevor says. "What happens if you do date her, and it does work out? Then Rory would get to see you happy, in a relationship with someone who already cares about her. To me, that sounds like a perfect scenario."

"I'm . . . honestly? I'm just too fucking scared I'm going to fuck it up. When Miranda left her with me, I told myself I would always put her first. Wouldn't this be me going back on my word?" I question.

"No, Rex. You don't need to turn into a monk just because you're a single dad. In fact, you'd probably be a lot happier if you had your dick touched more often," he chuckles.

I glare.

"I'm not a fucking monk."

"Having sex once a year when your parents take Rory to their cabin doesn't count," he counters.

"It's not once a year, fucker."

Trevor just stares with an annoyingly knowing look. I mean, I guess he's not entirely wrong. I haven't actually dated anyone since Rory, and I can count on one hand the number of times I've hooked up with someone since then.

And it only takes one finger to show the number of people I've wished I could hook up with again.

Sawyer.

She's the only one I wish I could see again. I enjoyed spending time with her outside of being naked, although I wouldn't mind doing that again with her either. But it doesn't change the circumstances. Besides, she still has that stupid fucking job.

"Trevor, think about all of the things against us, and the fact that she's still working at Atlantis. How am I supposed to bring a girl home to Rory who works at a strip club?"

"What is this, the 1800s?" Trevor challenges me. "Why does what she does for a living impact who she is as a person? Are you really that much of a dick that you would judge a person based on that? If she works at the daycare, getting an education, and has a second job to help follow her dreams, what is she doing wrong? It's not like she fucks a new guy every night for a living. She's a bartender. And besides, Cassie told me today that we were the only table she's ever served, and that *you* were the only person she ever danced for," he finishes.

That hits me right where it fucking hurts. I've never cared what people do for a living, especially when they're doing it to follow their dreams. I worked my ass off to get where I am today, but without my family supporting me, who knows what I would've had to do to get here. Do I even actually know why she does it?

"She was going on stage the other night," is all I am able to come up with in response, which Trevor must think is funny because his stupid ass grin is back, and his eyes are glistening with enjoyment, slowly taking over the seriousness that had just covered his face.

"And we know this how?" he asks.

"We talked the other night. She said she was at work and had to go. I might have told her to quit her job right before she told me that," I say with a cringe.

"And you believed her?"

"I mean, I don't know. Why wouldn't I?" I question.

"Would it change anything if she didn't?"

"If she didn't dance? I mean . . . yeah, I guess. I'm not too stubborn to admit that she's hot, and that I've enjoyed spending time with her. But that doesn't mean I hear wedding bells and all that bullshit," I grumble.

"No one has said that. It's called dating for a reason. It gives you time to figure all that out, but you have to take the first step and figure out your feelings. How did she handle it when you kicked her out?"

"She was hurt," I tell him quietly, remembering the look on her face when I told her to leave. She was crushed, and it was all my fault. Her gorgeous blue eyes were filled with unshed tears, crushing me. "I don't want me or Rory to get hurt. We've been abandoned enough."

"You realize that when you're the one refusing to try— refusing to open up—you're the one breaking your own hearts, right?"

I guess shutting myself off means I'll never allow myself to truly find happiness outside of my daughter. So, he's not wrong. But how do I fix it? What do I do to make this better?

"What do you think I should do?" I ask hesitantly, fear hitting me at the mischievous look that takes over Trevor's face.

"You go get her," Trevor says with a smirk. "We've got a couple hours until her shift. The guys will be here soon, then we go to Atlantis."

"And how do you know this?"

"Perks of knowing her besties. Especially besties that

also want to see her happy, and for some fucking reason, they think you're the key to that."

Grabbing my scotch, I down it right as the waitress comes over to ask if we want refills. Yes, please. In fact, bring over the whole damn bottle. Am I doing this? Am I really going to go try and talk to Sawyer? Maybe I should just text her. But she can avoid me that way. Plus, her face says everything her mouth doesn't, so I'd prefer to have this conversation in person so I can really know how she feels.

The next couple of hours go by stupidly slow. The guys eventually join us for dinner and drinks, then we all Uber over to Atlantis where they've reserved the same table we had before, right in front of the stage.

I look around, but don't see Sawyer anywhere—only the server that was here with her last time and another woman behind the bar. We take our seats, each grabbing a drink before getting ready for whatever show they're putting on tonight. I don't care what they do, my eyes are constantly looking for that sexy little thing who's supposed to be behind the bar making drinks.

The music starting should have been my cue to watch, but I don't.

When the lights dim even further, you'd think I'd stop looking for her and pay attention, but I don't.

When a guy is brought on stage and put in a chair, that should have been my sign, but I still ignored it and kept scanning the room.

But, when I finally looked at the stage, my heart stops. Sawyer is walking out from behind a curtain, making a bee-line for the gentleman in the chair, her eyes glaring directly at me.

"What the fuck is she doing," I growl at Trevor, who looks like he's hiding a smile. "Did you know about this?"

"Who me? Never." He smirks before turning his attention back to her. Which pisses me off even more.

Sawyer is wearing nothing but a red lace outfit, leaving nothing to the imagination. As always, this color is stunning on her. The man in the chair is about to put his hands on her, which is enough to make me feral.

The server from last time comes our way with more drinks, and pauses when she sees me, a slight smirk on her face as if she can read my thoughts.

"Sorry, she's a little busy tonight with a bachelor party, so you're stuck with me. I'm Serena," she says, her tone light, but a little too devious for my mood.

I feel like everyone is in on something but me and I hate it

"Go switch with her," I demand.

"No can do, grumpy man. She asked to go up on stage a few minutes ago, then she got to pick the guy. This is her show, I'm just here to watch."

"Fuck that," I tell her, standing up from my seat. Sawyer's still watching me as she comes up behind the chair and places her hands on the guy's shoulders. I expect to see the confident woman from the last show she put on for me. Yeah, I knew she was nervous, but from the outside she looked confident. This time, though, she looks nervous, as though doesn't want to do this but is going to go through with it for some dumb reason. Just as she's about to walk around to the front of the guy, I lock eyes with her and climb up onto the stage, causing her eyes to widen, but she doesn't take her hand off of him.

"Move," I tell the guy when I finally make it over to him.

"Excuse me? No," he says, before smirking at me. "Go find your own dancer. Maybe you'll get lucky, and she'll chose you next time."

"I already found my girl, so fucking move before I make you. I'm not going to ask you again," I tell him, grabbing the wad of cash from my wallet and shoving it into his chest. "Take this and get the fuck away from her."

The guy hesitates only for a moment before he realizes I just threw a couple hundred dollars at him. As soon as he notices, he quickly stands up and walks off stage.

"Rex, what the fuck," Sawyer starts, her eyes widening as I walk towards the chair and sit down, shocking us both.

"Go on, continue your performance," I tell her, hoping to see her confidence return but not exactly sure how to help her.

Isn't she just a bartender? Why is she even doing this? Glancing at our table, I see the server, Serena, talking to Trevor and Harris, all of them smirking, obviously proud of themselves.

These fuckers set us up.

"I, uh. I honestly wasn't exactly sure what I was doing," Sawyer says honestly, pretending no one else is here while we're on stage. "Serena asked me to do this. Said it was for a good cause or some bullshit. She put me up to this about ten minutes ago and said it was a performance for a group that wanted to watch." Her eyes narrow at me before turning to glare at Serena, who just winks as she turns to walk back to the bar.

"Bitch set us up," Sawyer says, as we watch Trevor and Miles pass money over to Harris. They knew I'd stop the show. At least Harris did. Well, if they want a show, I'll give them a show.

Pulling her towards me, she stumbles a bit as she straddles me, catching herself on my shoulders, her face just inches away from mine. I lean in, letting my lips brush the shell of her ear as I whisper quietly.

"No one gets to see you like this. No one except me," I growl, and stand up with her in my arms, my hands gripping her ass as I walk her off stage towards the back hallway, ignoring our friends annoying cheers as they watch our story unfold.

"Rex, stop, I'm supposed to be up there," Sawyer grumbles into my ear as she hides her face in my neck.

"No. You're not going up there, at least not unless you're the one choosing it. But I won't sit here and watch this whole club watch you on stage, and I sure as fuck am not going to watch them touch you," I tell her, gazing at her as she looks back to where Serena is already heading up on stage to finish the dance.

"Rex, put me down," Sawyer snaps, her attempt at sounding serious and tough nearly makes me laugh. "You've already made it clear I'm not good enough for you, so let me go."

"No," I say, going door to door trying to find a private room.

"What the hell are you doing, Rex?"

"Pulling my head out of my ass," I say, finally getting a room opened.

Carrying her into the room, I push her back against the door and slam my lips to hers, my hands gripping her ass as I hold her flush with my body.

She hesitates for a moment, but her fight quickly stops, and she kisses me back shyly. I gently begin nipping at her lip, teasing her until she's moaning into my mouth, urging me on for more as her hands start gripping my hair.

"I've fucking missed this mouth," I say, pulling back just long enough to let her catch her breath.

"Rex, really. What is this? You made it clear as fuck that I'm not good enough when you kicked me out of your place.

I'm aware I have enough strikes against me that this isn't going to amount to anything, so why are you doing this?"

"I know what I said," I whisper against her lips, refusing to allow too much distance between us. "It's all still true."

"Yet here you are," Sawyer mumbles, her words somewhere between a statement and a question.

"Yet here I am," I echo. "Unable to stay away. I could blame your perfect tits or these kissable lips, but it's not even about that. It's about you. I can't stay away from you. You've fucking dug yourself under my skin, making me feel things I wasn't even sure I could anymore. I was just being too fucking stubborn to realize it."

"I don't understand. What are you trying to say?" she asks.

"I can't get enough of you, and I don't want to. I don't care about Max being on my team. Yeah, I hate you fucking working here, but that's just because I'm a stubborn man who doesn't like to share what's his. The only thing I will say is that I of course want to protect Ro, but it doesn't have to be one or the other, at least I hope not."

She doesn't say anything. She just stares at me, the disbelief in her eyes slowly dissipating. When she leans forward, pressing her lips against mine, it's soft and sweet but full of truth. She wants this too.

Pulling back, she smiles. "I, uh, have to finish my shift, but are you going to stick around here for a bit?" she asks tentatively.

"I'll stay as long as you'd like me to," I respond with a soft kiss.

"You could always come home with me after. If you're free, of course. Cassie's going to some party tonight."

"Sounds perfect, come find me when you're done," I tell her, relieved I'm getting a second chance, as she slides down my body, a small smirk lifts on her face when she feels my obvious arousal.

"Maybe we'll find a way to take care of this little problem you have too." She winks as she gets to the door.

"Sawyer, I'm going to fuck you so good you'll never use the word little to describe me again," I growl, but Sawyer just smirks as she slips out of the room, leaving me and my hard dick waiting till she's off work.

Fuck me.

16

SAWYER

oly shit. He's here. Rex is here, at Atlantis, *for me.*

When Serena told me she saw him, I figured he was just rubbing salt in the wound, just out with his friends to party. So, I went along with Serena's idea, figuring I could at least make him a bit jealous. I quickly realized how wrong I was when he came barreling onto the stage, practically ripping the guy out of the chair.

Maybe that's a tad bit dramatic, but he did pay him to leave. Plus, I can't stop thinking about when he said, "I *already found my girl.*" Didn't he just kick me out of his house like two weeks ago?

"Well, that was fun to watch," Molly says as she walks over to my side of the bar. She doesn't *seem* mad, but I wouldn't blame her if she was. That's not exactly how that was supposed to go.

"Fuck. Molly, I'm so embarrassed. I'm sorry that happened," I start, but am quickly silenced by her waving her hand at me with a smile.

"I think you misheard me. I said that was fun to watch, and that's the truth. Was it a normal strip tease? No. Was it entertaining as fuck for our guests to watch? Well, yeah, and entertainment in any form makes money. So, you get a pass for this one."

Molly smiles sincerely, and that's one of the things I love about her. She's never fake and she's always supportive. It's one of the reasons I agreed to work here; I knew that I would be able to trust her.

"Besides, Sawyer, it's one thing to cause a scene like that just because you're in a shitty mood. What just happened up on my stage was not due to a shitty mood. That was some hot shit up there. That man is all kinds of possessive over you, and I enjoyed the show. Who am I to judge? I'm just fucking jealous you're going to be on the receiving end of all that fucking tension he was putting out," she sighs dramatically.

"Oh, shush. He did not look at me that way. You're ridiculous. And there's no tension, don't try to make something out of nothing," I mutter.

"Oh really? Then explain to me why he's sitting at the other end of the bar staring at you like he's watching his next meal?"

"What?" I shout, a little quicker than necessary, making her laugh. When I look down at the end of the bar, Rex is there, staring at me with hungry eyes that I can only imagine are picturing all the dirty things he wants to do to me tonight. Or at least I hope that's what's happening because ever since he kissed me, that's all I can fantasize about.

When our eyes lock, my thoughts must be written all over my face if his devilish smirk means anything. I feel my face heat up, which only makes him smirk more. Thankfully, he doesn't torture me too long before breaking eye contact and chuckles while looking down at his drink.

"Girl, go home. Grab that man and get the hell outta here. We've got this tonight," she encourages.

"I can't do that to you."

"Yes, you can. I just expect you to ride that man so hard tonight that you're not able to walk tomorrow. That'll tell me it was worth it," Molly says with a wink before shooing me away to grab my things.

As soon as I'm changed and have my things, I search for Rex and find he's already waiting for me outside the door.

"Hey," I say awkwardly.

"Hey. Molly said to meet you back here?" he asks, his eyes practically black with lust.

"Yup, I'm good to go," I say, breathless from just his stare.

"Good," he says before grabbing my wrist and pulling me out the back door.

"Where are you taking me, you brute?" I ask, doing my best to sound annoyed, but in reality, I love his possessive side.

"My car. Your apartment. Your bed. In that order," he growls.

"Well, slow down. It's not a race."

Rex stops and spins around so suddenly I don't have time to stop, and I collide with his chest. With his lips just a fraction away from my ear, he whispers, "Oh, but it is Sawyer. It's a race to see if we can get you home and in private before my control snaps and I fuck you senseless wherever we are. So, get in the fucking car. Unless, of course, you don't care if strangers watch me fuck you until you're coming all over my cock, then by all means, walk slower," his voice deep and raspy with desire.

"I can't walk any faster!" I yell.

In one quick motion, Rex has me lifted up and thrown over his shoulder, walking quickly to the car.

"Put me down!" I giggle, surprised by this sudden change of position.

"No. This is faster."

"Molly was right. You are a caveman," I squeal, playfully smacking his back.

He chuckles, but his free hand quickly smacks my ass in fake disapproval. "Not nice, Ms. Daniels. Just quiet your mouth before I do it for you."

He may be a caveman, but he's hot as hell and wants to do savage things to my body. Who am I to complain? As soon as we're in the cab, I pull out my phone to text Cassie. With my luck, she changed her plans and will be home all night. And while I'm pretty sure it wouldn't fucking stop me, it'd at least be nice to know ahead of time.

You're gone tonight, right?

CASSIE

Yup. Did you need something?

No, was just making sure you were out. Rex is coming back to the apartment.

CASSIE

Get it girl. Just not in my bed. No. Fucking. In. My. Bed.

CASSIE

You'll have to buy me new sheets if you do that.

But your room is closer ;)

I chuckle to myself before turning my phone off and putting it away for the night. The next fifteen minutes feel like a blur. Between paying for the cab, making out inside the elevator, and finally stumbling our way into my apartment, it feels like forever. Even though neither of us are drunk, we're both acting like it, our movements becoming sloppy, as if we're both on the edge of losing control. Leading him into my room, not stopping until he's against my bed.

Turning towards Rex, I drop my hands between us, immediately going for his belt as he leans in to kiss me. The kiss is slow and full of passion as one hand goes in my hair. Our tongues tangle between us, and he nips my bottom lip —*hard*—so hard, I taste a hint of metal.

My hand finally tugs his belt out, undoing it quickly. I make quick work of his button and zipper and have his pants sliding down his legs when he chuckles. "Slow down, baby girl. We're not in a hurry."

"Says you," I whisper against his lips, barely pausing our kiss as one hand grips his hard cock.

"Fuck, that feels so good," Rex groans as I stroke his cock.

Pulling back from the kiss, I spit in my hand before returning it to his cock, gripping it roughly as I begin to pump back and forth between us. Our kiss growing fierce, his teeth nipping and sucking like he's fucking my mouth

I drop to my knees, my eyes never leaving him as his cock is now eye level with me.

"You are seriously the hottest thing I've ever seen," he growls as my tongue presses against the head of his cock, slowly playing with his piercing as he slides both of his hands into my hair. He's not moving me or pulling yet, but his grip is firm.

This is the first time I've been able to get up close and personal with the piece of jewelry that has been staring in my fantasies lately. Opening my mouth, I slide him in, taking him as far back as I can until I start to gag.

"Open up wider, baby girl," Rex demands, his grip on my hair tightening until it's almost painful, but I'm too turned on to care. "Stick your tongue out."

As soon as I stick my tongue out, Rex is sliding his cock back into my mouth, all the way to the back of my throat, pausing just before I gag.

"Swallow, baby girl. Take my cock down your throat like a good girl."

I've never done this before, but Rex's commands are enough to give me the confidence I need. Swallowing as he thrusts his hips forward, I feel him hit the back of my throat before pushing down further with each thrust, until he's all the way in. Then he snaps. With his fists in my hair, gripping tightly, he slides in and out at a faster pace, no longer letting me have any control. He's using me, fucking my mouth, and it's the dirtiest thing I've ever experienced.

"You're such a good girl, Sawyer. Such a good fucking girl," Rex groans, his words have my thighs coated in wetness.

I let one hand fall away from his thigh and down between my legs to slowly rub my clit. Rex keeps going, thrusting wildly down my throat, his thumb gently wiping the tears streaming down my cheeks.

I love that he doesn't hold back; he can read my body language well enough to know that even with my tears, I want more. I feel like he's flipped a switch in me.

Hollowing my cheeks and sucking, I use one hand to grip his balls while the other hand starts rubbing faster circles on my clit, not even slowing down as he notices, his eyes widening with desire.

"You want to come, baby girl? Is my cock sliding down

your throat turning you on?" Rex's voice is low and raspy with lust, but I hear him loud and clear. Nodding fiercely, excitement fills me as I continue rubbing my clit, getting closer and closer to finishing.

"You'll come when I say. Not a second before. Understand?" He pulls out and waits for my response.

"Yes, sir." I nod, eagerly waiting for him to be back in my mouth. When he slides back in with no hesitation, I nearly come just from the look on his face.

Pure ecstasy.

"Now touch yourself. I'm going to come in this pretty mouth as you finish yourself off. Understand?

The thought of touching myself and making myself come while Rex watches is terrifying. I've never touched myself in front of anyone before. But . . . the thought of making myself come while he comes down my throat spurs me on. I start moving my fingers quicker, in firm circles, and my body slowly starts to shake as Rex's thrusts grow erratic.

"Not yet, baby girl," he says, his voice rough as he yanks my hair back, changing the angle for himself.

I'm barely holding on, whimpers attempting to fall from my mouth as my body starts shaking. Rex thrusts a few more times before looking down at me, and there's something different in his eyes. "Now," he says, as he thrusts into my mouth and his cock pulses as he pumps his release down my throat.

My whole body feels like it's on fire as I swallow his cum, my body shaking as I come so hard, I see stars. I'm trying to scream, but no sound comes out as Rex continues thrusting into my mouth.

It takes a moment, but he slides his cock out of my mouth, his thumb catching a small drop of his cum that I missed. In one quick motion, he slips it back into my mouth. "Suck it clean."

I do. I suck his thumb in my mouth like I'm sucking his cock again, making sure to give him a show. His eyes light up in obvious enjoyment.

"God, I could watch you do this every day," Rex whispers, his thumb rubbing my lips as he stares into my eyes.

The only thing I know is that at this moment, I feel like I belong right here, and that should scare me. But it doesn't.

I feel *safe*.

I feel *cared* for.

I feel *desired*.

"Then let's do it again," I whisper, pushing against his hand that has now slipped to my throat.

"No, we need actual food first. Come with me," Rex grumbles, but grabs my hand on his way out, bringing me along with him. It's cute.

When we get into the kitchen, Rex surprises me by lifting me up onto my counter and kissing me senseless. It's quick, but his body pressing against mine and our tongues caressing each other's has me wanting to try *really* hard to convince him that I can be his dinner.

Pulling back, he looks at me curiously.

"Anything you don't eat?" he asks quickly.

"Nope, I'll eat anything," I respond, shocked when he quirks up a suggestive brow. I can't help but laugh. "Hey, I'll try anything once. Besides, I can definitely cook for us." I wink, playing along a bit.

"You're going to be the death of me," Rex says as he turns toward my pantry. "Don't move, Sawyer."

Sitting here with this gorgeous man in my kitchen, about to cook me food, feels too good to be true. I almost feel like I need to pinch myself to make sure it's not a dream. But when Rex comes out of my pantry with ingredients for nachos, I pray it isn't one. This man is perfect.

Thirty minutes later, we're sitting on the patio, snuggled under a blanket because we're still naked, finishing up a tray of nachos. It's peaceful, perfect, but leaves my brain running, asking questions I need answers to. Now.

"Okay. Can we discuss the elephant in the room?" I finally ask.

"And that is?" Rex grumbles into my neck, his hands gliding over my core, pulling me back into him.

"What are we doing? What's changed?" I ask, annoyed at his obvious indifference.

"We're doing this," Rex says, dragging kisses up my neck. "Look, I wasn't lying; I can't get enough of you. I can't get you out of my head. At this point, I'm tired of fighting it, so I want to see where it goes."

"But what about your daughter? My brother? My job?" I stammer, trying to avoid the little kisses he keeps planting all over my neck. "There were so many reasons why you said this was a bad idea, but now that seems to be the furthest thing from your mind, and I'm confused." I say meekly.

"When it comes to Rory, I say we let everything happen naturally. We don't lie, but I don't think a big sit-down introduction needs to happen right now. It'll happen when it feels right." He shrugs, seeming more comfortable with this than I figured.

"My brother?" I question.

"Are you guys close?" he asks.

"Not at all. We barely talk. He doesn't even consider me family right now," I tell him, unable to completely ignore the pang of sadness at the thought.

"Well then, baby girl, we're not doing anything wrong. If it becomes a problem, we deal with it then. And about your work, there's nothing to even say about it. I was wrong before, it's not my place to have any input on what you do for a living. Do I like other men ogling at you? Fuck no. But I'm sure as fuck not going to stop you from doing anything that makes you happy. I think it's hard for me because I feel like you have way bigger dreams than what you're doing right now. It's just difficult for me to watch what you're having to go through to get there."

I can't do anything but stare at him. I'm not sure what exactly has changed, but Rex seems unbothered by the idea of these things, like we can overcome any challenge.

Gripping my jaw with his hand, Rex turns me back to face him.

"I do have questions, though," he says, his hand gripping my jaw. "What is the dream? Is it a specific dance studio? Have you had your eye on a particular one? Or is the goal just to do it all yourself?" he asks.

"I honestly never planned to do it all myself. My father, for as big a piece of shit as he is, left money for us when he left, but he also left money for our schooling. Unfortunately, the money was just given to my mother to 'be used for school,' but nothing was official," I tell him as my hand starts to play with his hair, trying to find any sort of distraction.

"It was all great until my brother and I had our falling out. After that, he somehow convinced my mother that I was making horrible choices for my life and that I was throwing away my education. So, she stopped paying. The fifty thousand dollars my father had given me could no longer be used to help secure a studio; instead, I used it to finish my education, so I needed to fund the studio in another way. This is where Atlantis comes in. It's a safe way for me to make a lot of money, fast. It's been so helpful, and Molly always makes sure I feel safe. I'm just doing it until I have enough money to be considered for leasing one of these studios. So no, I don't have a specific studio; I just have one in the city where I can help kids. I also don't care about doing it myself. I just didn't have a choice and wasn't going to roll over and let them steal my dreams from me," I finish with a sigh.

"I get it. I'm sorry all of that has happened to you, but it's so fucking attractive that you're not letting anything stop you. You're chasing your dreams and doing what you have to do to reach them. It's sexy as hell, Sawyer."

Before I can even respond or have an idea of what to say, he's kissing me, his hands gripping my hair like he's afraid I'll slip away. Pulling back, he looks at me, taking a moment before he finally speaks again.

"Look, Rory and I, we've both been through a lot. I'm not saying this will be easy. Hell, I can almost assure you that it won't be. I haven't been someone's boyfriend in a long time. But I can promise you that I'll try. For you. For this, whatever it is. Just be patient with me. It's scary for me to let people into our lives. But I'm trying."

I can't help the tears that well in my eyes, but I nod and mumble okay before kissing him back.

"Rex, I want to understand. I-I feel like I need to know what I'm up against before I can feel comfortable being all in," I tell him honestly.

I don't expect him to divulge everything about his life, but it would be nice to know a bit about what happened before Rory to make him so terrified to let people in. Even the smallest piece of his story would help me.

"What do you want to know, baby girl? I'll tell you anything," he says sincerely.

"I want to know what happened. I'll take anything you'll

give me. I'm just trying to understand, and fuck, I just want to be there for you."

Standing, Rex turns away from me and leans his forearms against the railing, staring off into the distance. I feel like he's shutting down. His jaw clenched, like I've upset him.

After what felt like hours but was probably only seconds, Rex turned back towards me, a smile ghosting his lips.

"I guess I'll start from the beginning. Well, the beginning of the end," he says, one hand running through his beard while the other hand remains on the railing, gripping it so tight like it's the only thing holding him up. "About five years ago, I got injured when I was playing for the NY Cyclones. It was my knee, and it was pretty bad. After surgery and going through PT, I ended up down in Texas to try some experimental treatments to try and get back on the ice. Needless to say, it failed, and I kind of fell off the deep end for a bit. A lot of drinking, pain pills, and, as much as I don't like to admit it, women."

Rex looks almost nervous to be telling me about his past, like he's afraid I'm going to duck and run if he says something I don't like. That couldn't be further from the truth, though, as I'm just happy that he's finally willing to share this piece of himself with me. Reaching out, I lace my fingers with his against the railing and squeeze.

"I guess one particular night after I found out my career was over, I went a little heavy on the whiskey and ended up hooking up with someone, and then surprise, nine months later she showed up with Rory and all the paperwork to sign her rights over to me. I had a daughter, and I didn't even fucking know it. I didn't know she was pregnant. Hell, I didn't even remember having sex with her." Rex pauses, his thumb beginning to rub gentle circles along my hand as if he's trying to calm me down, when in reality, I think it's helping him. "I was a mess. I was in no shape to be a father, and Rory's mom was fine just leaving her with me. My parents ended up having to come help me with her until I could get my shit in order. After that, it was just Rory and I against the world, and I promised myself that I would never let anyone hurt her again, because that's going to be a conversation, I end up having to have with her one day, when she realizes that many people have mothers and she's never even seen a picture of hers. Don't get me wrong, we have my parents and my sister, but that's her grandparents and her aunt; that's not a mother figure in her life and it kills me that she's missed out on that."

When Rex finally finishes his story, he looks equal parts relieved that it's out there and exhausted, as if he's gone through each of the emotions along with the story and now, he's just worn out. It's absolutely and completely heartbreaking knowing that this man has had to shoulder these emotions by himself for years, never really letting anyone in.

I just want to hug him and shoulder some of his burden, but all I can do is vow to be there for him and help him reach his dreams.

When he looks back at me, I have tears streaming down my face, unable to hide my emotions.

"Baby girl why are you crying?" he asks, cupping my face.

"I just hate it. I hate that you've had to go through all of this alone. I hate that she left you and Rory, but really, I just hate that I couldn't be there for you through all of this. I wish I could shoulder some of this for you, made you feel not so alone."

"You're here now," Rex says, his thumb gently wiping my tears away. "And to me, that's everything."

Unable to stop myself, I pull Rex down, our lips meeting in a kiss full of passion and raw emotion. Deep down, I know I'm lying to myself when I say there's no way it could be love, but there's no way either of us is ready to cross that bridge and admit that yet.

Nibbling his lip, I slow the kiss down before pulling back to look him in the eye. "I'm here now, Rex. You've got me," I tell him, laughing when he leans forward and picks me up with ease.

"Fuck the nachos. I'll clean it in the morning," Rex grumbles before walking back inside and carrying me to my room. "I'm going to spend the rest of the night fucking you, making you realize just how perfect you are."

And he does. Over and over until the sun finally comes up.

17

REX

S neaking into my own home this morning made me feel ridiculous, like I was back in high school trying to hide from my parents. Except now, I'm hiding from a cute little four-year-old and my nosy ass sister who stayed the night with her. Thankfully, when I got home, they were both still asleep, so I was able to slip into my room without an interrogation.

My sisters a smart lady, and she knows I've felt like shit ever since she caught Sawyer and I together. Why do I say *caught* like I was doing something wrong? If anyone would be thrilled about it, it'd be her. Hell, Stella is the leader of the pack in trying to get me to date again, she'd be over the moon. But honestly, I'm not quite ready for celebrations and confetti all over my apartment, so I'm avoiding that conversation for the time being.

Besides, today isn't about that. Today is all about Rory. I've planned it all out; it's our first daddy-daughter date here in the city. I figured it's been a bit of a transition with me working more, and it might be nice to get out and do something fun. I just need a quick shower, and I'll be ready to make breakfast with everyone.

By the time it's 8 a.m., both Rory and Stella are stumbling out of her room. Stella's grumbling, in search of coffee, while Ro makes a bee-line for me.

"Daddy! Morning, Daddy!" Rory says, immediately wide awake. "How are you? I missed you last night!"

"Hi, princess. I missed you too! Did you and Auntie Lala have a good time?" I ask, wrapping her in a big hug.

"Yes, we did, daddy. We watched movies and had popcorn...maybe a couple sour peoples!"

"Did you have a good night with Trevor?" Stella asks from her spot at the counter, obviously changing the subject. She has her coffee now, so she's much more civilized. Giving me a small smile, she adds on with a knowing smirk, "Do anything fun?"

Stella has hung out with me and my friends before, so she's aware that we are known to get into trouble. She thinks it's great, which was really fucking helpful growing up. Our parents listened to her much easier than us, so she got us out of a lot of trouble. It's probably why Trevor and she have remained close; there's a lot of history between the three of us, and we stuck together through it all. She may be a pain in my ass, but she's still one of my best friends.

Although, I'm still not ready to tell her about Sawyer.

"Just the usual. Had dinner with Trevor, but of course he invited the rest of the guys," I say, attempting to sound nonchalant as I clean up their plates from last night's dinner.

"Sorry about that. Rory and I fell asleep after we ate," Stella says.

"Wait. Didn't Cade make you guys dinner? I'm sure you knew all about their plans then, you brat."

She smiles, unable to hide it anymore. "Hey, Ro, go get your chef stuff from the playroom so you can help your daddy cook us pancakes, okay?" As soon as she runs off, Stella turns back to me. "Of course, I knew. Who do you think told them about that morning when you kicked her out right in front of me? I knew you wouldn't listen to me, so I enlisted reinforcements."

"Help with what! I didn't do anything wrong. I just didn't want Rory seeing Sawyer in my place," I exclaim.

My sister glares at me, it's unnerving as fuck. Sometimes I think she can read my mind or something because she can always get me to spill my deepest darkest secrets.

Just another reason she's a pain in my ass.

"I thought you were more concerned that Sawyer was Rory's dance teacher, who she loved so much. That not a concern anymore?" she questions.

"I'm not getting out of this conversation, am I?" I grumble.

"Nope, it's funny that you thought you would."

"Give me twenty minutes to whip these pancakes up with Ro, and I'll spill. Still don't need the little one knowing all about it just yet," I say with a serious look directed at Stella.

"Fine, I'll go shower." Stella stands and walks off to the spare room she stays in when she's here.

Grabbing the ingredients for pancakes, I start measuring everything out when Rory comes walking back into the kitchen. She's in an oversized chef's hat and an apron, with the biggest smile ever gracing her face. She loves her chef outfit.

"Ready to help me?" I ask, just loving how happy she gets when we cook together, even though we do it so often.

"Yes, daddy. Chef Rory is here to help," she announces.

Fifteen minutes later, we've mixed, poured, and flipped all the pancakes—well, I flipped, she poured. We've even put butter, syrup, and, of course, chocolate chips on them so everyone can be in a sugar coma by noon. By the time Rory was all set up in the living room with cartoons and her breakfast, Stella is back and practically frothing at the mouth for information.

"Here, grab a plate and dish up," I say.

"Whatever, just start talking," she demands.

"There's not much to say. Yeah, it bothered me that she was her dance teacher because I do have to think about what would happen if things ended. I, uh, I don't know exactly what changed, but after seeing her with Rory a couple times at the studio, it just kind of stuck with me. She is so good with her, and that's my main priority, but she's also so good with me," I admit.

"What do you mean?" Stella asks curiously. "I mean, I understand what you're saying, but what stuck with you?"

Before I can respond, my phone vibrates. When I see it's from Sawyer, it takes all my effort not to smile because Stella would love it too fucking much.

SAWYER

Good morning, Rex. I know I'm supposed to wait like three days, and let you text me first or some bullshit, but I just wanted to say that I had fun. Thanks for crashing my work . . . again ;)

Jesus Christ. It's hot as fuck that she doesn't feel the need to play games or like she has to follow certain social rules and is just doing what she wants. It makes me like her even more, and it also makes me believe that she's just as different as she seems.

> Nah, no need for all that nonsense. But
> you're right, it was fun.

> *Maybe next time we can plan something
> instead. Bet your boss would prefer that.*

Stella just sits there smiling, waiting for me to continue. "I guess I'm just realizing that maybe she's different. She puts up with me a lot better than most people I know. We all know I can be a grumpy motherfucker sometimes." I ignore her side eyeing me at my word choice, and just continue on, "I have fun with her, and she doesn't take offense to the fact that I don't wear my emotions on my sleeve. Plus, she also does so well with Rory and has gotten her to open up."

"I know. We could all see it. You've been different ever since you met her. Which, of course, is why we planned last night. We've all noticed a change in you, you're happier, or you were until you decided to be a dumb shit a couple weeks ago. So, spill, tell me how it went," she says with a broad grin.

"Uh, well, I didn't get home until six this morning," I say, rubbing my hand on the back of my neck nervously.

Stella smiles immediately. "I thought I heard something this morning! That has to be a good sign, right? You weren't in jail or anything?" she asks, narrowing her eyes.

"Yeah, it's a good sign, you goof. We ended up at her work, I'm not sure what all you know . . ." I trail off, waiting for her to fill me in.

"I know about Atlantis and that you tried to shame her for working there when, in reality, she was just doing what she had to do," Stella says in between bites. Her eyes say everything her mouth doesn't, which means I feel her anger, even if she isn't yelling at me.

The woman's pissed, and I deserve it.

Sawyer pointed all of this out last night. How I was a dick that day and how misogynistic I am if I believed there was anything wrong with her working at Atlantis. She pointed out repeatedly how fucked up it was for me to judge her for a job that she does, especially when that's how we met. She said if it was such a horrible and tasteless job, then I'm just as bad for being a customer. I shut her up by apologizing, then eating her out on the patio while having ice cream. There was something about hearing her scream my name outside with the cars driving past below us that turned me on.

I ended up fucking her against the patio railing in the morning while we both watched everyone below us. Secretly, I think she loved the idea of someone catching us, but that's a conversation for a different day.

"Yeah, I was a dick. But I apologized," I say.

"How did you apologize?"

Raising my eyebrows in question, I almost lose it when she blushes. "You sure you want me to answer that, baby sis? I can go into explicit detail if you'd like, a little step-by-step guide to apologizing?" I tease.

"You're disgusting, Rex. No thanks. But I guess that means you probably went home with her, right? And please, for the love of God, give me the PG version. I just want to know if you two are good," Stella says, and, of course, she's attempting her "serious face," but it's failing as her happiness is showing through. Stella has a difficult time being mean, but she puts on a good show sometimes.

"Yes, we're good. Really good, actually. I'm not quite ready to let Rory know about it, though. I want to give it some time and let it happen naturally. Maybe if it happens naturally, she won't completely hate the idea. It's only ever been her and I, so I don't want her freaking out by the idea of sharing me," I explain.

"Look, Rex. She's your daughter, I get that it's scary. But give her more credit; she's a smart girl. She wants what's best for you, and if Sawyer makes you happy, that little girl will be happy too. You have to trust yourself that you're doing things right. You always put her first. But you deserve to be happy too, don't completely forget about that."

"I know, and I agree. But I still think taking it slowly is the best idea. At least for now. We've spent weeks dancing around this, playing the will they, won't they game, and now that we finally are, I just want to live in that moment for a bit. Ya know?"

"I get it. I just want you to know that everything will be okay." Looking down at her watch, a quick moment of panic hits her. "Shit. I forgot I was supposed to be at the bakery twenty minutes ago to help with the cookies. Sorry, Rex, I've gotta run," Stella says, quickly grabbing her things.

"Not a problem, Stell. Thanks for watching Rory for me, and for, uh, talking," I tell her, ready to stop talking about my emotions.

"Of course, big bro. Someone has to watch out for you. You may seem like a big dummy, but you've got a big heart," Stella says with a smile. After a quick hug to Rory, she's running out the door.

Leaving me with my thoughts and the mess.

Luckily, clean-up is quick, and Rory and I were able to squeeze in a little pedicure before heading to Central Park for the rest of the morning. I don't have to be at the arena until four for the game tonight, so we still have some time to walk around.

"Daddy, where can we go next?" Rory asks as we cross the street into central park.

"I don't know, princess. We still have some time to kill. I figured we could walk around until we find something to do."

"Can we get dessert, daddy? I ate breakfast real good," she pleads, doing her best to bat her eyelashes. I really have to talk to my sister about teaching her this shit. I already have a hard time telling her no, and this makes it damn near impossible.

"Didn't you have enough sugar with Auntie Lala last night? Plus, we already had chocolate chips with our pancakes today," I try to argue, but in reality, I've already given in to her.

"No, daddy. Not enough. Ms. Daniels tells me about ice cream. Says it's by Auntie Lala's work, can we go?" she implores.

"We can try, but I'm not sure where it is. Did she tell you the name?" I ask as we start walking towards Stella's bakery in search of the mysterious ice cream cart.

"Nope. But we can find it. I believe in us," Rory says, a happy smile on her face at the fact that she gets ice cream before lunch. Hopefully some of her happiness comes from spending the day together, because I know that's why I'm happy.

"We can look for a little bit longer, but we don't want to go too far. Remember Grandma and Grandpa are meeting us to take you to lunch before daddy has his hockey game," I remind her.

My little girl's eyes light up like it's Christmas morning. She loves spending time with her family, which makes my job so much easier. I don't feel like an absolute asshole every time she can't sleep in her own bed because she's so excited to spend time with them.

Twenty minutes later, we've walked all around Stella's bakery and haven't gotten any closer to figuring out where this damn ice cream place is. The smell of all the baked cookies and cinnamon rolls has filled the air, and I'm to the point now that if I don't get some dessert soon, I might lose it.

I'm just about to break it to Rory that we have to give up when she stops walking suddenly and tries to pull her hand from mine.

"Ms. Daniels!" Rory squeals excitedly and runs in front of me before I even realize what's happening.

Looking up, I see a surprised Sawyer standing in front of us, her eyes quickly bouncing between Rory and I, probably having the same internal battle that I am.

What do we do? How do we act?

I try to remind myself that I told Stella I would just let everything happen naturally. At least that way, I won't feel like I'm forcing anything on Rory. Which is so much easier said than done.

"Hi, sweet girl! How are you?" Sawyer says, quickly recovering from her moment of panic.

As soon as Rory is in front of her, she leans down, wrapping my daughter in a giant bear hug. "Missed you, sweet girl. Are you out spending time with your daddy today?" Sawyer questions, looking over Rory's shoulder to sneak me a quick smile, which is enough to make me feel unsettled.

I'm not even sure if that's what I'm feeling. I feel anxious all the time, like I'm going to screw this all up. My stomach gets all fluttery every time I'm nervous or excited to see her.

I'm a grown ass man, there's no fucking way I have butterflies . . . *right*?

Yeah, there's no way.

"Yup! It's a daddy daughter date. Daddy and I made breakfast, then we went and got our nails done. I got purple and daddy got pink. I didn't know which one to get, so we each got one," Rory starts rambling excitedly, and I love the way Sawyer immediately gives all her attention to my daughter.

You don't always see adults giving their undivided attention to kids, *especially* when they aren't your own children. To watch Sawyer completely engrossed in what my daughter is telling her does something to me. It makes me feel shit that I wasn't even aware I could feel anymore. It's like she's awoken something inside of me that's been sleeping for a long, long time.

But now that it's awake, I want more. More time, more of her, just . . . more.

Fuck, what the hell is happening to me? It's always just been me and Rory.

"I love your color choice, Rory. Maybe you can pick out the color I do next time. I always have such a hard time picking it out, but you obviously have excellent taste." Sawyer smiles at her before turning to me with a devious grin. "Let me see it, Mr. Lockwood. Lemme see those pretty hands of yours."

"You wanna see my hands, huh?" I wink at her while Rory is distracted, happiness filling me when she smiles, her face and neck turning rosy from her blush.

"Oh, definitely. I want to see what shade of pink you got. Was it *daddy's princess pink* or *whipped pink?*" Sawyer smirks, thinking she's clever, but honestly, I don't give a shit that I'm walking around with pink nails. What Rory wants, Rory gets, and today she decided I needed a manicure and pretty pink nails.

"Nope, this is a special blend just for me. It's a nice combination of *spank me pink*, with one coat of *berry me deep*. I think it's a nice color, it kind of matches the blush on your neck right now." I smirk, leaning forward and letting my lips trace her jaw before whispering in her ear, "I'll still finger fuck your pussy so hard you'll forget your own name. Even with my hot pink nails. In fact, I think this shade of pink would look fucking delicious wrapped around your neck," I growl with a sharp nip at her jaw.

Her shiver is all I need to know that my comments hit their mark. I wanted to see if I still affect her, and I'm happy to confirm that I do.

"Rex, shh."

"She's not paying attention right now," I say just as Rory turns back to us from the flowers she was looking at.

"Ms. Daniels! I was telling daddy about the ice cream you told me about, and he said we could have some, but I can't find it. You can show us, right?" she begs.

"I, uh . . ." Sawyer is looking at me with pleading eyes, unsure how to answer. Hasn't she figured out that what Rory wants, Rory gets?

"Yeah, Ms. Daniels, would you have time to show us where the best ice cream in Central Park is?" I ask, giving her my best boyish smile to add to Rory's puppy dog eyes.

Sawyer rolls her eyes, immediately at ease. We didn't talk about how we would handle a situation like this, but we did say everything would happen naturally. This is natural, right?

"Of course, sweet girl. Let's go get some ice cream. But Rex?" She glances back at me, Rory's hand already in hers, her eyes alight with mischief. "It's the best ice cream in New York City, not just Central Park."

With that, Sawyer and my daughter walk hand in hand

ahead on the path, giggling away, leaving me smiling like an idiot. I've always wanted this type of relationship for my girl.

I'm sure I look like a lost puppy as I follow them, but I couldn't care less. It's so heartwarming to watch the way my daughter immediately opens up to Sawyer, acting like they've known each other for years. It's honestly a fucking dream come true, no matter how fucking lame that is.

"Here it is, sweet girl. The best ice cream in the city. You should try the chocolate peanut butter one, it's my favorite," Sawyer tells Rory with a wink, as Rory runs over to look at all the flavors, completely ignoring us.

"Are you not staying? The least I can do is buy you an ice cream," I say to Sawyer.

"Rain check, Mr. Lockwood. I'm meeting Cassie and Gwen in fifteen minutes. We're grabbing lunch before I head to the daycare center," she explains.

"Well, thank you for taking the time to get us here. It'll be the highlight of Rory's day, which I'm sure you'll get to hear all about tonight." I smile, loving the thought that Rory will get to spend more time with her today.

"I can't wait. She's the best," she says, smiling fondly at Rory.

Grabbing her pant loop, I pull her towards me, doing my best to not make it too obvious how close I want her.

"Well, baby girl you're quickly turning into one of my favorite things," I whisper.

Sawyer looks surprised when I pull back, but she hides her cheesy grin by turning to Rory for a goodbye.

"Bye, Rex. Bye, Ro! I'll see you later tonight." With a quick kiss on her forehead, I let her sneak out, watching the way her ass sways as she walks out.

Fuck, I miss her already.

It wasn't like we spent all day with Sawyer, but she fit

right in, immediately making Rory the center of attention. My daughter is crazy about this lady, and what's even more exciting? It seems like Sawyer just might be crazy about her as well.

I'm starting to think I might be crazy about Sawyer too.

18

SAWYER

He was right.

As soon as Rory came into daycare tonight, she has been talking nonstop about her ice cream. Apparently, Rex also loved it, and they ended up getting three different scoops to share.

"We got the chocolate peanut butter one, and you were right, Ms. Daniels, it was so yummy!" Rory says, talking so fast and excitedly that I can barely understand her, but the smile on her face tells me that her daddy daughter day was a huge success.

"I'm so glad you liked that one. What else did you get to try, sweet girl?" I ask.

"I picked the cotton candy ice cream! It was yummy. Daddy was boring and picked vanilla," she says, rolling her eyes in fake disgust. It's cute.

Scrunching up my nose, I can't help but giggle. "Vanilla isn't very exciting, you're right, but I'm sure it was delicious. I don't think they make an ice cream flavor that isn't incredible."

"I mean, I guess," Rory says, unconvinced.

"What else did you guys do?" I ask, at this point, we're just killing time till she gets picked up, which should be any minute now.

"We walked around and looked at all the pretty buildings. Daddy showed me where they do the Christmas ballet. The cracker one. I want to go see the pretty ballerina's twirl," she says excitedly.

"The cracker one? Are you talking about the Nutcracker?" I ask from the ground. We had been dancing before Bailey got picked up, so after that, Rory never got up again. I'm pretty sure she's exhausted from her long day of walking.

"Yes, Ms. Daniels. That's what I said. The Nutcracker looks so pretty!"

"I love the Nutcracker too. When I was younger, it was always my dream to be in it. I almost did it once, but then I got hurt and couldn't," I say, a hint of disappointment in my voice.

Rory looks at me for a moment before smiling. "You would have been so pretty doing the twirls. Maybe we can watch it sometime?" she asks hopefully.

"That would be fun, sweet girl," I agree.

"Auntie Lala is here," Rory says, jumping up to go hug her aunt.

"Hey, cutie! Your dad asked me to grab you. Said he'd be a little late but that he has a special surprise for you when you get home, so let's hurry!" Stella says with a smile. Rory immediately starts grabbing her things, now excited to be heading home.

"Yay! I love surprises!" she says as she hugs me goodbye.

"It was good seeing you, Sawyer. I'm sure I'll see you around soon. We've gotta get that drink we talked about,"

Stella says with a sincere smile. "I'll message you, and we'll plan something."

"Sounds good, you ladies have a good night," I say with a wave.

"Good night, Ms. Daniels," Rory shouts on her way out.

Once everyone is gone and I'm left alone in the studio, my thoughts keep slipping back to what Rory and I were talking about. Somehow, even with it being November, I've kept the nutcracker out of my mind, not letting myself think about it because the sadness and devastation that usually follow are never worth it.

But this time, sitting here thinking about it, I'm not hit with the sadness I usually feel. Instead, it's more nostalgic. Like I'm thinking about memories from a happier time, something I loved and enjoyed. It's nice not feeling the intense sadness I normally feel when I replay the moment everything was ripped from my hands because, honestly, the second I felt my Achilles tear on that last leap, I knew it was all over. Although hearing the doctors and my coaches confirm my fear, still fucking hurt.

My phone vibrates next to me on the floor, and my heart immediately starts pounding. It's been like this ever since I met Rex, and right now it's from of pure excitement that it's a text from him. And it is.

REX

Baby girl, thanks for taking such good care of my princess. Sorry it wasn't me picking her up today.

I smile. I know this man isn't the most outgoing with his affection or full of words, so the fact that he's messaging me and letting me know he's thinking of me means more than I care to admit to myself right now. Trying to keep it cool and not act like I'm in high school and my crush just texted me, I try to keep it short and simple.

> Of course, I love spending time with that sweet girl. Maybe you can pick her up next time.

REX

Or maybe I will send her home with Stella so I can show you what these pink nails can do ;) I think I can make your ass a nice shade of pink, close to my nails.

But I did want to let you know that we have games and late practices quite a bit this week, but I want to spend some time with you this weekend, ok?

I immediately clench my thighs at his dirty insinuation. I so wish what he was saying is what was happening. He must have done some magic last night, because his dick seems to be the only thing on my mind today, and the only rational explanation is dick voodoo.

> Promises, promises, Mr. Lockwood. I'll believe what those nails are capable of when I see it with my own eyes. And this weekend sounds perfect.

REX

Here's a promise, if you keep teasing me with that pretty mouth of yours, the first thing I'll do when I see you is fill it with my cock. Or redden your sexy little ass up for sassing me right now.

> Pinky promise?

REX

Oh, you dirty, dirty girl.

You don't even know. ;)

Good night, Rex.

REX

Good night, baby girl.

Standing up with my phone, I pull up the Nutcracker soundtrack and pick my favorite song. As cliché as it is, growing up, all I ever dreamed about was dancing to Tchaikovsky's The Dance of the Sugarplum Fairy, so it's obviously the first song I click.

The second I hear it, I feel the music in my body. My body is craving the movement that comes from dancing, and for years I've been too scared to feed this desire, afraid I would end up crumbling from having it all ripped away from me.

Honestly, I know it's pathetic, but without physically dancing and just having the knowledge that I think I can do it, I feel like I've kept my dream alive somehow. It's like if I don't try, I can't fail, and the thought of failing scares me.

I keep it safe, just allowing the music to move my body while making sure to keep my feet on the floor—no jumping for me. I'm not sure if I'll ever feel confident enough to try it again, although the temptation is always there, especially when teaching.

When the song ends, I'm sweating, just having spun, turned, moved, and danced around the floor until I'm breathless.

It felt *amazing.* It was just what I needed to solidify the smile on my face as I lock up and head home.

Damn, I missed dancing.

~

"Sawyer! Are you awake yet?" Cassie yells my name from the kitchen, obviously not giving a fuck that it's only seven in the morning. I've spent all week working at both jobs and cramming for finals, which are slowly creeping up. Waking up early today isn't something I'm really excited about.

Rolling over, I yank the blankets with me, covering my face from the world. Usually when I ignore her, she goes away, but apparently, I'm not that lucky today.

"Sawyer, wake the fuck up!" Cassie says as she opens my bedroom door.

"What if I was naked? Or even worse, what if Rex came over and we were naked in here and you just opened the door like that," I try to sound annoyed, but it just comes out whiny and tired.

"Then, I guess, I would get to see that sexy dad bod that you've refused to give me any details about. But you already told me he was busy this week." Cassie says, her face turning into a devious smirk. "Besides, I've seen you naked before, so that's nothing new, but I might've been able to sneak a peek at his dick, which you refuse to talk to me about. But this is important."

"What is so important that you have to wake me up on the one day my first class was canceled?" I grumble, my face still in my pillow.

"Gwen texted me last night. We were supposed to be going to the hockey game tonight, but apparently, she has the stomach flu or food poisoning. Regardless, she's not going to make it."

I hate that even with all the good things in my life—namely, Rex—I still hate the idea of going to the hockey game solely because of Max. I used to love going to hockey games. I definitely miss it.

"Cassie," I grumble.

"Sawyer, I know you hate the idea, but Max doesn't even have to know. Besides, I bet that hot coach with the big dick you're fucking would love to see you supporting his team," she says with a smirk.

"We aren't talking about how big his dick is. Nice try though."

"You've gotta give me something, the man is practically screaming with BDE. Come on Sawyer. Pleaseee. Let me live vicariously through you for a bit." She pouts.

"Nope, nice try though," I tell her, finally sitting up to look at her. "Why is this game so important?"

"It's not like it's that important," Cassie says dramatically. "I just told the guy from my communications class that I'd go to one of his games, and he got me tickets for this one. I was looking forward to watching it. Please? I'll buy the drinks after?" she begs.

"Don't say that like a question, and we have a deal. But I'm not getting bottom-shelf tequila tonight. If you're dragging me to my brother's hockey game, you better buy me top-shelf alcohol," I say sternly.

"Seriously? You'll come with me?" she asks, shocked.

"Yeah, just promise me I don't have to see my mother. I'm not in the mood for that bullshit when I've had a great couple of days," I sigh.

"I promise. We will just go to the game and get drinks after. Deal? Besides, if we see that ungrateful witch, I'll put her in her place. I haven't been properly laid for a while, so I'm feeling a little bit feisty."

"Fine. But I'm going back to bed, are we meeting there or going together?" I ask.

"Meet me there at seven? I have work till six, so that'll be easiest," Cassie says cheerfully, obviously happy she convinced me.

"Sounds good. Now go away. I still have a couple hours till my class," I say, rolling back over.

After Cassie leaves, I fall asleep in like 0.3 seconds, the exhaustion of this week finally caught up to me, even with the excitement of potentially seeing Rex tonight, even if it's just to smile at him from afar.

~

$\mathcal{B}$y the time the game comes around, I'm rested, have studied for two of my finals, and have finished a paper for my other class, but I'm still nervous as fuck. Walking into the arena, I can't help that I keep looking over my shoulder. Whether to avoid my brother or the possibility of seeing my mother, or maybe it's the excitement of possibly seeing Rex for a minute. I'm not sure.

Grabbing my phone, I decide to text Rex, letting him know I'm here as I head to my seat.

> Hey :) Just wanted to let you know I'm at the hockey game with Cassie. She dragged me with her.

Even though Cassie told me to meet her at seven, I got here an hour early. Anxiety will do that to you. I figure Rex is busy with the team right now so I'm surprised when my phone goes off before it's even back in my purse.

> REX
>
> Wait, you're here? Where?

> Heading to our seat. Apparently, we're down
> by the glass on the south side.

When the dots pop up immediately, showing me that he's already responding, I can't help the smile that takes over my face. It's nice knowing he's excited to talk to me.

REX

Do you know where the tunnel is?

> Tunnel? Huh?

REX

The team's tunnel. Down to the offices and
locker rooms.

> Yeah, I know where it is . . . I used to meet
> Max down there sometimes.

REX

I'll meet you at the bottom of the tunnel.
Come here, now.

*And don't worry, all the players are in the
locker room for the next twenty minutes, so
it'll just be us.*

Looking around, I'm almost to our aisle of seats, so the idea of going to sit down instead crosses my mind, briefly, of course. Rex is a smart man though, and he probably assumes I'd be on the fence since I already hate being in the arena, so he sends me a picture.

A picture I probably shouldn't have opened out in the middle of a crowd of families with their kids running around. It's definitely NSFW.

But that picture? That was enough to change my mind and start walking towards the tunnel immediately.

That picture shows me *exactly* what's waiting for me down in there.

I've been down in the team tunnels plenty before, so I know where they are. When I get down there, before I even see him, one of the office doors opens, and I'm quickly yanked in as it slams behind me.

"You took too long," Rex whispers against my mouth, his arms caging me in against his office door.

"I was on the other side of the arena. I had to walk all the way back," I say, frozen in place as he presses his hard cock against me, reminding me of exactly what was in the picture.

"Still took too long," Rex says, nibbling on my neck in between each word, leaving me breathless. "We don't have long. Come sit on my cock. I've missed you, and I want to watch these tits bounce as you clench around my cock before I go coach."

Dragging me over to his desk, he sits down in his chair, his legs sprawled out, and his lips just slightly turned up into a smile as his eyes gaze hungrily down my body. Staring at him, it's hard to believe that I'm capable of turning on a man like Rex, *especially* Rex in a suit.

Fuck, hockey men are hot. They can play like a boss on the ice, getting bruised and bloody, but then look hot as fuck in these suits with their boyish smiles, just proving they can be both. Good, yet bad as sin.

His hair is longer, with a slight wave, and it falls down across his face, making me want to run my fingers through it. His deep blue eyes haven't left my body as I slowly slide off my jeans, getting to what we're both craving. His hand pushes down against his cock before he undoes his belt and suit pants, pulling his cock out just enough for me to straddle him.

As I kick my jeans to the side and remove my shirt and bra, Rex undoes the buttons on his shirt sleeve and slowly starts rolling one side up his arm, uncovering the tattoos I love so much. There's something about a man dressed in a suit with tattoos covering large portions of their body that just makes me wet. I guess it's that good boy, bad boy vibe that's so fucking sexy.

I want someone to treat me like a queen and take care of me, just like most girls do. But when we're alone, I need him to fuck filthy.

The smug look on his face tells me he knows what I'm thinking and is well aware of what he's doing to my body. One finger is all it takes for him to summon me closer, then he's lifting me up to straddle his lap and slamming his lips against mine.

"I've missed this mouth," Rex says, his mouth barely leaving mine.

"I've missed you," I tell him honestly.

Apparently, it's the right thing to say as one of his hands grabs his cock and starts sliding it against my pussy, coating himself in my wetness.

"This is going to be fast and dirty; we don't have much time," Rex says, his breathing quickening as my nails dig into his shoulder and he pushes the tip of himself against me. Right as I'm about to start lowering my body and fully slide down his cock, a knock on the door stops us.

Motherfucker, we were so close.

Wait. Fuck. Is the door locked? Is someone going to walk in? Who is it? Shit. I start to think of every possibility, hoping to fucking God we aren't about to get caught having sex in his office. Rex's face shows the same uncertainty as mine, making me even more nervous.

Rex doesn't say anything, and just puts one finger up

against his lips, silently begging me to be quiet. Don't you worry, sir, I don't think I could talk if I wanted to. From being denied his cock as well as interrupted while naked in his office, I'm too overwhelmed to make any words. Sliding me off his lap, Rex stands up and adjusts himself before heading over to the door as I tuck myself away under his desk.

I can't see anything, so I just sit quietly, hoping it's a mistake or that they've finally gone away. As much as I'd like to stay in here and go sit on Rex's lap some more, the thought of someone catching us has completely ruined the mood.

I hear the door open quickly, my heart stopping as soon as the intruder begins to speak.

"Hey, Coach. You got a minute?" Max's voice comes into the room, making panic rush through me.

Fuck. It's my brother.

I knew this was a shitty idea, but Rex and his fucking voodoo dick somehow convinced me otherwise. I'm not going to let him use that cock for evil anymore if this is the consequence.

"Hey, Max," Rex says, his voice strained. "You, okay?"

"Yeah. I mean, not really. Just some family stuff. I wanted your advice," Max says, his voice getting closer as he walks into Rex's office. He sounds stressed. His voice is strained, and he seems tired.

As much as I try not to care about him after everything he's done, he's my brother, and I love him, so of course I still care. Max must've walked straight in and sat down, because Rex comes back around his desk, sitting down with his legs barely missing me as he scoots in.

"What's up, Max?" Rex asks cautiously.

"Honestly, I'm struggling. I'm watching a family member

spiral out of control and make a bunch of fucked up decisions while I'm supposed to sit back and watch. It sucks, and I feel like I'm the only one who can fix it, the only one who cares."

"I'm sorry, man. That sucks," Rex says patiently. A patience I'm no longer feeling after hearing Max talk about me like this. "I'm confused on what you need me for, though."

As Rex continues talking, I graze my hand up his pant leg until I'm pressing it against his still-hard cock, earning me a firm grip against my wrist and the pleasure of hearing his breathing catch when he speaks again.

But I'm not really concerned with getting caught anymore. That all went out the window as soon as Max opened his stupid mouth.

Now, I just want to have some fun.

19

REX

Fuck. Fuck everything. This is all a mess. What have I gotten myself into? I'm not sure if I'm more overwhelmed that I have a player in my office while a naked woman is hiding under my desk or if it's the fact that this player also happens to be said naked woman's brother.

The one quick glance I steal tells me everything I need to know. She's not stressed. She's feeling feisty and wants to tease me. It's difficult to pay attention to Max. However, I'm also aware that this is abnormal for him. He isn't the type to ask for help, so I need to listen.

"Sorry, Max. I just don't think I'm following. What is it that I can do to help you?" I ask, trying to keep my voice steady.

"So, apparently, I'm supposed to have dinner with them this Sunday, and I know we have mandatory practice to go over film, but I was just, uh, wondering if it would be okay for me to miss that practice," Max says, biting his cheek with obvious nerves. "Sir, I don't want you to think that this isn't important to me. It is. So important to me. There's just been a lot going on with my family, and I feel like I need to be there to try and help them see the error in what they're doing."

As soon as those words fall from Max's lips, Sawyers hand grips my cock through my jeans, sliding back and forth as she attempts to jerk me off through my pants. The small tremors that start shooting through my body tell me she's going to succeed. I feel her fingers attempt to pull at my zipper and grip her wrist. That's a no-go. There's no way that I can sit here and talk to Max while she plays with my bare cock.

Jesus Christ, this woman is going to be the death of me.

I'm half tempted to pull my cock out and shove it down her throat for daring to tease me like this with someone in the room, but that would defeat the purpose.

"Are you asking me if you can miss the practice Sunday evening?" I ask.

"Yes, sir," Max says tightly.

"Not a problem. If there's anything you need to go over, I can meet with you the following week. Take care of your family," I tell him.

"Really?" Max asks in disbelief. "Thanks, sir. I really appreciate it."

"But do me a favor, okay?" I tell him, standing up and knocking Sawyer's hand off my cock in the process.

"Yeah, anything," Max says as he stands up as well.

"Go get your head on straight. Head back to the locker room. You have thirty minutes till show time. Make sure you leave everything off the ice."

"Of course. Thanks again, coach," he tells me with a smile before slipping out the door.

The door has barely shut before I'm locking it and practically sprinting back to my desk before Sawyer can even stand up, a devilish look on her face.

"Ms. Daniels, what am I going to do with you? Did you miss me this week? Or just my cock? Is that what this little display was about? You're desperate for my cock?" I question. "I should punish you for teasing me like that."

"Yes, sir," she nods, unaware of what those words do to me.

"Baby girl don't say things like that to me unless you're ready to face the consequences. Hearing that word from your mouth has me wanting to stop being so gentle and use you like my dirty little slut. Do you want the consequences? Is that what you want?"

Her eyes glisten with desire, her thighs clenching at my words. She doesn't say anything right away, but her body language says it all. She wants that.

"Hands on my desk, turn around. I want to see that pretty ass of yours."

Her breathing picks up as I walk closer, the anticipation building. I haven't even touched her yet and she's already panting.

Undoing my belt and pants, I slide my cock back out before stepping behind her, my cock lined up, pressing beneath her ass. "Is that what you want? For me to use you? Turn you into my dirty little slut until you're boneless and spent beneath me?"

"Ye . . . Yes."

"Interesting," I whisper. "I'm going to fuck you quick and dirty. We're out of time to take it slow, but I'm desperate to feel your tight little cunt suffocate my cock. I need you to be quiet for me, okay?"

She nods, her hands gripping my shoulders as I line up my cock, my hand coming down on her ass, hard, as I slam all the way in with one quick push. Her moan is enough to spur me on. I don't give her even a moment to adjust to my size before I'm pulling out and slamming back in over and over, driving us both to the ecstasy we crave. One hand caresses her ass I just spanked as my other hand grips her hip, holding her still.

I don't stop or slow down the entire time, our bodies using each other as our orgasms begin to build.

It's not long until she's coming around my cock, her orgasm pushing me over the edge, my cock filling her with cum as she muffles her cries into my neck, her entire body shaking around me. I slow my thrusts but don't stop completely until I've milked my orgasm to the very last drop.

"Jesus Christ, you're perfect," I groan as I pull out of her. "I could watch my cum drip out of this pretty pink cunt forever. I love the thought of you sitting in the stands with my cum filling you up. Fuck."

With one finger, I gather my cum and shove it back inside her, thrusting it in as the sensation overwhelms her.

"Rex. Please. I can't take anymore," she begs, her voice catching as I stroke her clit before bringing my fingers up to her mouth.

"You can, and when I finally have you alone, I'm going to prove to you what your body is capable of. I'm going to fuck you so hard. You'll beg me to stop as I use your body like the dirty little slut you long to be, watching as you enjoy every fucking moment. Now, suck."

She doesn't hesitate, her mouth opening and allowing my fingers, wet with my cum, to slip past her lips, her tongue caressing my fingers as she drinks me down.

Every. Last. Drop.

"Such a good fucking girl," I growl.

I don't miss how her eyes light up at my praise. My girl likes it dirty.

She just might be perfect for me.

"I'll meet you guys after the game, just let me know where you and Cassie end up. Deal?" I ask.

She just nods as she finishes dressing. Her eyes still blown out from desire, and her hands still shaky. With a quick peck on the lips, she's slipping out of my office before we actually get caught this time.

Standing in my office and thinking about just how close we were to getting caught, I realize I'm not sure I give a fuck anymore because I'm falling hard for this woman.

Sawyer is quickly taking over my mind, burying herself so deep inside of me that I'll be lost in the dark without her.

But it's just casual . . . right?

***

The game takes forever, or at least it feels like it does. It was a rough game, but we were finally able to secure another win. We ended up going into overtime before finally winning in the shootout. It was a hard-fought win, and luckily, some of the changes we made seem to be working. We're getting a lot more shots on the goal, which is obviously helping us win games.

It took a bit to get out of the arena, between talking with the players and scouts. But two hours after the game ended, I'm walking into McCully's to meet everyone.

It's a popular pub, and the lighting is dim, so it's hard to find everyone. There's music playing through the speakers, setting the mood, and people have already started to crowd the dance floor. It looks like the celebration of our win has already begun.

I see hands waving me over from a back booth by the dance floor, so I head in that direction, ignoring the looks some of the college girls give me. I know that look; they want me to know "they're a sure thing." But I don't care about them. I'm walking over the only woman who has held my attention in years. I'm known to be the "one and done" kind of man, but with Sawyer, I don't want to be done. Ever.

When I make it over to their table, I realize it was Trevor and Miles calling me over. Guess the whole gang came out tonight.

"Hey, dude. Helluva game tonight," Miles says, leaning across the table for a fist bump.

"Thanks, I thought you guys had practice tonight?" I question.

"Nah, got canceled last minute. I guess a pipe burst or something, so we're free tonight. Cassie had told us that they were going to the game, so we all met up here to watch. Figured this way we could all hang out."

"Besides, you haven't been around lately to give us an update. What's going on with you and Sawyer?" Trevor asks with a knowing smirk.

"You just want to hear me say it, don't you?" I groan.

"Yup. It'll feel like a sweet victory to hear those words come out of your mouth. I love knowing the big, badass hockey guy is falling for the cute ballerina."

"Who's a cute ballerina?" Cassie asks, carrying a tray of shots up to the table.

"Oh, no one," Trevor says, adding a playful wink.

The man is a flirt, always has been. But according to him, he hasn't been with anyone for quite a while. He has options, plenty of them, but none of them the girl he wants."

"Sure," Cassie says with a giggle. "Hey, Rex. Nice win tonight."

"Thanks, where's Sawyer?"

"Oh, she's at the bar waiting for more of the drinks. I'm heading back to help her," she says.

"No. Don't. I've got it," I tell her. She's obviously satisfied with my answer if her bright smile tells me anything.

Fucking women and their sappy emotions.

Looking over at the bar, there's Sawyer, innocently talking with the bartender. The male bartender. I have no problem with her talking to him, but I'm immediately punchy as I watch him shamelessly fucking flirt with her.

Clenching my fist, I have to remind myself that I would have to deal with Bernard if I had assault charges, and that's not a conversation I'd wish on anyone.

I lean up against the bar behind Sawyer, who's busy on her phone, and gesture to the bartender.

"Just a moment, I'm helping this pretty lady out," he snaps rudely at me before turning back to Sawyer, who's oblivious to the whole situation. Sawyer must be waiting for Cassie to come back to help carry these trays, and this bartender is talking her ear off.

"Me too," I tell him, passing him my card. "Put all of these on my tab."

"She already opened one," he says.

"Then close it. She's mine, and I always take care of what's mine," I grumble, but Sawyer notices me before I can continue, her whole face lighting up, erasing all of my frustration. Well, most of it, but that's better than anyone else has done before, so that's saying something.

"Hey, you!" She beams, not hesitating to lean in for a hug.

Wrapping my arms around her, I ignore the bartenders glare at my interruption of their "moment."

Motherfucker, she's mine. I'm sure of that much. What exactly that means? I'm fucking clueless.

"Hey, baby girl," I whisper, leaning down to kiss the top of her head. "I missed you."

Looking up at me, her bright blue eyes staring deep into my soul. I see the moment that she truly believes my words as her eager eyes darkened. "You just saw me a couple hours ago." She beams.

"I know I did," I grumble in her ear, turning her till her front is pressed against me. Using one finger, I lift her chin until she's staring into my eyes again. "But it was a long week, and I hated that I didn't get to see you more."

I can't help myself any longer, and I lean in, brushing our lips together in a quick kiss.

"I missed you too," Sawyer whispers quietly, her teeth gently biting into her lower lip.

"Let's grab these drinks and head back to the table, I'm ready for a drink," I tell her, ready to be in a place where I can actually sit and talk to her. Grabbing the trays, we turn around, leaving a very pissed off bartender. Leaning forward, I whisper quietly in her ears, "Oh, and quit biting your lip. It makes me want to lay you out on his bar top and eat you out while everyone else in this bar watches you squirm beneath my mouth."

I smirk at the blush that begins on her neck and rises all the way up to her cheeks. I love watching her squirm, even when it's just from my words.

"You're incorrigible," she grumbles, turning her face and trying to hide her smile.

Getting back to our table, more of the guys have gotten here, so everyone's made it. Grabbing a drink, I sit in one of the chairs at the table next to their booth. We have a large group, so spreading out has become necessary. As soon as Sawyer grabs her drink, she tries to slide into the booth next to Cassie, but I shake my head. "Come here."

Grabbing her drink, she walks over and sets it down before going to sit in the chair next to me. Before she can, I grab her hips and pull her back into my lap.

"Sit," I mutter, ignoring the way the others look at us, like they're just dying to ask questions but afraid they'll fuck it up or something. It'd be almost humorous if it weren't so annoying.

"That's what I was doing, you barbarian," Sawyer giggles, not minding at all as she wiggles her way back in my lap, grinding along my quickly hardening cock with every move she makes.

"Stop wiggling," I whisper in her ear. "Or I'll make good on my promise from earlier. I'm always prepared to eat dessert."

Her eyes darken, and I can tell she's turned on by the idea of people watching us. Her next words come out in a sassy, joking way, but when she says, "Yes, sir."

I nearly come on the spot.

"Stop being difficult. I'm trying to spend time with you out in public, not just get you naked every chance I get, even if it is my favorite thing to do," I groan.

"Fine." She pouts but turns her body in my lap so she can see me better, a smile on her face. "Then how was your day, sweetie?" she asks.

"It was fucking phenomenal until this hot little pain in my ass kept teasing me," I joke, tickling her sides quickly. The giggle that falls from her mouth is pure joy. It's interesting to me just how quickly we've fallen into this . . . relationship? Situationship?

"No, to be honest, it's been a great day. I spent some time with Rory before she got picked up by my mom for the weekend. I planned a lunch with my mom for tomorrow, then I had a little fun before the game, which, as you know, we won. So, all in all, it's been pretty perfect if you ask me. Even if you are a little tease."

"I'm not sure what you mean, I'm just sitting right where you put me," she replies, doing her best job at feigning innocence.

"Hey, I wanted to ask. Are you okay after what you overheard in my office?" I ask.

Sawyer takes a moment, thinking over my question before smiling. "Yeah, I'm good. It's frustrating, but I'm trying not to let his opinion of my life impact me. It's his issue, not mine."

"That's hard to do when it's your family, but I'm glad you are. You're too fucking badass of a lady to let someone tell you otherwise," I tell her, surprising both of us.

"Apparently, I'm meeting Max and my mother for Sunday dinner this week. I guess I'll find out for sure what that conversation was about," she says with a sigh.

"Are you two going to keep whispering sweet nothings in each other's ears, or are you going to share with the class? We're all sitting here on pins and needles," Cassie practically shouts from the booth, causing the guys to laugh.

"I'm more than happy to share with the class, Cassie. I was just—" before I can finish my sentence, Sawyer has her hand over my mouth.

"Yeah, not happening. Moving on," Sawyer tells us, her face heating with embarrassment.

"Ooh, must've been juicy. She rarely blushes," Cassie adds on.

"Who's down to come play pool? We can play teams?" I ask everyone, trying to draw attention away from Sawyer as soon as I sense her discomfort.

"I'll play," Miles says, sliding out from the booth.

Looking around, I see that Cassie and Cade are listening

to a story Harris is telling them, while Trevor is messaging someone on his phone. He's in a whole different world.

"Yo, Trevor," I shout, getting his attention. "You're up. We're playing teams."

"Yeah, I'll be right there. Go set it up while I finish," he says, nodding towards his phone.

Walking over to the pool table with Sawyer, I can't help but pull her close to me, loving the feeling of her melting into my side like it's carved out just for her. The smile on her face as she leans in should be a warning sign. A red flag. My normal sign that it's time to move on. Instead, it has me making plans.

"Are you free tomorrow morning?" I ask as she starts to rack the balls.

"Yeah, what were you thinking?"

"I was thinking I'd like to take you on an actual date. We could do breakfast?"

Sawyer stops what she's doing and walks over to me, surprising me with a kiss. "I'd love that, Rex. Just tell me when."

"Stay with me tonight. Rory's gone. We can head back and watch a movie, then do breakfast in the morning."

Sawyer bites her bottom lip, thinking for a moment before nodding her head yes.

"Yeah, that'll work. I just need to make sure Cassie gets home safe," she says.

"I've got that handled," Trevor says, openly eavesdropping. "Sorry, I just walked up and couldn't help but overhear. It's no problem for us to get her home. It's not like it's out of the way. Rex, I know you don't get a ton of free nights, so enjoy it."

"Thanks, man," I smile, turning to watch as Miles prepares to break.

We play two games, both of which Sawyer and I completely destroy Trevor and Miles, resulting in the others refusing to play against us again.

Fucking sore losers.

By the time we finish Sawyer is yawning and leaning against me a little harder.

"You tired?" I whisper in her ear as she leans her back against me.

"Yeah, a bit. I worked last night, so I'm a little sleepy. But don't worry, I stayed behind the bar," she says with a smile.

"Good girl," I tease. "Let's go tell everyone we're leaving. It sounds like the couch is calling our name. We can order some takeout."

"A man after my heart," Sawyer says with a smile, like she doesn't realize how much I love hearing those words.

~

*A*n hour later, we're back at my place, with empty Thai food and sushi boxes around us as we attempt to watch a movie curled up on my couch. Attempt is the best word to describe this situation. We ordered takeout before we even left the bar, so it was ready for us by the time we made it to my place. After eating more food than either of us needed, Sawyer passed out with her head in my lap while we tried to watch a movie she picked. She fell asleep within five minutes of us finishing the food, which has to be some sort of record.

Selfishly, I want to cuddle her in my bed, so I carry her there, being careful not to wake her. As soon as she's in my bed, I quickly shower and throw on sweats before snuggling up against her, loving the soft sounds she makes as I pull her in tight.

As much as I love fucking this woman, knowing she feels safe in my arms and is happy to spend time with me outside of sex makes me feel even better than an orgasm, and that's fucking impressive.

I don't remember falling asleep last night, but the sun light coming through the window tells me it must be morning.

"Good morning, sleepy head," Sawyer's raspy morning voice whispers.

"Who are you calling a sleepy head? I'm not the one who fell asleep within minutes of starting the movie."

"I had just eaten half my body weight in sushi because you ordered enough for an entire hockey team! I was in a sushi coma. Look it up. It's real," Sawyer says, cutely defending herself.

"Excuses, excuses," I grumble. "What time is it, anyway?"

"It's just after eight."

"What? Really? I never sleep in this late. I must've been comfortable," I say in shock.

"Yeah, you looked too adorable to wake up," Sawyer says, turning her body to face me before planting a kiss on my lips. "On a serious note, I'm sorry I just came over and fell asleep. I'm sure that wasn't very fun for you."

"It was perfect. We were both tired from the week. If I'm being honest, I enjoyed spending the time with you, even if it was just cuddling up."

My words must turn her on because, in one move, Sawyer's straddling my hips, grinding herself along my cock.

"As much as I'd love to fuck you right here, we have reservations at nine, and I know the owner will kick my ass if we're late," I say.

"Wait. I don't have any clothes. I don't even know where

we're going. I can't wear this out!" Sawyer says, pointing at her clothes on my floor from last night.

"Don't worry about that. Let's go shower, then we can worry about getting you in clothes." Gripping her hips, I thrust up, brushing my cock against her. "Besides, right now I'm more concerned with getting you out of my clothes, even if I like the way you look in my shit."

"Lead the way, Mr. Lockwood."

Picking her up, I throw her over my shoulder in a quick move before turning towards the bathroom.

"What's with you carrying me like a caveman!" she squeals.

"It's faster this way. Oh, I forgot to tell you that Cassie and Trevor dropped off a bag for you last night. It's already in the bathroom."

"You think of everything, don't you?"

"Sometimes, but not always. But, let's go shower. You can thank me in there."

~

*W*e walk into Stella's bakery with just three minutes to spare, which I'm thankful for. We were cutting it a little close after a very eventful shower that took twice as long as I had planned for. Although, I would have been late for that shower in a heartbeat. Stella's wrath does not compare to Sawyer's fucking mouth.

Walking up to the hostess stand, I don't recognize the woman working—I'm assuming she's one of Stella's new hires—but she immediately smiles as she greets me, completely ignoring Sawyer's existence.

"How may I help you, sir?" she asks with an even bigger smile, if that's even possible.

I feel Sawyer's grip on my hand tighten when the hostess addresses me as sir. Looking at her, I see she's shooting daggers at the hostess. My girl is a tad possessive of me. It's hard not to let myself smile at that thought as I turn back.

"Table for two. It's under Lockwood," I tell her, offering a small smile to be polite to my sister's employee but nothing more.

Her eyes immediately light up.

"Of course, Mr. Lockwood. Your table's ready for you already. Follow me," she says.

The hostess grabs the menu, brushing past my arm unnecessarily close as she walks by to bring us to our table. The entire time she talks to me, she completely ignores Sawyer. I would say something about it, but it's fucking cute watching Sawyer fume.

She's all possessive and stabby over me, and I fucking dig it.

Sitting down across from Sawyer, I can't help but smirk at her as she pours herself a cup of coffee and begins drinking it.

"Why are you smirking?" Sawyer snaps.

"Because you're mad," I tell her flatly, unable to stop smiling at this beautiful crazy woman across from me.

"And that makes you smile because?" she pushes.

"Because it's cute that you're mad over me," I tell her, leaning forward on the table. "But I'll let you in on a little secret, she didn't stand a chance. I only have eyes for this blue-eyed little psycho." I wink.

Her face eases into a smile, no longer looking like she's about to commit murder.

"I just can't help it. You're so damn hot, and she was practically ready to drop to her knees in the middle of the bakery and suck your cock. *That* makes me grumpy. You're *mine* to look at like that," Sawyer says like it's a known fact.

"I like that. Besides, you're the only one I want on their knees for me." I grin.

Watching her blush might be my favorite thing to do, especially since Cassie let slip that she doesn't blush often. I like that my mouth and my actions can cause that reaction in her.

Reaching across the table, I grab the coffee and pour myself a cup, smiling as Sawyer looks at the menu. Stella walks up, smiling and giving Sawyer a hug before finally coming to say hi to me.

"I already have a little bit of everything going for you guys. I'll bring it out a couple at a time, then you can get a taste of everything we have," Stella says, smiling over at Sawyer.

"Thanks, that's so sweet of you. I'm starving," Sawyer says.

"I wore her out," I add, unable to hold back from teasing her more. I don't expect the smack on the back of my head, although I shouldn't be surprised when I'm around Stella.

"Don't be crass, big brother," Stella retorts, ignoring Sawyer, who's glaring at me. "I'll be back out when the foods ready. Enjoy your coffee and the Danishes."

As she walks away, Sawyer's attempt at being angry fades into a smile. It seems she might enjoy her time with me just as much as I do her.

"Okay, Rex. I have an important question that'll decide if you're in the doghouse," Sawyer says.

"This must be serious if that's my penalty."

"Oh, it's the most important questions I'll ever ask. Pancakes or waffles? Which one is superior?"

"Superior? Neither," I deadpan.

"Excuse me? Wrong answer. Doghouse," Sawyer grumbles.

"No, I just think French toast is superior. By a landslide. There's something about the cinnamon and the butter and the drippy syrup that's just delicious."

"That's not fair. That wasn't a choice," she says, rolling her eyes.

"Stupid rule. The best breakfast food—that's sweet, that is—is French toast. Just wait and try my sisters, it's fucking incredible.

We spend the next hour trying item after item, each one somehow more delicious than the last. When the French toast comes out, I love watching her eyes light up when she tastes Stella's French toast. I think she may be enjoying it a bit too much, though.

"So, what's the verdict?" I ask, already knowing the answer.

"Holy shit," she moans.

"Yeah, let's not make that sound out in public." I glare, adjusting myself under the table.

"This is the best thing I've ever tasted. So much better than waffles," she says, her mouth full.

"So, I have two questions. First question: how's it going with the studio hunt situation?" I ask.

"It's not. Pretty much anything I can afford is taken right now, so I'm just going to keep saving and see what comes up."

"Makes sense. Same location or branching out around the city a bit?"

"I'd love if it were close to the city, but at this point I just want the opportunity to teach kids how to dance, so I'm open to anything," Sawyer says, sipping her coffee between bites. "Second question?"

I love being here with her, sitting across from her having breakfast. I could get used to this, which prompts my next question.

"How would you feel about telling Rory about us?"

The whole time she was sleeping in my arms last night, I couldn't help thinking about how much I loved feeling her next to me. I love spending time with her, and she's amazing with my daughter. The more I learn about this woman, the harder I fall for her, but in reality, I'm already hers.

"Are you sure? What happened to taking things slow?" Sawyer asks curiously.

"I mean, I'm all for taking things slow. But I want to be out in the open with you. I want Rory to know you'll be spending time with us. I just don't like hiding us, even if it's just from a four-year-old," I tell her.

"You know that means the whole preschool will know, right?" she asks.

"Yup, still don't care."

"Then, deal."

We spent the next hour walking around Central Park, obviously stopping at her favorite ice cream place before having to part ways. Thankfully, we're just about to enter the playoffs, so things will slow down for a while, and we can spend more time together, especially if my plan for getting her a studio works out.

20

SAWYER

"What happens if you just don't show up?" Cassie asks from my bed, where she's made herself very comfortable under the covers.

"You know my mother. I'm pretty sure she'd come haunt me in my dreams or something. She's not a nice woman." I glare from my closet as I finally get dressed.

My mother picked the restaurant, so of course it's some fancy steakhouse that's going to serve tiny portions of subpar quality. But that's her, she'd prefer the name and the clout over things of quality or substance. This just means I had to dress up, which I hate. Thankfully, after dinner I have no plans, so I've been thinking about heading to the studio to dance.

I'm not sure what's been different lately, but I've been feeling lighter, less weighed down by my past, injuries included. I've even been considering dancing again.

"That's putting it lightly, Sawyer. I'm sorry to say it, but your mom's a bitch," Cassie says, not worried about offending me because we both know it's true.

"I mean, yeah. It just feels shitty to say sometimes. I feel like people should like their moms, and not think they suck."

"Yeah, well people shouldn't have moms as crazy and manipulative as yours."

"Fuck. Is it really 5:00? I need to get going if I'm going to be there at 5:30," I say, shoving my feet in my boots and grabbing my purse.

"Text me after, okay?"

"Promise. Heads up, though, I might go to the studio depending on how the dinner goes," I say, surprised when Cassie hugs me.

"I'm really happy to hear that. Let me know how everything goes."

"I will."

The walk doesn't take as long as I thought it would, so I'm walking in at 5:15. Heading up to the hostess desk, I leave my mother's name, expecting to be the first one here.

"Follow me. Ms. Daniels is already seated," she tells me, already turning to walk me to the table.

Fuck why is she already here?

"Hello, Sawyer. It's so nice of you to join us. Hope this wasn't too early for your schedule," my mother says.

"Obviously it wasn't. I'm here early."

"Hardly. I said 5:30. The least you could do would be to show up at 5:00 to have our table ready," she snaps, like I've wronged her in some way.

This is why I avoid her. In absolutely no time, she's already started to argue with me and try to bring me down.

"Do you hear yourself? Or are you just so delusional that you think it's okay to speak to me like this?" I question, finally standing up to her.

I'm tired of taking this from my own family. Rex has helped me see that I'm worth so much more than letting them bring me down. They don't have to agree with every-thing I do, but the least they can do is support me. But no, they want to treat me like shit, and I'm done taking it.

"Enough," Max growls from my mother's side. I'm not sure who he's speaking to, but we both quiet down. "Stop acting like children. Sawyer, why did you want to meet us?" he questions.

"Excuse me? Mom called me and told me to be here for dinner 'or else.' I figured I should show up to find out what it was about."

We both turn to face our mother, who just stares at Max.

"Max, I did this to help you, silly. That whole scandal you've gotten yourself involved in isn't going away on its own. One of the coaches said it would be best for you to have your family by your side. We can't let your dreams die just because you made some poor choices. Sawyer will help us," she claims confidently.

"Excuse me? Max, I'm not really interested in whatever shit you've gotten yourself into, it's not my problem anymore. But, mom, do you really expect me to be a united front with you two? Max has made you believe so much bullshit about me that you were willing to stop paying for my schooling. Mom, you even went as far as trying to get my trust fund dad set up switched to you somehow. How selfish are you two to think I would play happy family with you guys when you can't even support my dreams? No one was there for me when I lost dance, and now you refuse to support me when I let that dream evolve into something I'm still able to do. So, I'm opening a studio regardless of your help, even if I've had to work two jobs to do it," I snarl at my mother before turning to Max. "And fuck you, Max, for convincing her that I'm a fuck up and that she shouldn't pay for my school. Real fucking manipulative, bro," I finish, breathing deeply.

Max's jaw drops in surprise, probably at the fact that I finally got the courage to stand up for myself. But the look on his face is a mixture of hurt and confusion, like he wasn't quite expecting me to say those things. My mother, on the other hand, just looks pissed.

"I never did that, Sawyer," Max says, looking between my mother and I in disbelief. "Any of it. I'm not sure what games you're playing, but that's ridiculous."

"Are you joking, Max? You really thought you would get me to come to dinner and all the things you put me through or said about me would just disappear, and I'd help you like the good big sister I am?"

"Sawyer, enough. Stop being such a drama queen. We are your family," my mother snaps.

"Mother, stop saying that. We aren't family because I'm no longer acting like your pawn." standing up, my mother stares at me in shock. "Max, I'm sorry you've gotten yourself into some shit, but it's your turn to man up and figure it out on your own. I'm not willing to put myself through pretending to be a happy family just to help people who constantly throw me under the bus."

Looking at Max, I expect him to be staring at me, but he's just looking at my mother, frustration and hurt all over his face. It looks like they've got some talking to do, but that's not my problem anymore. Turning around, I grab my things and walk out, ignoring my mother's protests as I finally stand up for myself and walk away from those two.

Pulling out my phone when I get out of the restaurant, I text Cassie.

It was a shit show. They still suck.

CASSIE

What happened? Do I need to kick
their ass?

> I'm going to head to the studio for a bit. I'll
> tell you about it when I get home.

CASSIE

Deal, be safe.

As I head to the dance studio I sometimes use on campus, I can't seem to stop myself from overthinking the dinner. It's fucking infuriating that they think they can continue to manipulate me into doing things for them, especially when my mother has completely cut me off. What do they think they have to use as leverage to get me to help?

Letting myself into the studio, I'm thankful it's empty. It might be the release I need. I've been craving movement lately, feeling the need to dance in my bones, and I finally feel like I'm ready to take the leap, literally.

I set my phone up to the speakers and press play. Sia's "Chandelier" starts blaring through the speakers. I slowly start to move, letting my body flow with the music and doing my best not to think. My favorite type of dancing has always been when I turn off my brain and just let the music move me.

I'm able to not think about my movements, but I can't stop thinking about everything else going on in my life. From my feelings for Rex to the pain and hurt my family has caused me to the dream I have to open a studio, none of it will stop. Before I realize it, tears are streaming down my face, but I can't stop dancing. It's cathartic and cleansing, almost like these emotions have been begging to come out and they're finally able to.

It's painful. I feel heartbroken but also fresh and happy, like this is a new leaf turning over. I keep dancing as the songs change until I feel myself struggling to stand, but that doesn't stop my body from wanting to make the leap.

For the first time in years, I go to jump but can't. Collapsing to the floor, I start to cry, really cry. The tears seem unending, like the pain from the last few years has become so overwhelming that I'm not sure what to do.

It's here on the floor that Rex finds me sometime later and brings me into his arms.

"Do it again," he whispers into my ear. "I want you to try again. Jump to me."

I stare at him like he's speaking a foreign language, but eventually I just nod as he helps me stand up.

"Remember, I'll never let you fall, baby girl. Trust yourself and trust me. You've got this. I remember getting back on the ice for the first time. I was sure I was going to get the same injury again, but our bodies know our sports even if our mind tries to forget. Just believe, okay?" he implores.

Is he really here right now? Is this man really helping me pick myself up, believing in me when I barely even believe in myself? With the music still going, I start to move, tears still streaming down my face, but I keep my eyes on Rex, his gaze never straying from mine.

The music keeps going, and I keep dancing, moving towards Rex. He's standing in one spot, his feet spread apart, his hands out in front of him, ready to catch me when I fall. It's in this moment that I realize I've already fallen. Harder than I ever would have if I jumped. He's made me see a part of myself that I've kept hidden for a long time, all while supporting my dreams and reminding me just how much of a badass I am.

This realization makes the tears come faster.

When the moment comes for me to leap, Rex's hands grab my hips, lifting me up in the air above him. It feels like a movie as he begins to spin with me still in his hold. He spins for a moment, letting me feel the music and the relief of finally taking that leap again. But most importantly, it's the time I craved and that I needed to feel the love I feel for this man, even if I'm too afraid to admit it, even to myself. As he brings me down chest-to-chest with him, his hands on my lower back holding me up, I fall into his body and cry.

"Sawyer, baby. You're okay. I've got you," Rex murmurs into my hair, one hand rubbing small circles on my back. "What's going on, baby girl?"

But I can't talk. All I can do is cry, so I let the tears fall. I let them fall for the little girl who lost her dream of being a ballerina. I let them fall for the young woman who lost her whole family when they turned their back on her. I let them fall for the woman who believed she was unlovable since no one ever stayed permanently in her life.

Rex picks me up in his strong hold, turns off the music, and carries me out of the studio, not even putting me down as I locked up. By the time we get to his car, I'm all cried out.

"I'm sorry," I murmur as he drives, his hand resting on my leg in a comforting way.

Turning to face me, Rex looks sad—vulnerable even—and I can't quite figure out why.

"No, Sawyer. You don't get to be sorry. You don't get to apologize for this."

I'm taken aback by his bluntness, especially directed at me. What?

"I—"

"No, Sawyer, you don't understand. *You* didn't do this. You shouldn't be the one apologizing. I'm sorry that you were raised to believe that you needed to apologize for showing emotions and for needing someone. You should never feel that with me. I'm with you every step of the way," Rex says, his hand gripping my thigh as he watches the road. "Right now, I'm really fucking pissed Max is on my team because I wish I could teach him a fucking lesson."

"I'm okay, Rex," I tell him, realizing I may actually be telling the truth. I had a ton of emotions hit me all at once. Some were sad, some were painful, but some were filled with so much happiness and love that I wasn't sure how to process them. Apparently, my body decided tears were the answer.

Turning towards me, the smile on his face is filled with the same love I feel deep inside. I'm not sure if it's his eyes, his face, or the passion radiating from him, but I think he might be feeling the same as me, and we're both just too afraid to admit it.

"It's fine. I'm just glad Cassie told me I should swing by after practice," he says, squeezing my thigh.

"Me too. Cassie knew you guys had practice? That's weird. I wasn't aware she was that involved with the hockey team," I tell him. It is weird because she's not much of a sports girl. She's always been more interested in athletes outside of their work. Rex shrugs, seeming as unsure as I am.

"I have Rory tonight, so I can't be gone for too long. But is it cool if I come up and hang out for a bit? I'm not quite ready to leave you yet," Rex says as he parks his Jeep in our apartment garage.

"Of course. If you don't have time, I'm okay to be alone. Don't feel like you have to take care of me."

"I don't feel like I have to do anything, Sawyer. I *want* to take care of you. There's a very big difference, baby girl. Now let me grab your things and let's head up," Rex says as he hops out and grabs everything himself.

We ride the elevator in silence, but it's not uncomfortable. It's rare to find those people you can be with, even for short periods of time, and not feel like you need to fill all the space with conversation. For someone who gets exhausted after too much peopling, it's refreshing.

That moment is shattered the second we get inside my apartment, though. It's no longer just the two of us. I had expected Cassie to be inside. I mean, she lives here, but I hadn't expected the visitor who is currently in a yelling match with her in the kitchen.

Max.

My brother is in my kitchen.

"You need to fucking go, Max. It's not fair for you to show up here," Cassie yells in Max's face.

"I don't fucking care, Cassie. Don't sit here and tell me what the fuck to do after I've had the kind of day I've had. You don't know the shit that's happened," he yells back.

"No, I don't. But I also know that you guys treated her like shit. You are such a fucking dick. Sometimes I can't believe I—" Cassie says, but suddenly stops when she sees me and Rex in the doorway. "Fuck," she mumbles.

Max turns, following her gaze, his eyes immediately changing from cold to a surprisingly sad look when he sees me. Which, of course, immediately changes when he sees who's standing directly behind me. His coach.

"Sawyer, what the fuck is this?" Max yells, his fists white from clenching them, and he refuses to look away from Rex.

"No, Max. You're in my apartment. You don't get to fucking ask questions first," I snap, catching him off guard. "What the fuck are you doing here?"

"We'll get to whatever the fuck this is in a minute," Max

says, glaring at Rex before turning back to me. "I came here after I dropped mom off at her place. Well, after I made her tell me everything. Apparently, she's not as great a person as I thought she was," he says, sounding defeated.

Cassie doesn't try to hide it one bit as she starts laughing. "I could have told you that, you moron. Your moms a fucking bitch," she adds, shrugging her shoulders like it's common knowledge.

She's not wrong.

"That doesn't explain why you're in my apartment."

"I came over and knocked on your door. Cassie opened it . . ." he trails off.

"Is that really the story you're going with?" Cassie asks, turning to me. "No, your brother came over and was banging on our door like a barbarian, refusing to leave till the door was open."

"That's not the point. I wanted to fucking talk to you. But I didn't expect to see you with my coach. So, care to enlighten me on what the fuck is happening here?" Max shouts, hurt coating each of his words as he starts mumbling something about seeing me near the tunnel and it finally making sense.

Not surprising, depending on what he learned about our mother dearest, he might feel like he just lost everyone.

Rex walks into the room then, standing beside me as we face my brother, neither of us talking as he starts connecting the dots.

"Wait. No. This can't be. Are you fucking my sister?" Max yells at us. "That day that you were in the tunnel, Sawyer? I tried to talk to coach. You weren't . . . you weren't there, were you?"

"Max, stop. We aren't having this conversation," I say, trying to remain calm. Rex's hand goes to my lower back in comfort, which just pisses Max off more. Wrong move apparently.

"Answer my fucking question," he snarls.

"Yes, Daniels. I'm dating your sister," Rex says, unease flowing out of him.

"No."

"You don't really get a say in that, Daniels. She's your sister, not your pet."

"Fuck you. This is so fucked up. How could you do this to me, Sawyer?"

"Do what to you? Date? Sorry that it's cutting into your hockey life, but I didn't do anything on purpose," I respond.

"I won't allow this," Max says, an edge to his voice that I almost don't recognize.

"I'm not sure why you think you have any right to choose who I date," I snap.

"No, but I have control over if I play in the playoffs, and from what I hear, your little boyfriend might have a good shot at an NHL coaching position if we make it all the way. It would suck for him to lose that opportunity if his lead scorer decided not to play," Max shrugs, his tone easy like he has no worries in the world.

Manipulative fuck.

What job offer? Rex hasn't told me about any offers. Shouldn't he tell me something like that?

"Are you always this much of a prick, Daniels?" Rex asks.

"Maybe not, but it works. So, what'll it be, coach? My sister, or your dream job? From what I heard tonight, you have a good shot at the New York position, which would be perfect for Rory. Not having to move again," Max says, manipulating Rex by bringing Rory into this.

Turning to look at Rex, he pauses, obvious tension filling his body, his eyes weary like he's weighing his options.

When a sad look falls in his eyes as he starts to talk, I nearly crumble.

But I cut him off. I refuse to let Max force Rex into choosing between me and his career. That's not fair. It's taken him years to make his way back. What kind of person would I be if I actually made him choose? So, I'll choose for him. I'll be the one to make the choice for him, because when you care about someone, you always put them first.

"Max, stop," I shout, tears falling from my eyes. I look at Rex and see his eyes are filled with pain and torment, and I'm positive I'm making the right decision. "You win," I whisper, barely audible. I'm shaking so bad.

"The fuck? What are you saying, Sawyer?" Rex asks, turning to face me.

"I'm saying no. I'm not worth it. I'm not worth losing your dream over, so Max wins."

"Sawyer, that's not your fucking decision to make. You don't get to tell me what I think is worth it," Rex snaps.

"But it is. I've had my dreams taken from me before. You've watched me claw my way out of that mess, helping me along the way. I won't sit here and let my piece of shit brother take that away." I tell him, doing my best to remain strong, but the tears keep streaming down my face. "I'm sorry, Rex. You're better off without me."

It's feels like time stops. I thought I had everything, but with one last look, Rex just stands there for a moment, watching me and taking everything in.

Our last moment.

Max is forcing our hand, taking all of the power out of our hands, or at least it feels like that."

"Plus, Rex, Bernard probably won't take too kindly to finding out you're dating my sister. I mean, she does go to the university you coach at, isn't that against policy?"

Rex still doesn't say anything, just stands and watches me, understanding finally registering on his face.

"I guess it makes sense. The first time I let myself care about someone, they leave again. I should have seen it coming," Rex says quietly before turning to Max. "You may be right that both our dream jobs ride on this decision, but it wasn't my only dream. Here I was thinking I'd help pull some strings for you and get you on your dream team after that little situation you put yourself in," Rex says, shaking his head in disbelief. "But yeah, you can go fuck yourself," Rex tells Max, before turning around and walking out, leaving me broken and Max's jaw dropped.

When the door slams, I crumble to the floor, Cassie rushing to my side.

"Max, what the fuck is your problem!" Cassie shouts as she cradles me in her lap.

I can't think. I can't talk. All I can do is feel my heart breaking into a million pieces. I was about to tell him I loved him, and honestly, I thought he felt the same. But I saw the look in his eyes, and I watched him let go.

"My problem? Are you kidding me? He's like twenty years older than her, and he's my coach! Besides, Cassie, I don't think you are really in a position to talk about the little situation I'm in," Max shouts, his tone full of venom as he and Cassie just glare at each other.

"Don't be so fucking dramatic, Max. We're not kids. No, this is about you needing to control everyone and everything under this fake impression that you know what's best. Reality check, you don't, and you just fucked up something that actually made your sister happy when all you've done lately is make her sad. Now I'm telling you one more time. Get. The. Fuck. Out. Of. My. Apartment," Cassie growls, her protective instinct kicking it up a notch.

If I were in any other state, I'd probably smile at her, but I'm too broken to care.

I vaguely hear the door slam, but I don't move as Cassie lets me sit in our kitchen and cry.

If I thought I was broken before, I was dead wrong.

Without Rex, I feel empty, like a shell of who I once was.

21

REX

Fuck. It doesn't matter what I do, I can't bring myself to care about playoffs. I can't seem to bring myself to care about anything, well, except Rory, of course. She's been my only saving grace these last couple of weeks, the only reason I'm not holed up in my apartment like I was in Austin.

Damnit, I hate this. I hate that I can't talk to her whenever I think of something I want to tell her about. That I can't pick up Rory from daycare and sneak a kiss from Sawyer. Or our late-night talks after I'd tuck Rory into bed. When we would stay up late talking about everything and nothing all at the same time, I miss sneaking her ice cream when I would pick Rory up from daycare, all because I loved seeing that look in her eyes. I've never seen anyone so animated with excitement over ice cream, but I loved seeing it.

But most of all? I miss having Sawyer on my team. It felt like I'd known her my whole life, not just a couple of months, and that alone scared the shit out of me. But we fit together so well that now it feels like a piece of me is missing. To make matters worse, I could tell she truly cared about Rory and me. She was the first person I let into our lives, and she was there for us, rooting us on. I liked it, and it fucking sucks that it's gone.

But she made her choice. And how could I blame her? She's spent so long handling her life on her own that if her brother wants to try to be in her life, what kind of person would I be if I stood in the way of that?

I think it just pisses me off that she made the choice for me. When her brother told me it was her or him on the team, I wanted to tell him to fuck off and not play if that's how he felt. But if I know Sawyer, I think she was scared I would choose her and resent her for not following my dreams. What this woman doesn't realize is that following my heart leads me directly to her.

Every. Single. Time.

Regardless of everything that's happened between me and her, I'm on my way to meet with my mom to propose an idea about one of their vacant buildings in the city. We may not be together, but that doesn't mean her dreams don't matter to me.

By the time I make it to the little café she picked, I'm happy to see she's already at her usual table.

"Hi, honey, it's so good to see you," my mom says, leaning up to kiss my cheek as I lean down to give her a hug. She's dressed up, far more than this place requires, telling me she probably came straight from work. For someone who's supposed to be retired, she's as busy as I am.

"It's good to see you too, mama. Thanks for coming to meet me. I know you've been really busy lately."

Sitting down, I realize just how long it's been since we've done this, just the two of us. It's always either the whole family or Rory is with us. As much as I look forward to those days, even as a grown man, sometimes it's nice to get some one-on-one time with your mom.

"So, I ordered us some appetizers. I know you're pretty much always hungry. They should be here soon," my mom says with a smile, but her eyes give her away. She's already homed in on the fact that something's off.

There's something about moms that, even as a grown ass adult, they have this way of pulling information out of you, regardless of whether you want to talk about it. It's ridiculous. The woman is like a damn leech, but it's all out of love. That's why her spidey senses must be going off, or whatever bullshit power she has to pull this shit.

I want to be mad, but it's fucking impressive.

"Spill," my mother all but demands. "Son, I know you like the back of my hand, and I know something's different —off—I can tell you're down, so start talking."

"I don't want to," I grumble, knowing damn well there's no chance she's letting that slide.

"Rex Michael, start talking, or I'll just call Stella. We both know that girl couldn't keep her mouth shut if her life depended on it. So just tell me what happened."

I shiver at the thought of everything she'd find out with that one phone call. Stella does actually know what happened and is currently pissed at me for "letting Sawyer make this choice." She's been trying to convince me that it's obvious it's not what she wanted, that she was doing it for me. I'm having a hard time believing her or even finding it in me to care. Moral of the story is: she's gone.

"I don't even know where to begin, mom," I tell her quietly. Sitting up, I run my fingers through my hair before looking her in the eye. "It's a long fucking story."

"Start at the beginning. I've got all afternoon," my mom says as she grabs the attention of our server walking by.

"Can we get a bottle of Pinot Noir and two glasses, please?"

"Of course, Ms. Lockwood. I'll have that right out," he says politely before heading towards the bar.

Fifteen minutes later, I've told her the story of how we met, how we stopped talking, and then started dating, only to have it blow up in my face. Basically, I told her the story from start to finish, minus the things no mom wants to hear about their kids. She sat quietly through the whole story, casually sipping her wine while I spilled my heart out. Once I finished talking, she just watched me, probably leeching more information out of me somehow—things I'm not even aware of.

"Are you stupid?" are the first words out of her mouth. In fact, they're the only words out of her mouth as she sits and stares at me with a look of pure bewilderment.

"What? What the heck, ma? Did you listen to anything I said?"

"Yes, I did. Every single word. Are you really so dense that you can't see how much that woman loves you? It's fucking clear as day, and it seems like you're being too fucking stubborn to fight for her."

If anyone else said any of that to me, I would probably be pissed, but hockey moms are built different. They drive a bunch of boys around, listen to us shit talk and get in fights on the ice, so they learn to fucking dish it. And my mom? She's perfected it.

"Are you kidding me? I didn't do any of this! She broke up with me, all because her brother decided he wanted to be a dick. Do I want to coach in the NHL? I mean, yeah, but it's not like I don't have plenty of time. If he wants to throw his dream away because he's throwing a bitch fit, I say, let him," I shoot back, frustrated that she's trying to turn this on me.

"She broke up with you because she knows you. She knows your past—about everything with hockey and Rory —and if she loves you like I think she does, then she would want to make sure nothing else got in your way, including her."

"She's too smart of a girl to do something as fucking stupid as that."

"Love makes people stupid, son."

"Love? What?" I say, dumbfounded.

"How are you so blind to this? Did everything with Rory and her mom really do this bad of a number on you that you can't see what's right in front of you?"

"I . . . I don't know. I'm not sure I know how to trust, mom. I'm not only trusting for myself anymore, but I'm also trusting for Rory now, too."

"I don't think that's actually the issue with Sawyer," she says wisely.

"I don't know, mom. I really don't." Looking at her, I try my best to smile. "Honestly though, she is what I wanted to talk to you about today. I just didn't expect it to get quite so personal," I grumble, which she just rolls her eyes at.

"I thought you wanted to talk about the charity?" she questions.

"Yeah, I wanted to talk to you guys about that space you've been trying to figure out what to do with that your foundation has. You know, the one in the city."

"Oh, I know the one you're talking about. The one we've been trying to get someone to take over for, like, an activity center for the kids. What about it?" my mom asks, her eyes lighting up with curiosity.

My mom might be a little older, but she's feisty and a hard worker. She'll do anything for kids.

"I have an idea, and honestly, I just want you to hear me out for a minute. As you know, Sawyer is Rory's daycare teacher. She's also the one who's been teaching Rory ballet in the evenings while I'm at hockey games," I begin.

"Okay?" my mom says. "I'm not quite sure what that has to do with the space."

"I'm getting there, patience woman," I tell her, joking of course. "She has a dream of opening up her own studio, and she's about to graduate with her master's in business this May. I was thinking that the space might be perfect for her and a way for you to finally get it filled. I don't know, maybe we can find a way to lease it or sell it to her. I know this is coming out of left field, especially with everything else you've learned today, but you've always told me to trust my gut, and I think this could be a really great thing."

As soon as I'm quiet, I look up to see her smiling, the wheels obviously turning as she sits in silence thinking.

"You're right, this is coming out of left field, but I'm not entirely against it. Like I said, I'm team Sawyer right now. Well, that's not entirely true. I'm obviously team Rex, I just think it's clear to anyone that's not a big dummy that she's what makes you the happiest. But I think your idea has promise and definitely works with the charity and our goals," she rambles on, lost in thought, making me more and more anxious.

"I'd like to meet her, but that's just a formality. I just feel like I should meet the woman I'm giving a dance studio to, but don't worry, with everything you've told me already, I'm already rooting for her," she says with a smile.

"Are you serious? You'll really think about letting her use the studio? Even with everything we talked about?"

"Honey, I want to let her use the studio because of what you've told me. Besides, this would benefit us too. It's costly as hell for us to keep the studio in our name since it's not being used. This way, we can just write it off as a charity donation. I'll talk with her about all this when I meet her, but if she's the kind of girl I think she is, it'll be a piece of cake."

"Thank you. This means a lot. She'll be really happy," I say, happiness overtaking me.

"But Rex? I have one condition."

Oh fuck, here it comes.

"All I'm asking is that you take some time and do some thinking, some soul searching, or whatever the fuck you need to do to pull your head out of your ass before it's too late. Because I guarantee that if you stopped being so stubborn, you'd realize you love her too."

I have nothing to say, so I just nod.

We spend the next half hour bullshitting about the city, her charity, and the hockey team. Thankfully, my mother let the conversation about Sawyer die down. At least this way, I can sort through my thoughts before talking to her about it more.

Is Sawyer in love with me?

More importantly, am I in love with her?

***

This last week has been the most exhausting week of my life, which isn't surprising as playoffs have officially started, so we've been practicing a little extra. Honestly, I'm thankful for the distraction. Having to drop off and pick up Rory from daycare has been torture, but thankfully, I've only had to see Sawyer once.

It was hard not to pull her close to me or sneak a kiss while Rory grabbed her things, but she did a good job of keeping it professional. I lasted until we got home before calling Trevor to come over and have a drink with me while I bitched about this situation like a teenage girl.

But now I'm at practice, trying to fix some of the team's issues before they cost us another game. We've already gone over the footage of the last game and are about to start drills. Something's missing with the team, and I've been keeping an eye on Max ever since the last game. He's been off, but I have no idea why. He's angrier than usual, yelling at his teammates, and just being a dick to everyone around him, although some deserve it for being lazy fucks.

It's not like he's going to willingly talk to me about anything. He's effectively given me the silent treatment except for quick one-word answers. It's fucking irritating, but I'm not exactly in the mood to argue with him. He's at least being somewhat polite.

Turning around, I see Trevor and Bernard making their way over to me from the offices. As much as I love seeing them, I'm not in the fucking mood for their cheery attitudes today.

"Fuck," I mumble under my breathe, giving them a quick wave. "Daniels, come here," I shout, ignoring his obvious eye roll as he skates over.

"Yes, coach?"

"Have the team split up into two teams, we're going to do a scrimmage. Let's see if the tweaks we've made to the lines help us," I tell him.

"Okay. Anything else?" Max grumbles. Apparently, he holds a fucking grudge.

"Nope."

Max nods before turning to Bernard and Trevor, who

just walked up. "Hello, Mr. Adams. Nice to see you again, Trevor." With pleasantries out of the way, Max skates back to the team and starts getting them ready for the practice game.

"Think they'll be ready, son?" Bernard asks.

It's no secret that the last playoff game was atrocious. They weren't working as a team and couldn't score a goal to save their lives. Quite honestly, Max also played like shit, and when your lead goal scorer doesn't score and has only has a single shot on the goal, you're probably going to lose. Which we did.

"I think we've done a lot of work and fixed some of the issues, but who knows until we play the game," I tell him honestly.

"Agreed. Did you fix the issue with Daniels?" Trevor asks.

Bernard must know about everything that's happened because he just keeps watching the practice, not shocked by Trevor's question.

"Not exactly. He hasn't had too much to say to me, and if we're being honest, I think it's pretty fucking childish that he's acting like this and letting it impact his job. If he wants to throw away his NHL career over something so dumb, that's on him," I say.

"Does he truly understand what he's going to lose? Does he understand what's going to happen if he doesn't get his shit together?" Bernard asks, turning to join in on the conversation. "Look, I get it. Years ago, I too fell in love with someone I shouldn't have, so I understand the drama that often follows. Just talk to Max and tell him your side. Things usually aren't as bad as we think they are once we learn the facts."

"Want my opinion?" Trevor asks. He must take my

silence as a yes because he continues on, watching Max in the scrimmage, again missing a shot opportunity. "Go grab Max. Take a walk and make this shit go away. Make him understand. This next game is too important to lose, so he's gotta grow up. Cyclones scouts will be there tomorrow, and from what they've told me, he's their number one choice."

"Yeah, son. I think that's the best plan. We've got some time; we'll help run the rest of practice. I always like to watch the practice every once in a while, anyway," Bernard says.

"Yeah, fine," I grumble before turning back to the ice. "Daniels!" I shout, getting his attention. "Come with me." He skates over, throws on a pair of slides, and stands up with obvious confusion on his face.

"Let's go," I say, turning to head towards my office.

"What's going on?" Max finally asks as I shut the door and take my spot at my desk.

"Apparently we need to talk, and I guess it needs to happen now," I tell him as I sit down at my desk.

Max stands up, anger already crossing his face. "Coach, with all due respect, I don't want to fucking talk to you right now."

"Sit down, and I'm curious where the respect was in your statement, but I get it. You're pissed, and you're willing to throw everything away because of it. Unfortunately, this request comes from Bernard, who's not willing to throw away winning these playoff games."

"I'm not sure what you think I'm throwing away. I'm still playing well," he grumbles.

"You're about to throw away your NHL dreams, or at least your dreams with the Cyclones, if you have a repeat of last night's game," I snap. "You played like shit; don't pretend you actually think you played well. You had one shot on the fucking goal. One! When you average at least five a game. That's horseshit, Max, and you fucking know it," I snap.

"What the fuck do you expect from me?" Max yells. "You were fucking my sister behind my back while I told you all about my family problems! My sister, the one who hasn't wanted anything to do with me in fucking years, was fine warming your bed and being your little plaything. It's fucking disgusting, and it hurts that you both did this to me. So, no, I'm not playing well because it's hard to want to be successful when I know it also benefits you."

"Do you hear yourself? Do you even know the reason your sister stopped talking to you? You and your mother dropped her as soon as she got injured. Like she was a burden now that she wasn't going to be a professional dancer. And when she decided to go after her dreams and try to open a studio instead, you both told her it was stupid and stopped paying for her college. If you're really fucking shocked that she doesn't want anything to do with you, you're an even bigger idiot than I am."

Max sits there, eyes turned towards his lap, processing everything I've said. His knuckles are white from clenching them so tightly. After what feels like forever, he looks up. His jaw flexing. "Are you telling me that our mother really stopped paying for her fucking college? That wasn't Sawyer being dramatic?" he asks, his voice small.

"She's been working two jobs just to make sure she can afford school and still use the money from your father for a studio. Unfortunately, she did have to tap into the funds a bit, so she's still going to have to wait a while for the studio. But she worked her fucking ass off to make sure she's better off than she would have been," I finish, proud of everything my girl has done for herself.

"That fucking bitch," Max growls.

"Look, I want to get this shit over with you as calmly as we can," I tell him, taking a deep breath. "But if you call her a bitch one more time, I promise you I'm going to fucking knock your ass out and give you a reason to sit on the bench for tomorrow's game," I growl, unable to push down my anger any longer. He sits up, eyes wide. "She's absolutely everything you're not, everything we should all dream of becoming. In those few months that I was lucky to know her and have her in my life, she made it infinitely better for myself and my daughter. You should feel lucky she's giving you a chance, even if it takes a while. She made her choice, so stop throwing a bitch fit at me when this whole situation is on you."

"I was actually talking about our mother. She had me so convinced that our father was controlling Sawyer. So convinced it's not even funny. But I never knew that she stopped paying for her school. She's been on her own all this time . . . everything that happened was because of that horrible fucking woman. But you're right. Sawyer has always been a good person. She has the best heart, always so giving. I hope she actually does give me a shot."

"You need to tell her the whole story. She loves you, even if right now she hates you." I shrug. "But from now on, you've gotta leave this off the ice. The Cyclones will be at the game tomorrow. I know it's your dream to stay in New York, and they're coming to watch you. They're interested, so play like the Mad Max we all know and love, and everything will fall into place. Your sister is an amazing woman. I'm sure once she sees you're making an effort she'll give you another shot," I tell him.

"Coach, you know the same goes for you, right?"

"What are you talking about?"

"If you make the effort, she'll give you another chance," Max says, standing up.

"No, she won't. She made her choice, and she chose you, which I understand, you're her family."

"But she didn't choose me. She chose you. She was fucking livid that I threatened your career, which is why she made the call. She wanted to see you follow your dreams. But don't worry, Cassie has made sure to tell me all about how I've fucked everything up." He looks at me, contemplating his next words. "I hated the idea that someone was closer to her than I was. She was always my best friend, and I lost that. But I guess I also thought you were just fucking her. Now, though? I can see that you're in love with her."

"Max, no—" I start, but he cuts me off.

"She's in love with you too."

"I'm not so sure that's true."

"I am. Everything she did, she did for you," Max says, like that's the answer. "I know my sister, she'll do anything for the people she loves, and you are definitely someone she loves. She gets the same look in her eye when she sees you that she got when she was dancing, like she's finally found her peace. Fight for her. I won't stand in the way, and I'll make sure she knows that. It still doesn't mean I like the idea of you with my sister, especially because you're old as fuck." He winks, knowing I can't hit him, so I just glare.

"But I know you'll take care of her, and that's more than I've done in a long time," he says, sounding disappointed in himself.

"You're right. I do love her, but sometimes that's not enough." Standing up, I walk over to Max, handing him an envelope. "Please find a way to get this to her. It's important."

"Give it to her yourself," he tells me.

"No, this needs to happen right away, and I'm giving her the time she needs to figure out what she wants."

"Okay, coach," Max pauses. "Just think about what I said. I shouldn't have acted the way I did without knowing the whole story."

"It's fine. Like I said, just keep it off the ice next time."

"I will," Max answers. "But coach? Just remember that she's worth the fight. It seems like our family might've fucked up a lot for her. Just please don't let it stop you from fighting for her."

I just nod.

"Let's go finish out practice," I tell him, gesturing him out of my office and back to the ice.

Miraculously, the rest of practice went exactly as we needed it to. Which impresses Trevor and Bernard, thank God. Apparently, Max just needed to clear the air a bit and hear things from an outside perspective, because now he's playing like the crazy son of a bitch we all love.

Through the rest of practice, though, the only thing that came to mind was Sawyer and thoughts of how she was doing.

Why is she still the only thing I can think of, and what the fuck do I do now that I've finally realized it?

I'm in love with Sawyer.

22

SAWYER

W hat are you supposed to do when it feels like your heart has been ripped out and stomped on?

Even worse, what do you do when you're the one who caused it? I've been going on autopilot these last few weeks, barely doing anything outside of my typical routine. I'm either at school, daycare, the club, or in my bed hiding from reality. I haven't had the energy to socialize with anyone lately, regardless of Gwen and Cassie trying to kidnap me a couple of times.

I don't want to do anything. I only want these feelings to go away. I'm so confused. So anxious all the time about everything, and I don't know who to turn to. It's been weeks since Max found out about me and Rex, and it still hurts the same as it did when it happened. It's been a week since I ended things with him, and that pain is only getting worse. I feel empty. I miss him. I want to take it all back and be lying in his arms, warm and safe, but I can't. I'm still not willing to risk Max following through and ruining Rex's chances for a career with the NHL.

Rolling over, I attempt to fall back asleep, but I hear a

knock on my bedroom door, followed by Cassie letting herself in. I've been holed up in my bed after I got sent home from Atlantis earlier tonight. Molly was adorable and totally supportive, but I just couldn't snap out of my bad mood. Molly said people don't tip well when there's a sad girl around, so I came home and crawled back in bed. At least here, I can cry without ruining someone's boner.

"Hey, Sawyer? Are you awake?" Cassie asks quietly as she sits on my bed.

"Yup," I mumble, my face still puffy from crying.

"Uh, Max is here, and, uh, he has something for you."

I stiffen at the mention of his name and the memory of the last time he was here. When everything fell apart.

"I don't want to talk to him, and I sure as hell don't want anything from him. Tell him he can go straight to hell. We'll talk there."

"Whatever he has, it's from Rex," she adds. "Look, he's in the living room. He's refusing to leave until you give him at least five minutes. I tried, but he won't budge. Fucking stubborn mule."

Those two are like oil and water, always have been, probably always will be.

"Fine. But if I go to jail, you're bailing me out," I say.

"Deal. Although I'd probably be sitting next to you, so I'm not sure how much good that'll do."

I throw my covers off and stand up. I'm in the same sweatpants that I've worn for the last week, an old t-shirt that looks like it has wine on it, and I haven't washed my hair in over a week. I look every bit the hot mess that I feel, but I can't seem to bring myself to care. Following Cassie out of my room, I'm not sure if I'm angry that I have to talk to Max or nervous about what he has for me.

Something about this feels weird. Max hates Rex, so

there's no way whatever this is could have been given by him. What the hell is it?

When I see him sitting on my couch, I get angry all over again, but something about the way he's looking at me stops me from screaming at him.

"What do you want Max? I'm not exactly in the mood for this shit. The thought of having a heart-to-heart is making me a bit stabby," I say, arms crossed over my chest.

He just looks at me, slowly taking in the state of my appearance. I look like shit, and I know it. Honestly, I'm embarrassed I let it get this bad.

But when I look at Max, really look at him, I see a broken man. There's so much devastation and sadness in his eyes that it's hard to look at.

But nothing surprises me more than the first words out of my brother's mouth.

"I fucked up, I get it," he states, his tone hushed, almost solemn. "I, uh, made mom confess a lot of shit to me. I still don't think I know it all, but I put two and two together when I started thinking back on things that happened. She's manipulated me a lot over these last few years, and I'm realizing how fucked up it's made me."

I don't think I ever expected to hear this from him. Max has *never* been the type to admit fault. He was always the one who would be fine just ignoring it and waiting for it to blow over. "Where is this coming from?" I stammer, holding back tears. Hearing this apology, one I never expected to get but so desperately needed, is hitting me with emotions like a freight train.

I'm doing everything I can to keep the tears from falling.

"Honestly? I sort of played like shit last game. Like really fucking bad," Max says.

I hear Cassie mumble next to me, "That's the fucking

understatement of the year." Which earns her an impressive glare from Max before he turns back to me.

"But, uh, I talked with coach, I mean, Rex. He filled in some of the gaps for me. Told me some shit I didn't know," Max says, looking away for a minute and biting his cheek like he's nervous. "I fucked up. I should have never thrown our relationship away like I did. She fucked with my head so badly that I truly believed everything she said. I regret everything so much. I regret that everything I did cost me my relationship with you. I just hope you can one day forgive me. I don't expect it to be right now. Just please understand how sorry I am."

I stare at him in disbelief, tears streaming down my face.

Before I realize it, I'm walking toward him. Whether to slap him or hug him is still up in the air. But when my arms fling around him and I sob into his chest, I'm not sure who's more surprised. Max immediately hugs me back, a single tear streaming down his cheek as Cassie slips out of the living room, giving us a moment.

Pulling back, he looks at me. "I'm so sorry, Sawyer. I'm so sorry. I hope you can forgive me and that somehow, we can go back to how we used to be. You were my best friend, sis," he cries into my shoulder.

"Honestly, dude, I get it. She's so manipulative, so I understand how you could have been brainwashed by her. She was like that with me and ballet, even after I was injured. But hearing you apologize means a lot. I don't think I realized just how much I needed to hear those words from you."

Reaching into his back pocket, he pulls out an envelope with just my name on it and passes it to me.

"What's this?" I ask.

"I have no idea. Rex gave it to me at practice and asked if

I would make sure you got it," Max says, looking a little embarrassed. "Apparently, you've been ignoring his calls and messages or something. Probably something to do with your prick of a brother."

I must look confused because Max starts to chuckle. "Yeah, I know. It felt awful saying it out loud, but even I have to admit when I royally fuck something up," Max says before turning serious. "You do realize that man is in love with you, right?"

I just roll my eyes. There's no way that man is actually in love with me. Yeah, he cared about me and wanted to date. But love . . . there's no way he feels the same.

"I'm serious," Max says.

Looking down at the envelope, I see my name written in Rex's blocky handwriting. What could he possibly have to say to me that he couldn't send in a message or phone call? I mean, I guess that would require me to actually answer them. I've done a good job avoiding him completely these last few weeks.

Unable to wait any longer, I rip the envelope open and slide everything out. Inside is a letter and some paperwork. Opening the letter, I immediately drop to the ground after reading the first line, my legs shaking too badly. Tears immediately start flowing until I'm practically sobbing on the ground, the letter laid out in front of me.

"What is it, Sawyer? Are you okay?" Max asks, keeping some distance as Cassie comes barreling out of her room, probably expecting to have to kick his ass.

"What the hell is happening? Is she okay?" Cassie asks before glancing down at the letter. She doesn't hesitate in grabbing it to see what it is, unlike Max. "Holy shit," Cassie says as she sits next to me.

"He found you a studio. It says, *"It's an old studio and will need some work. But it's going to be yours. Mom's charity found a way they can donate it to you, as long as you align it with their goals,"* she says as she looks through all the paperwork for me. "His mom wants to meet you in the next couple of weeks to get everything started."

"Sawyer, the date on all of this paperwork was just this week . . . he did all of this after you ended things," Cassie says it like that should mean something to me. "Max is right. That man is in love with you."

Everyone keeps saying this, but I can't bring myself to believe it. But the more they tell me about Rex, the more I realize just how in love I am with him.

He was so against even dating me, there's no way he could be in love with me. But then what does all this mean? And if he is in love with me, have I fucked everything up? Fuck, these are questions I'll never know the answer to, and there's no point in even wasting my time thinking about it.

But, I mean, he did make all this effort and pull a bunch of strings to find a way to get me a studio. That has to mean something, right? Plus, he's been trying to reach out, and before everything with Max happened, we were doing great.

"God damnit! I think I ruined everything," I practically whimper.

"No, I did," Max protests. "But I don't think everything's ruined, Sawyer. At least I hope not, because honestly, this is on me. I talked to him, though. I told him I'd stay out of the way. It's not my place, and I had no right to tell you who you could date. I shouldn't have gotten in the middle of you two. I just fucking hated it and acted like a child. I'm not saying I love the idea of you two together, but I can see that you both truly care about each other."

"Well, I hope you're right, because I think I love him too," I reveal.

"I have an idea, but you'll have to trust me, okay?" Max flinches at his own words. "I know that's a terrifying thought, trusting me and all, but on this one, please just give me a shot. Come to our game tomorrow, we'll go out after. Plus, I'd also really like to have you there. Uh, the scouts from the Cyclones are coming, and I'm nervous as hell about playing."

I look at him, about to tell him an immediate no, when I stop myself. I would like to be there for Max, especially because playing for the Cyclones has been his dream since he was a kid. Besides, maybe I can talk to Rex, send him a text, or something.

Or I could go to the game and see what this plan is that Max has.

"Maybe," I tell him, too nervous to fully commit. "It's not a no, but I'm still not 100% sure."

"I'll take what I can get. I'll make sure that there are tickets for you at the front," Max says before turning to look at Cassie in annoyance. "For both of you."

"Thank you. And, Max, this means a lot. You coming here and talking to me. I've missed my brother. I've needed you," I tell him sincerely.

Max pulls me into a hug, squishing me against his solid frame. "I need you too, sis." Pulling away, he just smiles as he turns towards the door. "See you both tomorrow. And Sawyer? Think about what I said."

"I will. But not until tomorrow. Right now, I'm going back to bed. I need a good night's sleep. I'm wrecked," I tell them as I smile and walk to my room, leaving Cassie to walk Max out. For the first time in a long time, I feel at peace. Hearing everything Max said, I finally feel like we're going to be okay. And if Max is right, there might also be a chance for me and Rex too.

I'll always miss my mom, but this has been her choice, not mine. You can't force someone to love you or be in your life.

Even your own mom.

~

Waking up this morning, I realized for the first time in weeks that I slept past sunrise. I've been struggling to sleep since everything happened and usually get up before the sunrise. But not last night. Last night, I slept the best I have in weeks, probably the best I have in months.

Pulling myself out of bed, I finally take a shower and get ready for the first time in what feels like weeks. When I finally make it out to the kitchen, Cassie is already sitting up at the bar eating breakfast.

"You're alive!" she jokes, but there's a tiny bit of concern still in her eyes. "I thought I was going to have to go in there to check your pulse or something. And you're dressed! Is everything okay?"

"Yeah, honestly, everything is better than okay. I feel the best I have in a while. Figured I'd get up and get ready for the day," I tell her.

Cassie sits in place, still staring at me like she's seen a ghost. "You sure you're feeling okay? I expected you to be a little bit of a mess after everything with Max."

"I thought I would be too. But it felt good to hear him say all those things, and I can only hope I really get to have my brother back. As for Rex? I've decided I'm going to trust Max for once. So, I'm going to the game and will see what happens." I shrug. "Either Max has somehow worked some magic, or I just get to enjoy the game. Either way, I'm refusing to let myself be sad today."

"Well, I guess I'll take this as a good sign. I'm just glad your brother finally realized everything your witch of a mother was doing. It doesn't excuse everything he did, but it's something," she states.

"It is. Right now, it's enough," I admit.

"You going to let me get you ready for tonight? I've got an idea," Cassie says with a smirk that has me wanting to run for the hills. But, I mean, why the hell not? I guess I'm just trusting everyone tonight.

Hopefully this all works out, but even if it doesn't, I might as well look hot. Especially because I promised myself that if I see him, I'll tell him how I feel. I don't think I could face Rex again without telling him I love him. Even if he doesn't feel the same. Even if I've destroyed what we had past repair, at least he'll know he was loved.

Both him and Rory.

"Give me everything you've got, girl. I'm all yours tonight."

23

REX

It's the final game.

Two periods down and one to go. Thankfully, we're ahead three to one. I should be excited. It's my first year as the head coach, and we're about to be champions. Well, as long as we can hold this lead through the third period.

Max invited the team to a bar down the street to either celebrate or drown our sorrows, depending on how the rest of this period goes. I promised I'd be there.

Yet, even with all of this happening around me, all I can think about is checking my phone again to see if she's messaged me.

Max told me he gave her the letter last night. Wouldn't she have said something by now?

Thankfully, I have an amazing assistant coach and great captains because my mind is so fucking far out of the game it's insane. I don't think I've ever sucked more at compart-mentalizing my thoughts than I do right now. I've been thinking about what I'll do if I see her again. How I'll convince her to give us another shot. I'd tell her that I love her. That I love her so much that even if she's not quite there yet, I'll wait because I think she's exactly what I need. She's what I want and love more than anything in this world.

I've looked around the arena and at the seats that the team uses for their family, but I still haven't seen her anywhere. At one point, I thought I saw Stella and Cassie heading down one of the rows, but I lost them in the crowd.

When that final buzzer goes off, the crowd goes crazy.

We just won. Five to two.

I look around, loving how the excitement of the crowd has taken over the entire arena as the red and blue confetti floats down from the rafters into the stands. The entire team is out celebrating on the ice while our opponents slip off to head into their locker room.

Fuck. We really did it.

We won the fucking championship! I didn't think it would feel this exciting as a coach, but it's exciting as hell knowing I helped get them here.

Max skates over, beaming like a kid in a candy store. "Think that did it, coach? Think I might've impressed 'em?" he asks, knowing damn well that unless they're blind or stupid, they're impressed.

Three goals.

Max scored a damn hat trick in the final game of the championship.

"Fuck, yeah, I do. But I gotta tell ya, as much as I know you like the Cyclones, think about your options. I know there was at least one other team checking you out tonight, and they might just be local as well," I tell him, so damn proud of what he's done tonight.

He looks genuinely interested and excited, which is great because I've been working on a little something of my own with the New York Ice Hawks. Trevor and the guys were a little bummed when I told them, but honestly, I don't think I could handle coaching all five of those fucking morons.

"I'll keep that in mind," he says with a smile. "I'm going to get back out on the ice with the guys for a bit. I just wanted to say thanks for everything. Also, remember, tonight. Nine o'clock."

"I told you I'd be there. And don't thank me. Y'all did the hard work. You earned this," I tell him as I turn around. When I look up and start heading over to media, I see her.

Sawyer's here.

I can't focus on anything else in this building except the woman who's already smiling back at me.

Holy shit. She's here. Sawyer is actually here.

And goddamn does she look fucking good.

The woman always looks amazing, but tonight it looks like she went all out. She's wearing thigh-high boots and a blue and red Brooklyn U hockey jersey that goes just below her ass. God, I miss that ass. The jersey looks familiar, which is weird because it's not a typical jersey, but I can't see it well enough to figure out why.

Sawyer smiles wider when she realizes I've noticed her, giving me a small wave before turning back around to talk to someone. As much as I love watching her walk away, that's not what I'm looking at right now.

As soon as she turned around, I realized why I recognized the jersey. The name on the back says Lockwood #17.

She's wearing my jersey.

I've never cared about seeing a woman in my jersey until now. And right now, I'm wondering if I'm ever going to let her wear anything else ever again. If I didn't have to go talk to media for a bit and sneak in one last quick meeting with the Ice Hawks, I would be chasing her down.

But I can't, not yet at least.

Does this mean what I hope it means? Fuck, it's gotta mean something that she's wearing my jersey, right?

Time to fly through these next meetings so I can go find out for myself.

~

By the time I make it to the bar, it's 9:06 p.m.
I *hate* being late.

Walking into the bar, I expect it to be busy, but this is another level. It feels like everyone from that entire arena has tried to pack themselves inside this fucking bar, making it difficult for me to see anyone.

Even with the crowd as dense as it is, I can hear them from here, smack dab between the pool table and the dance floor. Some of the guys spot me and wave me over.

These boys like to party. Empty bottles of champagne and tequila are scattered around the table, with a waitress currently bringing them more, along with a couple of mixed drinks that I can only assume are for their girlfriends.

Thank fuck the seasons over because they'd all be useless at practice tomorrow.

I quickly find Max and pull him aside. I've been keeping a secret from him, but now that the seasons over, I can finally tell him.

When we get away from the music, I turn to Max and hand him an envelope.

"What's this?" he asks, looking confused.

"It's an offer letter. If you're willing to drop out of the draft, there's an offer in that envelope to follow me to the Ice Hawks. I understand it's not the Cyclones, but I made a deal when they recruited me. I told them I'd only be willing if they gave you a competitive offer. I like your style. It reminds me of myself."

Max's face is blank, not showing any emotions, like he hasn't quite registered what I'm saying.

"Take a look at it whenever you want, but I think you'll like what you see inside," I tell him.

He finally cracks a cocky smile. "You wanna take me with you, huh?"

"Oh, Jesus Christ, don't get all fucking emotional on me. It's hockey, not a slumber party. Keep your damn clothes on."

Max gets almost giddy as he rips open the envelope, looking at his offer.

"FUCK YEAH!" he screams, fist pumping the air. "Looks like you're stuck with me for another five years, coach." Max smirks.

Thank fuck. I worked hard with the Ice Hawks to force them to see his worth. I made sure they came today because I had a gut feeling, and I was right. I'm excited to see where Max's career takes him.

"Is this official? Like, as long as I sign it?" Max asks.

"Yep," I tell him, chuckling when he signs it before running off in search of someone in the crowd, the letter still in his hand.

"What's he all excited about?" a voice says beside me.

Turning to look, I smile, already knowing who that soft voice belongs to.

Sawyer.

"Oh, nothing. I just told him I'm the new Ice Hawks head coach." Her eyes widen with excitement. "But I also gave him an offer letter for a five-year contract with us, so he's a little excited."

"Wait?! Does he need to sign?"

"Already did."

Her squeal of excitement is fucking adorable. Even more adorable is her wrapping her arms around me and hugging me with excitement, for her brother and, I guess, for me.

It feels good to have her back in my arms. It feels like it's supposed to feel when you've found your person. That's what Sawyer is to me. She's my person.

She pulls back, looking a little nervous. "Sorry about that. I got a little carried away," she says as she tries to pull herself out of my hold, but I don't let her.

Gripping her chin in my hand, I tilt her head up until she's looking at me.

"My jersey, huh?" I smirk as she blushes, cute little wrinkles forming as she scrunches her nose in embarrassment. "Baby girl, I like it. No, that's not true. I fucking love seeing you in my jersey. I want to—"

"Rex, I . . . I, uh, have something I need to say first," Sawyer says, looking me square in the eye. Shit, that alone almost makes *me* nervous. "I made the wrong choice. I, uh, fucked up. I . . ."

Her momentary pause is all I need before I'm slamming my lips against hers. She immediately melts into my touch, kissing me back before her hands finally make their way into my hair, pulling me even closer into our kiss.

I'm lost for a moment in a kiss that I wasn't sure would ever happen again. An overwhelming feeling of happiness courses through me like a wave. Nothing around me matters. The only thing I care about right now is this woman in my arms. So, when she pulls back from our kiss, I want to argue, but the look in her eyes stops me.

"I love you, Rex. Like, I really, really love you. Even though you don't think ice cream is a major food group and you think *Die Hard* is a Christmas movie, I still love you, even if you're wrong. I love you for the studio. Holy shit, I can't believe you did that. I love you for everything you do. But I don't expect you to say it back. I know I fucked up a lot, but I just wanted to make sure you knew how I felt." She takes a deep breath before finally looking up at me.

"First off, *Die Hard* is a Christmas movie, and you can't fucking tell me otherwise. Second, we need to discuss your sugar consumption if this is going to work. But, I mean, I guess the NHL does have good dental," I tell her, enjoying watching her squirm. "And third, I love you too, baby girl. The studio wasn't contingent on that. I just want you to have your dreams. I wouldn't say you fucked up, but I will promise you that if you ever pull anything like that again, I will handcuff you to my bed and fuck you until you finally see the truth of the matter. You're my person. We belong together, Sawyer." I'm not sure who leans in first, but next thing I know, we're making out again in the middle of the bar, not giving a fuck about anyone around us. My hands grip her ass as she leans into my kiss, moaning when I suck on her bottom lip.

"Fucking, finally," I hear Harris say from somewhere near us, but I don't stop kissing her. "I thought I was going to have to make a move and kiss her, you know, to get you to pull your head outta your ass. Kind of bummed you did it yourself," he laughs.

I lift one hand to flip him off, which only makes him laugh harder.

"Hey, that's my fucking sister, you asshole," Max grumbles, but I don't stop. I don't know if he was talking to me or Harris, but either way, I don't give a shit.

"Don't act like you don't know what they're about to do," Harris deadpans.

"Shut the—"

Right then, Sawyer pulls back, laughing, and turns to face the boys with a smirk. "Hey, Max, wanna see if I can still kick your ass at pool?"

"You're on, sis. Teams?" he asks.

"I'm in," I say. "But I'm on her team." I point to Sawyer, who's already walking over to the table.

Cassie walks over right then with a tray of drinks and passes them out. When she passes Max his, he grabs his arm and pulls her towards him. "Deal. But Cassie's on my team."

"Uh, you know I'm fucking awful at this game, right? And why are you touching me? Get off," she sneers, but keeps walking towards us.

"Doesn't matter. I'll do all the legwork, you just reap the benefits, princess," Max responds with a wink. "Besides, we're playing against a man who has bright blue nail polish. I'm pretty sure we can beat them," Max laughs, throwing a jab at me.

I honestly forgot that my nails were still painted after my last daddy-daughter date, but again, I really don't give a shit as long as she's happy.

I just shrug. "Eh, whatever, man, Rory's a persuasive little thing, and at this point I just do as I'm told. It's much easier that way. You just wait until you have daughters. I'm sure you'll have your hair in pigtails and makeup all over."

"Shit, Rex. I'll put makeup on him. I bet he'd look so pretty," Cassie laughs as she pinches his cheek.

These two are fucking wild, it's entertaining as fuck.

When we get over to the table, Sawyer already has it set up and passes a cue to Max to break.

"Wait, wait!" Cassie shouts. "If y'all are making me play, let's at least make a bet. Hmm, Max, what should we bet? Drinks?"

"Nah, boring. Losers have to give a lap dance to a song of the winner's choice," he smirks.

"Fine, but the guys are doing it this time," Sawyer says with a wink.

"Ew." Max cringes but starts the game. He immediately gets three solids in right off the break, and within the first round, they have all but two balls in, one of which is the eight ball.

The rest of the game doesn't last long.

At all.

While Sawyer may be fucking killer at this game, Max is a goddamn pool shark and within two rounds finished the game without breaking a sweat.

"That was fucking impressive," is all I manage to say.

"I told you he's how I learned how to play," Sawyer says, like she's used to it.

"Time to pay up, suckers. Sawyer, sit," Cassie demands, and surprisingly, Sawyer actually listens. "And you, big boy. Get ready."

Why am I immediately regretting this?

When the song starts, I don't immediately recognize it, but Sawyer and Max both start laughing. That is until Max glares at Sawyer for the TMI. *Latto's -"Big Energy"* starts coming through the speakers, and Cassie can't hold in her laughter, especially when Harris and the guys join in on the little watch party.

"Come on, big boy! Dance for us. Show your woman all your moves," Trevor jokes.

"Shut it, man. At least let me get used to it before you start making fucking sex jokes," Max growls.

"Oh, pull the dildo out of your ass, Max," Cassie says, defending Trevor. "Don't be so fucking uptight. People have sex. We all do. It's fucking fun."

I see the moment she regrets her statement as Max looks like he's caught between choking her or kissing her—or maybe both at the same fucking time. Either way, I can tell that they've definitely fucked before. You know it's obvious when even I can tell.

Walking over to Sawyer, I climb in her lap, loving the way she giggles when I touch her.

"What a switch in roles, baby girl," I say as I grind my cock against her. "I will admit, I'm partial to the first version, but I'll take any chance I can to rub my cock against you", I tell her with a wink, making her blush.

Leaning forward, I whisper in her ear, "We'll take Rory out for ice cream tomorrow. We can talk to her then. Tonight, you're all mine."

"Always. Now dance for me, handsome."

We all start laughing as the "BDE" jokes go around

I never would've thought that moving back to New York, back to the place where I lost everything, would bring me such peace. I never imagined that this place would be where I would find everything I never knew I needed but now can't imagine living without. Sawyer is the missing piece of me, the reason I smile, even if it doesn't look like it. She's the reason I'm willing to crawl onto her lap and dance in a crowded bar, not giving a fuck who watches. Because I have her.

Sawyer and Rory are all I need.

Who would've thought that I would be giving a lap dance in a bar to fucking "*Big Energy*" with the woman of my dreams, while all our friends make jokes around us?

Not me.

But I'd make every fucking wrong turn again, as long as it led me straight to her every time.

It doesn't matter what mistakes either of us have made or what we've done. None of it matters.

In every version of our story, she's my happy ending.

EPILOGUE

REX- THREE MONTHS LATER

If you would have told me a year ago, even six months ago, that I'd be lying in bed next to the hottest women I'd ever met, I would have called you a fucking liar. I probably would've told you to go get your head checked.

But here we are, in that exact situation.

The only difference is that Sawyer isn't just the hottest woman I've ever met. She's also my favorite person, and the love of my life. Well, my favorite *adult*. My favorite little person is currently fast asleep in her room, probably dreaming about whatever sugar concoction Sawyer's convinced her is appropriate for breakfast.

As much as I want to get annoyed about that, it's hard because I've loved seeing Rory and Sawyer's relationship develop. It's everything I could have ever imagined for my little girl. Sawyer adores Rory and it's obvious my daughter feels the same way. We were both so nervous to tell Rory about the two of us, but it went so much better than I thought possible. She acted like it wasn't a big deal, just a part of everyday life, which I guess to her it was.

Sawyer and I kept waiting for the other shoe to drop and

for her to freak out, but she never did. Stella and my mom just laughed at us, apparently Rory told them all about us at their sleepover, but they made a deal to wait for us to tell her.

"Stop staring at me, you're creeping me out," she mumbles, turning her face to nuzzle deeper into my chest.

"I can't help it, you were making these soft little sounds, almost like you were snoring. It was cute."

"I DO NOT SNORE," she warns, her eyes immediately snapping open to glare at me.

"I didn't say it was a bad thing, they're cute little sounds," I smirk.

"It's decided. I'm never sleeping here again," Sawyer says as she flips over to face away from me.

"I thought they were cute. But your little moans and whimpers while you dream? Those turn me the fuck on. I just had to wait for you to wake up so I could find out if you'll make those same sounds while I tongue fuck you," I growl as I slide my body over hers, holding myself up on my arms as I stare down at her.

"You could have done that anyways," she mumbles, still refusing to look at me, but an adorable smirk is now peeking out.

Holding my body still, I lean in so my mouth is right next to her ear. "But then I wouldn't have gotten to watch your face as you came all over mine."

"I'm still mad at you," she says, her voice breathless as I continue down, pressing kisses along her jaw, pausing when I reach the juncture between her neck and collar bone. She's so sensitive here, and as I nip and suck, she moans and her body lifts up towards me as her hands grips my hair, pulling me in closer.

Sawyer joking about how she'll never sleep here again

gives me the motivation to talk to her about something—something I've been thinking about for awhile but have been way too chicken to bring up. You'd think I'm a teenage boy getting ready to ask a girl out on a date, but here I am, a fucking thirty-seven-year-old dad acting like a little bitch about this.

So, I'm not going to play fair.

Sliding down her body, I stop when I reach her perfect breasts, cupping one with one hand, as my mouth latches onto her other, gently nibbling and sucking her nipple. Switching back and forth between the two, I don't stop until she's squirming beneath me, practically begging for more.

"I have a question for you," I say as my mouth pops off of her nipple with a loud *pop*.

"Really, Rex? A question for me right now? My vote is that your mouth stops talking and instead starts eating me out. It's a more productive use of our time."

Cocking an eyebrow, I look up at her. "Oh, is that so? I'm only good for my mouth?" I whisper quietly, before blowing against her clit, just hard enough to drive her wild.

"Stop teasing me, Rex," she whines, her hands pulling my hair trying to place my mouth exactly where she needs it. "If you don't touch me soon, I'll do it myself."

Grabbing both her wrists, I put them in my left hand, holding her still while I lean forward until my mouth is right next to her ear. Gripping her jaw with my free hand, I hold her still, demanding her attention. "Like fuck you will, baby girl. You play by my rules and you'll get what you want, I promise. Fight me and I'll bring you right to the edge before pulling all of the way back. Then, I'll do it over and over until you think you can't take it any longer. Do you understand me? Are you listening?"

Her eyes are wide, but not with fear. Sawyer gets off on

me demanding things from her and her body. She especially loves when I demand orgasms from her. But right now, I'm withholding orgasms until she talks.

"Fine. I'm listening," she responds after what feels like minutes, but was probably just a few moments.

Taking a deep breath, I move back down her body until my mouth is back between her legs. Pressing kisses down her thigh, I kiss down to her knee before back up to her hip, holding back a laugh when she protests, but she waits patiently. She knows the game.

"I like you here, in my bed," is all I can muster out, my tongue flattening as I press it against her clit in a long, languid swipe. Keeping it up, I slip one finger inside of her cunt, sliding right in. "You're so fucking wet. Is this all for me?"

"Was that your question?" is all this infuriating woman is able to moan out, as I angle my fingers to hit her g-spot, my tongue still working her clit.

"Stop being a pain in my ass. Move in with me," I growl, staring at her, loving the moment realization hits her at what I just asked. Pressing firmer against her clit, my thumb rubs slow, circles against her clit, bringing her closer and closer ever so slowly.

"You want me to move in here?" she asks, a huge grin already showing on her face.

Relief hits me when I see she's actually smiling.

"Yes, baby girl. I want you to move in with Rory and I. You're the piece of us that we didn't realize we were missing until we found you."

"Of course I'll move in, Rex" She jumps forward, right as I latch onto her clit, finally giving her the orgasm she craved.

Fuck I'm crazy about her.

"Move in this weekend."

Snapping her head up, she looks perfectly content from an orgasm, yet shocked.

"This weekend? Are you crazy? My lease goes until August. I'll move out then. I'm not going to leave Cassie."

"That's five months. That's too long. Two months," I grumble. I don't want to wait that long to have her in my bed every night. I want her toothbrush in the bathroom, her scent on my pillow. Fuck I even want her goddamn hair everywhere, because then she'd be here. She'd be mine.

"Four."

"Sawyer--."

"Three. Final offer. I'll move in at the beginning of July. That'll give Cassie time to figure out if she wants to stay there and get a new roommate."

"Fine. At least you're moving in here." I can't help the smile I have, I probably look like I'm ten, but I don't give a fuck. I'm so excited to have this woman in my life and can't wait for her to move in. Just then I hear a light knock on our door, Rory's awake.

"Come in, sweetie," Sawyer says as she slips on the last of her pajamas.

"Hi daddy, hi Sawyer," Rory smiles as she walks further in the room until she's standing at the edge of my bed. "I want pancakes. Can we make pancakes? Please daddy, my tummy is hungry and I just want pancakes."

"Okay, sweet girl. Why don't you put cartoons on while I get up, then I'll come make pancakes."

"Okay, daddy. But can we have sprinkles? Sprinkles make the pancakes taste so yummy."

"She's not wrong, sprinkles make everything taste better," Sawyer says with a smile.

"Fine, we can put sprinkles in," I do my best stern voice, but it falls flat based on the smiles my girls have on.

"Let's go to the couch while we wait for your daddy to get up, I need coffee," Sawyer says, waiting for Rory to lead the way.

As I watch my girls walk out of the room, I can't help but be thankful for every mistake, problem and wrong turn I've made in my life because it led me to this moment. Right here, this is exactly where I'm supposed to be, with my two favorite girls.

I just can't wait for her to be here all the time. I can't wait to tell our friends about this next step, tonight when everyone is here.

It's permanent. She's mine.

EPILOGUE

SAWYER

"Ro, are you sure we can't do clear? I mean, hell, even a blue color without all that glittery shit?" Max groans from the floor.

"That's a daddy word, you're not supposed to say that," Rory tells him nonchalantly, not even looking up as she sits across from him on the floor painting his nails. "And no, Uncle Maxy. The glittery *sparkles* make the color, besides it's sooooo you, don't you think?"

Harris and Cade start laughing, obviously enjoying the 'torture' Max is enduring at the hands of a cute five year old. Rory had her birthday party last month, and unfortunately for Rex, she wanted all of us to go out and get manicures. So the three of us went and she picked colors for each of us. I got a pretty teal, she got purple and of course she picked out bright pink for Rex. His friends, specifically Max, never let him live it down, so the guys are enjoying watching this.

Rory has taken to calling Max her uncle which is probably the cutest damn thing I've ever ever heard. Watching them bond and get close makes my heart happy, even if he is still a huge pain in my ass.

"I think he meant an adult word, I think it'll be okay, Ro," Max tells her, patiently watching as Rory does her best to paint his nails.

"Stop moving, Uncle Maxy. I'm getting the color everywhere."

"Sorry, little Ro," Max says, embarrassed to be getting scolded by a little girl. Looking up, he scans the room, searching for something or someone. When he catches sight of Gwen, Stella and Cassie curled up on the couch talking, he smiles as he watches the three of them for just a moment before quickly looking away. Weird. Max and Cassie have honestly never gotten along in all the years we've known each other, but I don't think their hate runs as deep as he believe it does. But that's for him to figure out when he's ready. I love seeing Max this calm and carefree, he seems so happy.

This isn't just a found family for me, Max lost our parents too so I'm thankful he has them too. It's also nice that his new best friend happens to be the cutest little five year old that he'd pretty much do anything for. She's got all these big bad ass hockey players wrapped around her finger. I hope she realizes that none of these men will let her get attention from any boys until she's at least thirty.

We've been sitting here in Rex's living room since we finished dinner, just laughing and watching some random movie they put on TV. It's moments like this that I realize just how far everything has come, and none of it wouldn't have happened had I not been at Atlantis that night. I'm the happiest I've been in as long as I can remember, and it's because of Rex.

We decided to have a little get together before all the boys started back up with the NHL preseason. Rex and my brother have already started to get to know their new team, had a couple of practices but nothing official. They both seem really happy to be there, even if they will be rivals with their friends. But hey, that just makes it more interesting, right?

Rex walks up behind me, his arms wrapping around my waist, pulling me in close to him. "You okay? Want another glass of wine?" he asks, whispering in my ear, his breath tickling my neck.

"I'm perfect," I smile, truly believing my words. "But I'll never say no to another glass of wine."

Pressing a kiss on my cheek, Rex chuckles. "Of course, baby girl. By the way, your ass looks delicious. I want to bite it," he says as he swats my butt as he turns to walk away, smiling at us as he walks away. "Your nails look beautiful, Max. You should always have sparkles, maybe do the Ice Hawks colors next, I'm sure the guys would dig it."

Max just laughs, shaking his head while Rory smiles proudly. As soon as Rory looks back down, Max flips him off with a laugh.

I love these people. This feels like home, and soon, it will be.

I thought I would feel a piece of myself missing when I finally cut my mother out of my life, but instead I feel a sense of peace.

It takes time and growing up to realize people that actually *want* to be in your life and who will make the effort.

"All done!" Rory exclaims proudly, her smile wide and her cute little face beaming. "Uncle Maxy, go show everyone your pretty nails. They'll love them so much."

Standing up, Max looks down at his nails which are *definitely* blue. She did paint his nails, but she also painted around the nails and the tips of his fingers in the process. He does a good job of telling her how much he loves them though, which only makes her happier.

Max walks over to the guys who all make a big show of oohing and aahing at his nails. When he gets to the couch where the girls are sitting, I watch as he and Cassie start whispering to each other. She looks annoyed while he just sits there with a smug grin on his face. He's obviously said something to annoy her, which tracks.

I don't even realize I'm still staring at them until Rex hands me my glass of wine, startling me.

"Easy there, baby girl. Daydreaming?"

"Something like that," I murmur, taking a sip of my wine.

"Should we tell them?" Rex whispers.

"Yeah," I smile. "Cassie and I talked about it before everyone else came over. She's bummed, but happy for us."

"Ok," he smiles before turning back to the room. "We want to tell you guys something, we have some news."

"You're knocked up?" Harris shouts out, which earns him a smack on the back of his head from Max.

"My sister doesn't have sex, you asshole."

"No, you idiot, she's not pregnant." Rex grumbles while I laugh. "It sounds silly saying it out loud, but I just wanted to let everyone know that Sawyer is going to be moving in here this summer."

Grabbing his hand, I smile. Rex is so proud, telling our friends and family we are planning this next step in our lives. It may not be a wedding, it certainly isn't a baby yet, but it's a step for us to start building our lives together.

"That's awesome, you guys!" Miles says with a smile.

"Couldn't get away from this asshole, could you?" Harris says before giving me a hug. "But in all seriousness, I'm so happy for you guys."

"I'm so excited, Sawyer! I've always wanted a mommy to live with me! Daddy, daddy! Does this mean I have a mommy?" Rory says as she jumps up and down filled with excitement.

"Sawyer will eventually be your step-mommy, but you're more than welcome to call her whatever you two feel comfortable with, okay Ro?" Rex says proudly.

I can't help the tears that well in my eyes. I love this little girl with my whole heart and soul, and to hear her talk about me this way, it brings me so much joy. Leaning down, I give her a big hug.

"Can I call you mommy?" Rory asks, her hands gripping my cheeks in an adorable way to keep my attention, not that she needs the help.

"Sweetie, you can call me whatever feels comfortable for you. If you want to call me mommy, I'd be honored."

"Yes!" Rory fist bumps in the air before running off to go play.

Looking up at Rex, he has tears in his eyes as well.

"What about the apartment?" Trevor asks.

"Gwen was going to move in, but they won't let her break her lease. Figured I'll find someone to sublet it until the lease is up then figure it out." Cassie says with a shrug.

"You are absolutely not having some random person living with you."

Turning to look at who said that, I'm surprised to see it's my brother.

"Excuse me?"

"I said, you are not having some random person move into your home. Fuck that."

"What, are you my daddy now?"

"If that's what it takes to get you to listen to me, then sure, I'll be your daddy. But I'm not going to let you be the idiot that gets murdered in her sleep.You've seen those crime shows, it happens."

"You do watch a lot of *Criminal Minds*, he's not wrong about it being sketchy." I add, which earns me a glare from Cass.

"Can we talk about this later? I want to celebrate your news," Cassie says with a smile.

"Yes princess, we can and we will," Max says before stomping off to the kitchen leaving Cassie and I just staring at each other in disbelief. Max is headstrong, but never usually in a way where he tells people what to do.

Apparently that changed when Cassie became involved.

"He'll get over it. I'm grabbing another glass of wine then we can put the next movie on."

As she walks away leaving me alone with Rex, part of me wonders if there's more to the story with Max. Why is he being so...bossy and possessive over someone he claims to hate.

"Stop thinking about it. It doesn't matter tonight," Rex says quietly. "Tonight, we celebrate. Tomorrow, we deal with the bullshit."

"Deal. Now get me drunk, sir. I want lots of celebratory sex tonight."

"You got it, baby girl. I hope you're ready for the rest of our lives, we're about to be a power couple." Rex adds a wink at the end, obviously having overheard the girls and I talk about celebrity power couples.

"I am. With you and Rory? Always."

Who knew that landing in Rex's lap one night would be the power play I never saw coming.

∿

Keep reading to take a glimpse into the Adam and Vanessa's story:
The Mistake (The Maxwell Family)

Prologue, Adam

She's gone.

She's already moved everything out of our place and even put her engagement ring on the kitchen counter as if this were a movie or something.

Four years. That's how long we've been in this relationship, and she just threw it all down the drain, and for what? I don't even recognize who I am anymore.

Everything lately has been done for Holly; we're always going out with her friends and only ever doing what she wants to do. I even distanced myself from my family because she didn't want us to spend so much time with them. Worse, I gave up my dream of starting my own tech company and shut down my cyber security business because she thought it would take too long to be financially successful and wanted me to have "a safe source of money," which is how I ended up working for my father and will eventually help open a new branch in Chicago.

I've loved New York, but I'm always the happiest when I'm near Chicago, whether it's the city or our family farmhouse. That's my happy place. Holly always wanted to visit the farmhouse because she would hear Amelia, my sister, talk about it. Somehow, I always found excuses to not bring her.

In reality, I think I knew that I didn't want her to taint the place that made me so happy.

But what was the point? Luckily, I work with my family, so I get to see them. But I changed so much of my life just to make her happy, and now I'm alone while she's off doing whatever she wants with her latest victim.

The worst part is the only thing I really wanted was someone to share my life with. Someone I could discuss successes and failures with and, at the end of the day, support each other and have each other's back.

I guess my mistake was thinking that person was Holly when all she really wanted was a puppet to get her where she wanted to go in life.

Seems I'm stuck with the bachelor life now, because I'll be damned if I ever make the slip-up and open my heart up to someone again.

Instead, I'll just get lost in someone for a night and move on.

Love was a mistake, and it's one I'm not willing to open myself up to again.

Chapter One, Vanessa

"I can't do this," I say into the phone as I'm rushing onto the subway. Luckily, there's a seat right by the door, and I sit down right as the doors close.

"Does this mean that they offered you the job?!?" Blaire squeals into the phone.

"Yes, everything got messed up though. We couldn't have an in-person interview because their plane was delayed, so it ended up just being over the phone. Plus, instead of having a little time to prepare, I told them I had already quit my other job, so they asked if I could report on Monday. I guess the cyber-attacks have been more frequent.”

“I’m not understanding what the issue is then. It’s great that you got the job!”

“Yes, I just wish I could have been able to do an interview. That way, I would feel like they hired me for me. Now I just feel like they hired me because of my references, which unfortunately had to include someone from my father's company, which makes me not want to take this job. I don’t want to get a job because of him after what he did to me”.

Although we don’t speak about him much, Blaire knows that my father helped me get started in this industry and that he was also the reason I nearly left the industry. Things between my father and I are . . . complicated, to say the least.

“You don’t really have a choice now, do you? This is your dream job, what you’ve been waiting for. Who cares if he somehow had a hand in you getting the position? He has nothing to do with it now, so now is the time to prove it to yourself,” my best friend says into the phone.

I know that she’s right. I mean, I have been dreaming of this job ever since I can remember, but a job at Maxwell Investments is a big deal, and I’ll be working directly with the CEO of the company to help change their security over to their newer branch here in Chicago.

“I know, but that doesn’t make this reality any less scary. I wish I had gotten to meet them in person. Why do I have this irrational fear that I’m going to walk in on Monday and it’s all going to be a big joke and my father will be there laughing. I just feel like if that’s why they are hiring me, then they should know the whole story, or maybe they do know the whole story and that’s why they’re hir—”

"Whoa, whoa, whoa! Stop. We are not going down that path. It's Friday night. You don't start until Monday morning. We can sit here and overanalyze everything until we're blue in the face, or we can go out and celebrate and get you laid," Blaire laughs.

"Blaire, just because your job has loved you from day one, does not mean it's going to be that easy for all of us. You love your job; you were born to be a model. Ugh. I'm going home and going to bed. I will not be discussing my sex life with you," I whisper, looking around, realizing I'm still on the subway.

Thankfully, no one is paying attention to me. The lady next to me has her nose in a book, and the guy next to her has his headphones in and is watching Rick and Morty loud enough for me to hear. Pretty sure neither of them have even noticed I'm here.

"Ness, sorry, but discussing your sex life would mean that you have a sex life. And, before you try to convince me that sex with yourself counts, it doesn't. Sorry, but we need to get someone else in charge of your orgasms for once."

"Oh my god. You are the worst," I whisper into my phone like that'll stop everyone from hearing her.

"We're going out and finding you a man. Not someone you'll have to talk to tomorrow, just someone who seems like they might be able to give you an orgasm or two. If nothing else, this will at least help take your mind off of everything with the new job for a little while."

She's right. On all accounts. And that's the worst part. I'm able to admit that it has been a little while for me. Three years to be exact. That's what happens when someone you're supposed to be able to trust takes advantage of you. It's easy to forget who you are, and sometimes you end up single and lost.

It's been even longer since I've been in an actual relationship, everything that happened has just made it so hard for me to trust anyone.

Days turned into weeks, months, and then they began turning into years. Trust is something that is hard to give back to anyone once it has been destroyed. Which is why it's been so long since I've had sex. I've only had two one-night stands ever, and they were hard for me. I've always wanted a connection with someone, and it felt unreal to think I could have a connection with someone that quick, even just for sex.

But maybe she's right . . . maybe it's time to go have some fun, even if it's just drinks. And if sex happens, great. Maybe even an orgasm? Even better.

"I'll agree to the drinks, as long as I can borrow your black Jimmy Choo's," I say with a sigh, knowing there really is no way I'm getting out of this tonight.

"Okay, I'll be at your house at eight. I'm picking out your dress as well. No arguing. See you soon!"

She hangs up.

I look down at my watch and see it's 6:45. I have just over an hour to get home, eat, shower, and be ready for her intense energy.

Bring on the tequila.

***

It's 7:45 when I hear my apartment buzzer go off. Blaire is here, early as usual. I look down at my robe as I walk over to let her up. At least I had time to shower and eat something, but I'm not ready.

"You're early," I grunt into the speaker as I buzz her in.

"Yes, but I brought the shoes and I can help you with your hair. Oh! And I have tequila," Blaire says.

"You should have led with the tequila," I grumble into the speaker as I she comes up the stairs. I walk over to the door and let her in.

She's smiling as she walks in with bags in hand, bumping into me as she tries to give me a hug. She's cheerful, but not the normal cheerful that I'm used to from her. She's surpassed normal. She's practically bouncing with energy.

"What's happened?" I ask, looking at Blaire as she continues to set her stuff down in my living room.

"What do you mean?" she asks, with a perplexed expression like she doesn't understand.

"You're happy. Like cheerful. And smiling. Why? What's happened?"

"It's nothing! I'm just excited to go out tonight. It's been a while since we've been out. I know just the place too!" Blaire says, way too excitedly, as she pours us each a shot of tequila.

"Why do I feel like I'm not going to like where this is going?"

"Oh. Well, remember that guy from last week? From the modeling job?"

"Yeah . . ." I say, still looking at her confused.

"Well, it took him a couple of days, which was making me nervous. But he finally reached out and wants to meet up with us tonight at Lucky's."

Blaire looks up at me with a smile, and I know there's no way I can be annoyed with her. It's just that she knows I hate going out in larger groups and having to socialize.

"I know I said tonight was all about the two of us going out and celebrating, and finally finding you a man, but I was just so excited I didn't know what to say to him when he asked!"

"So, wait, now I'm going to be the third wheel? No thank you, Blaire!" I shoot my tequila back and grab a lime from the bowl. "I'll stay home, you go out."

At least this way, I might actually get to stay in for the night. She doesn't need me for a date.

"Nope! It's perfect! He's going to be there with some of his friends who are in town for a bit. I'm sure they'll be fun! Besides, out of towners? What better way to have a one-night stand?" Blaire jokes. "Are you mad?"

"Blaire, I'm not mad. Just hadn't prepared myself for a group event. It'll be okay though, totally fine. Just give me a minute, and more tequila. I mean, at least I get to meet this guy you keep talking about. But I'm sure as hell not hooking up with one of his friends." I look at her, expecting her to argue with me, but she just smiles.

That's the look she gives when she's planning something she knows I'll hate.

Fuck.

Grabbing the tequila, I pour us each a shot. She starts talking as I take mine, so I grab hers and take it as well. If she expects me to go out tonight with what she has planned, I'll need the alcohol more than she does.

***

Two hours and two more shots later, our cab pulls up to the curb of Lucky's. As we hop out of the car into the chilly fall air, I'm happy we took all of those tequila shots before we got here. The gentle numbness my body is feeling and the warmth in my tummy is helping battle the coldness of a Chicago night in October.

With the dress Blaire brought over for me, the warmth is necessary.

She tried to convince me that just because something has sleeves, that means it's appropriate for this time of the year. But it's backless and it's short. Very, very short.

"I can't believe you got me to wear this tonight," I say, as I tug the dress down over my ass again.

"What's wrong with your dress?" Blaire asks.

"Besides the fact that it's missing half of it." I deadpan.

"Stop it, Ness, you look hot. Your legs look fucking amazing in that dress. And with those shoes. Damn. I'd bet every man in this line is imagining what your legs would look like wrapped around their neck."

"Oh my gosh," I say, as my face heats up.

Blaire has no filter, and as always, she chooses the most inappropriate times to say things. Looking up, I notice a group of guys being escorted in through the VIP door directly in front of us.

I can't help but stare at them. Each is wearing a perfectly fitted suit that highlights their builds nicely. Definitely not just pulled off the shelf.

The last one to enter the club turns back around just in time and winks at me with a knowing smirk. Normally I'd be embarrassed, but I can't help but stare at him as he smiles my way, his eyes the most stunning emerald green I have ever seen.

Blaire interrupts my staring just in time for him to turn around and walk inside.

"Oh, please, everyone here is thinking it. Besides, anyone that is here is drunk, or will be. No one will remember any of this tomorrow, so who cares?" Blaire says as we walk up to the bouncer at the VIP door. She gives him our names and he lets us in. I guess it pays to be friends with Blaire.

"Did you see that group of men outside the club?" I ask nonchalantly.

"No, I didn't get a good look at them. This is a pretty high-profile club, so it wouldn't surprise me if there were celebrities here tonight."

"He didn't seem like a celebrity, he seemed . . . in charge, dominant. I don't know, something about the way he looked at me just made me feel like that's who he is."

"I'm confused. Are we talking about a group of guys, or one?" Blaire asks as we head towards the bar.

"It was a whole group of guys, probably four? But the guy at the end, I think he heard what you said. As they were heading in, he turned back around and winked at me. But hot damn, he was something else. The way he looked at me, I nearly melted right there," I tell her as we squeeze our way up to the bar.

Once we get up there, she grabs the attention of the bartender and orders us two shots of tequila each, which we immediately slam back one after another.

"Was he hot? Let's go look for him. If something is making you notice, it's worth finding out. You haven't been interested in anyone in . . . hmm . . . years."

Quickly, she pays for the drinks and grabs my hand, leading me away from the bar.

"Nope! We are not searching for him. We came to get drinks and to meet your friend. Let's go over there. Maybe we'll run into them later on the dance floor or something."

Blaire pauses for a minute, obviously weighing the decision. She must realize I actually don't want to go looking for a man because she finally nods.

"Isaac has a table over in the corner; we can go there," Blaire says, smiling from ear to ear. It feels like she's genuinely happy to be out with me, which is nice. I've been a little different lately with everyone except for Blaire, but it has made me more introverted.

It's hard not to feel a little sad at the loss of who I was. I can't help but think about this as I follow Blair. She pulls me through the crowd of people, walking towards a group of four guys, one of whom I assume is Isaac.

"Hey! You guys made it!" He quickly jumps up, giving Blaire a longer than necessary hug, proving just how happy he is that she made it.

Thankfully, I have a little liquid courage in me, which makes it less painful to be at a club on a Friday night, meeting new people, and wearing a dress that is much shorter than I like.

Isaac looks over at me, giving me a quick hug before turning back to sit down with his friends, pulling Blaire to sit next him.

As Isaac starts to go through introductions, I sit down in the only chair available. I barely notice the names Isaac is saying until he gets to the last guy. Sitting directly in front of me, with bright, emerald-green eyes and a sly smirk, is the man from outside the club.

"Finally, this is Adam." I realize that Toby must have been talking that whole time, and has just now finished his introductions, but honestly, I can't remember a word he just said.

The man, who Isaac just introduced as Adam, is sitting across from me at the end of the table, holding his scotch in one hand while the other rests on his chin.

His cocky smirk from earlier has returned. This man screams confidence and power, and although it shouldn't, it excites me.

Since Blaire is sitting down at the other end with Isaac, I realize that I should probably try to make conversation.

"Hi, I'm Vanessa," I say, having a hard time making eye contact with the man. Looking around for our server, I'm relieved when I see her at the table next to us, slowly making her way over. A quick distraction will be nice.

"I know. Isaac did the introductions," he says, and when I look up, he's staring at me with that irritating smirk still on his face.

It's unnerving. It feels like he can read my mind and knows my deepest, darkest thoughts. We've only said like five words to each other, but it feels like he's already seen too much.

As the waitress passes by our table, I notice him grab her attention. Quickly stopping at our table, she ignores me completely, giving Adam all of her attention.

"What can I get for you?" she asks in an almost seductive way.

"The same thing I had last time, another scotch," he says with an unamused smile. "But I stopped you because my friend here would like to order," he tells her, pointing to me.

I'm not sure what to focus on. The way this man can disarm me with a simple smile, or how he's standing up for me with the waitress who clearly just wanted to flirt. I don't miss the way she brushes his arm accidentally as she turns to look at him again.

"Oh, I know, handsome. You just flagged me down, so I was seeing if there was something else you needed my help with." Leaning forward, I notice she whispers something in his ear.

Instead of being excited, or even liking what she said, he appears annoyed.

"That won't be necessary, Maria. Now, if you wouldn't mind, take a step back and continue doing your actual job. You know, taking everyone's order. Don't forget to start with

Vanessa here." Adam commands the words as he says them, gaining every one's attention at our table.

I have literally spoken two words to this man, yet I can't help but feel a wave of possessiveness after watching the server with him, as well as a slight excitement that he isn't feeding into it.

What's even more unnerving, though, is the way he hasn't stopped staring at me this entire time, almost like he's watching to see how I'll react.

"What are you having?" she asks me rudely. "A white claw? Cosmopolitan?"

"I'll have the same as him," I reply, never once taking my eyes off of him.

"Are you sure?" She looks at me in disbelief. "You want to drink Macallan?"

"Yes, I do. Now, do you only have the fifteen year that they ordered?"

"Fifteen year what?" she asks.

"Macallan. Do you only have the fifteen year? Or do you have the fifty?"

Adam just smiles, obviously enjoying this.

The waitress's face flushes red, embarrassed that she's the one who looks dumb now instead of me like she wanted.

"Nope. Just the one he has. Would you like to start a tab?" she asks, still snippy.

I go to reach for my clutch, but Adams voice stops me.

"She's with me, just add it to mine."

Everyone can hear her audibly scoff, but she surprises me by keeping her mouth shut. Finally moving on, she takes everyone's orders, keeping her eyes down on her notepad. After she's finished, she heads back up to the bar without a second glance.

It took a moment for everyone to start talking again, and

during that time, everyone's eyes were on Adam, while his eyes never left mine.

Needing to break the ice, I reach across the table. Adam looks surprised, thinking I'm going to hold his hand or something.

"Gimme," I tell him as I reach for his drink. "If everyone is like that around you guys, I need more alcohol, like ten minutes ago."

Chuckling under his breath, he slides me his glass and just watches me with curiosity.

It's always funny what people assume about others. He's probably thinking the same thing as the waitress but isn't bold enough to say it.

Picking up his glass, I never take my eyes off of him as I take a sip.

I see the moment he realizes I actually enjoy it.

"You weren't joking around with her? You actually like scotch?"

I turn to look at whoever said that, and I realize I still don't know their names.

"No, I wasn't playing around. I was introduced to scotch when I was twenty, my grandfather loved the stuff. I guess it grew on me."

Adam doesn't say anything, he just leans back, listening to my every word.

"I'm sorry, I feel terrible. I didn't catch everyone's names when Isaac was doing introductions. I was a little over-whelmed."

I hear laughing, and his friends are looking at me with a knowing smile. Their smiles say a lot, and I know they're not trying to be rude at all. Instead, for some reason, their smiles seem welcoming.

Adam steps up to do introductions again, causing his friends to share a quick smile.

"Vanessa, these two are my brothers. This is Caleb."

"It's nice to meet you, Vanessa," he says, smiling while shaking my hand.

"And this, this is Connor. My youngest brother."

"Hi, Vanessa, it's been so wonderful getting to meet you. You've brought an interesting change to our evening," Connor says with a wink.

I look over at Adam to see him glaring at his brother, which just seems to make Connor laugh harder.

"I must be missing something," I say with a laugh, while looking around, hoping our server will magically appear with our drinks.

I look over and see Isaac has his arms around Blaire, and she has moved into his lap.

Hoping to ease the tension at the table, I decide it's time to go dance. I stand up, getting the attention of Blaire as I do.

"Let's go dance!" I tell her with a smile.

Just then, our server returns, quickly setting down our drinks and walking away. Smiling at Blaire, I hand her the drink she ordered, and we quickly shoot them back.

"Alright, come on! I love this song!" She jumps up, and I watch as Isaac gets up as well.

Isaac grabs ahold of Blaire's hand and starts to lead her away from the table and toward the dance floor. He turns around to look at where he left me, to see that Adam has yet to move from his seat. He gives me a quick smile and I wave them on.

"That's our cue," Connor says, smiling. Both he and Caleb stand up and head towards the bachelorette party out on the dance floor.

"Are you coming?" Caleb asks.

I look back at Adam to see that he's still sitting down, staring at me.

"Well . . ." I say, right as Adam swallows down the rest of his scotch. Unable to take my eyes off him, I watch as his throat contracts when he swallows. He sets down his glass and stands up, all the while one last drop of scotch goes sliding down his lip.

Unable to stop my thoughts, I watch the drop of scotch, wondering what it would be like to taste it, the scotch, or him. I'm not entirely sure. But as the drop slides down his lip, I get the urge to trace it with my tongue and follow it down his throat.

Adam stops the drop, catching it with his thumb, before grazing his thumb ever so gently along my bottom lips, freezing me in place. Leaning forward, he brushes his lips over my ear and whispers, "You're thinking too loud." He smiles.

"If you wanted a taste, all you had to do was ask," he continues to whisper in my ear, before grabbing my hand and leading me out to the dance floor, passing his brothers, who both look shocked.

Embarrassment floods me as I realize that he was able to read my thoughts so easily. I have never been so transparent before. I'm usually able to hide my emotions, but the memory of his thumb against my lips causes my whole body to send tingles straight to my core, turning my embarrassment into desire.

ACKNOWLEDGMENTS

First off, I want to thank you, my readers! I wouldn't be anything without you all. I love this community more than anything and as a new indie author, I wouldn't be anywhere with you! I love connecting and interacting with you all so feel free to say hi or let me know what you think!

To my Alpha readers, Candice and Emily. You ladies are fucking incredible, thank you for sticking by my side through not only my debut, but this book as well. Your support and feedback and been invaluable and I love that you believe in these characters and their stories just as much as I do. You ladies rock.

To my Beta Readers. Again, y'all are incredible. Lauren, Caroline, Erin, Danielle H., Hannah, Danielle, Shannon, and Allie. Thank you for all your feedback and help turning this story in to what it is now. :) Hearing the love you ladies have for Daddy Rex and Sawyer has been everything.

To my badass editor, Matti. This would not have happened without you. You're incredible at what you do and this book would be nothing like it is without you. Thank you for dealing with my stressed out self and always pushing me, you're a rockstar editor and friend.

To my family, thank you for supporting me even though you've been forbidden to ever read my books. You're always so excited about the details I share and I love that. If you've read this, that means you failed. ;)

To my husband, thank you for holding down the fort and never complaining when my face was in my laptop for hours on end. You're my rockstar, my book boyfriend come to life, and I couldn't have done this without you. You believe in me enough for both of us.

ABOUT THE AUTHOR

Lexi James lives in Washington with her husband and their two little boys. If she's not at work, you can find her out adventuring with her family, exploring trails, or curled up on the couch with a steamy book. She began reading after the birth of her kids when she needed something 'just for her' and since then she's read every day.

She's a daydreamer who always has characters and their has stories running through her mind. With encouragement from her husband and family, she sat down to write a book, giving a voice to her imaginary friends.